TRIAL OF THE BERS[

PRIMAL FURY

NOËL TRAVER

Primal Fury: Trial Of the Berserker (Book 1)
Copyright © 2023 Noël Traver. All rights reserved.

No part of this publication may be reproduced, distributed, or transmitted in any form or by any means, including photocopying, recording, or other electronic or mechanical methods, without the prior written permission of the publisher, except in the case of brief quotations embodied in critical reviews and certain other noncommercial uses permitted by copyright law. For permission requests, write to the publisher, addressed "Attention": Permissions Coordinator at the e-mail address: noeltraver1@gmail.com

Any references to historical events, real people, or real places are used fictitiously. Names, characters, and places are products of the author's imagination.

Cover Illustration: Taekseo (@Taekseo_art) on Twitter

Cover Design: MiblArt

Worldwide rights

# Chapter 1

The hammers of the forge rang out in a steady beat beneath the thrum of the chanting shamans, a sound that shivered through flesh and rooted itself deep in Orsin's bones. He nodded unconsciously along with the rhythm as he made sweeping and decisive lines with the stick of charcoal clutched delicately in his paw.

He'd learned the hard way that if he held too tightly to the stylus, his claws would chip it or his grip would pulverise it to dust, and while his fur was already black and the charcoal dust hardly visible, the smiths would growl at him for wasting another writing implement, and Orsin dared not risk their wrath, not when he was so close to needing the forge to craft his weapon for the Trial.

"What are you doing still working on that? An axe is an axe. Sharp on one end and a solid grip on the other. Done. What more could you need?"

Orsin bared his fangs in a broad grin in spite of himself. The voice belonged to Torben, his foster-brother and best friend. Orsin turned to watch the other Fursja approach, the heat of the forge—even here at the very edge of it, practically in the street—beating at his back even as the sharp and frosty chill of the winter air bit at his face. Or tried too. Orsin's fur was thick, and he hardly noticed the cold within the city walls.

Torben stepped into the light of the forge, the fire adding a russet overtone to the rich brown of his fur. Not that Torben needed any help looking good. He was an impressive specimen, rising a full pawspan above Orsin's own five-and-a-half meters of height, and his sapphire eyes were always sparkling with good humour or mischief.

"I need a weapon I can rely on for the upcoming Trial, not just some weak stick of wood with a spit-honed edge on the other end."

"Are we talking about your weapon or are we talking about your *weapon*?" Torben leered at Orsin and waggled his brows suggestively. "One of those is definitely regularly spit-honed."

Orsin laughed. He couldn't help it. Torben was outrageous.

"You should spend more time worrying about your own weapon," Orsin said when he'd recovered. 1

"Oh, I do. I really really do," Torben assured him with yet another shit-eating grin.

"Seriously! Your smithing could use some work, and if you're not careful it won't be you swinging your massive weapon around, it'll be some Herd beast using you as a sheath."

Torben's eyes flickered, and he grimaced. With the Trial looming, even Torben's boundless good humour ebbed a bit. Soon they would be facing life-and-death struggle against their people's greatest enemy, alone. It was a sobering thing, even if it offered an untold chance at glory and honor.

But not even the harsh realities awaiting them could keep Torben's confidence down for long.

"Bah! What are the Herd against the might of a Fursja warrior? We may not be berserkers yet, but we're more than a match for anything the herd can throw at us!" Torben boasted.

"Even a Herd Prince? Or a Queen?" Orsin teased, knowing how much the idea of the Herd Queen unsettled Torben.

His friend quickly made a sign to ward off evil and changed the subject.

"Come one! The Opening Ceremonies are about to start. We'll miss them if we don't hurry."

Orsin squinted up at the sky. It was so hard to tell the time in this season. Everything was so grey.

"That late already?"

"We'll both be late if we don't hurry," Torben said, turning to move away. "As in mudor will kill us for missing Warlord Ursahre's speech!"

The she-Fursja who had whelped him and taken in Torben as her own after his parents died was a force to be reckoned with. There was no way Orsin was risking her wrath. Better a whole host of the Herd and him without a weapon!

Orsin stowed his design and followed Torben away from the forge and into the streets of Velegard. The massive ursine forms of his fellow Fursja sailed through the streets, their towering forms moving through the seasonal gloom like ships sailing ponderously through the fog. At this time of year, the tundra that made up most of Svanhalor's terrain was hardening with the oncoming winter and fading sunlight, but the residual warmth seeped into the air and sent thick banks of fog drifting across the chilly expanse of the land.

The city was a sprawling thing, curving and knotting streets coiling about one another, stone longhouses set out in long rows, regular market squares scattered throughout like the pieces of a child's game. The two Fursja moved though it with the ease of long practice, however. This was their home, and they knew it well.

"This way," Orsin said. "It'll be faster if we take the shortcut past Old Bale-Eye's place."

"Is it actually faster or do we just move more quickly because we don't want the old bear catching us anywhere near his place after we got in trouble nicking his crutch when we were just cubs?" Torben grinned and strode through the fog, trying to outpace his friend.

Orsin just snorted and increased his own pace.

They made it through the alley without incident, passed three market squares, then turned to walk along the Plaza of Weihlaris, pausing just long enough to mutter a quick prayer to the God of the Fursja, of battle and unyielding fury.

The center of Velegard rose around them as they passed the plaza and moved deeper into the city. The buildings were larger, older, and more impressive, rising high above the tall stone longhouses of the outer districts. The towering keep that was the heart of the city was clearly visible, built ages ago by their ancestors as a refuge from the predations of the Herd, then a bulwark of the fight to drive the abominations back, and now a memorial to that time of ancient glory.

More and more Fursja surged around them, drawn to the heart of things for the Opening Ceremonies. Cubs ran growling and roaring with excitement as their parents chased after them. Enterprising vendors had set up temporary stalls selling dried fish on slim skewers and deep tankards of warming ale and small flasks of stronger spirits. The *svagringe*, a large, circular stadium that warriors of the Fursja often used to stage training and mock battles to prepare themselves to face their hereditary enemies, was just ahead.

"Mudor and Vador should have a space saved for us," Torben said, quickly pushing through the crowd and into svagringe.

Orsin followed him, craning his neck to search for their parents.

"There!" Torben pointed. "About a third of the way up the second section over."

The two of them pushed through the crowd, climbing the massive stone terraces until they reached the space their parents had set aside for them.

"Sit, sit!" Their vador gestured at them. "You've already missed the entrance of the warriors."

"The skalds are about to begin," their mudor added. "Listen well! You never know what bit of lore might come in handy for your Trial!" She softened her words with a small smile, however.

Practical as ever. Orsin and Torben settled onto the cold stone, their fur protecting them from the deep bite of it. As they did so, the skalds—the wise storytellers, the poets and historians of the Fursja—began to sway in their formation, their regalia moving with them. Antlers and fangs, feathers and animal skins, the totems of the natural world which symbolised the Fursja connection to nature and the pure purpose of the divine war against the herd, were their hallmarks. Then, as one, they began to chant.

It began, as it always did, with the legend of how the world came to be, and the hand that Weihlaris took in shaping everything. Then came the legend of the Herd, how greedy humans from the Kingdom of Herkalbosch came to these lands under guise of trade, but in reality sought a hidden power that could make them invincible. Instead, they found and released the herd, allowing the abominations to sweep over the land, shattering the Fursja nations of old and driving them back until, under the guidance of Weihlaris, the berserkers were able to shatter that advance and buy time for the creation of the legendary wall, Vaeggdor, behind which the Herd remained penned to this day.

Then came the sagas, which differed year to year. The skalds chose tales of mighty warriors and berserkers of the past, tales which the auguries suggested might be helpful for the hopeful cohort attempting the Trial to hear.

Orsin listened as Warlord Ursahre launched into his speech. It was the same one he gave every year at this time, but every time he heard it the words never failed to stir his blood. To his right, Torben watched with rapt attention, hero-worship in his eyes. To his left, his mudor and vador listened with coiled and controlled intensity. They had heard the speech many more times, heard the ones given by Ursahre's predecessor even, when they were cubs. And still they were caught up in it all, in the purpose given to the Fursja, to guard the world from the predations of the Herd.

And soon he would cross the wall and take up arms in that battle, the centuries-long war for the survival of the world itself. The same one that Warlord Ursahre was describing now, in brutal and bloody and glorious terms. If Orsin was strong enough, if he was worthy, he would return with many trophies and receive a mark from the hand of Weihlaris himself, perhaps even one that might rival that borne by Warlord Ursahre! This was the dream of many of his cohort, who faced their Trial this year. This was their purpose! The thing they had been born to do. Protect the world and win glory in the doing.

Orsin's dreams of glory were shattered by a roar from the crowd all around him. Ursahre had reached the climax of his speech and the blood of several thousand Fursja was beating as if driven by a single heart and a single purpose.

"The Herd will be destroyed! Glory to the Fursja! Glory to Weihlaris!" Warlord Ursahre roared.

The svagringe roared back in approval.

"Now let the celebrations begin!"

# Chapter 2

The world around Orsin was a bleary roar. Fursja were mighty in battle, but they were just as skilled in celebration and song. Skaldic apprentices were chanting, and drums pounded throughout the arctic night. Torches flared, driving back the gloom, and great bonfires burned casting warmths and dancing light across the many squares and plazas they had been kindled within.

But the fires were not the only thing to drive back the chill. Great casks and butts of ale abounded, brewed from the thin and sour wheat that managed to survive in the harsh tundra. Rarer but more potent were the prized ice wines and the three-honey mead brewed by the Weihlaran monks of the Order of the Lattice and Vine.

The three-honey mead was so strong a single sip was enough to get a berserker roaring drunk, and to knock out a regular Fursja. Torben and Orsin had been trying to get their paws on a few sips of that mead all evening, to no avail.

Grunin, their mudor, was settled at a nearby table, smiling as she watched her husband, Ljorn, making a fool of himself dancing around the fire. Ljorn, unlike his sons, *had* managed to snag a sip of three-honey mead, and was a mighty enough warrior that it didn't fell him in the drinking.

It did impair his judgement a bit, though, as evidenced by the merry laughter that followed his antics.

Orsin, however, had more pressing concerns than his father's drinking escapades. Torben had more than his fair share of ale and was prowling around the fire, boasting in front of the other young Fursja about the might of his weapon. Bright Bijask, always competing with Torben for the largest laugh drunkenly egged the warrior on while next to him solemn Sengetiid just shook his head at their antics. And several young Fursja maids giggled at them all.

"Yes, your weapon sounds mighty indeed," Higrun said, eyes dancing in the firelight.

"If indeed it is as mighty as you say it is," Mathajara, her friend, teased.

Bijask snorted. Sengetiid simply took a long pull from his tankard. Orsin knew better than to try and wade into the verbal conflict.

Higrun and Mathjara were of an age with Orsin. The four of them had grown up together, but they'd grown in different ways the last few winters. Higrun and Mathjara had risen and broadened, filling out and blossoming into fresh and vibrant sprigs of she-Fursjahood. Torben fancied Higrun. He'd always liked her, but recently that like had taken a whole new dimension.

Too bad for Torben that Mathjara, Higrun's best friend, thought he was an idiot.

"'That's true,' Higrun agreed with her friend. "So often in tales monsters are made much bigger than they were in reality."

"Yes! Remember the head of the ljindwurm Dathorr brought in last year after his Trial?" Mathjara laughed gaily. "You'd think the thing was too big to fit in the city gates, yet when we went to see it on the Field of Glory afterward, *tch*—" Mathjara made a dismissive sound, "—it was hardly bigger than my hand! Nothing at all to brag about."

"Hjarsurung is nothing to laugh at!" Torben was in the blustery stage of drunk. "He is the mighty hammer that strikes with the force of two blows for every swing!"

The she-Fursja in front of him giggled.

Orsin wanted to laugh as well, but it was bad luck to name your weapon before you forged it.

Of course, that probably depended on *which* weapon Torben was bragging about.

Orsin waded in before his friend could blow any chance he might still have with Higrun or Mathjara.

"Torben! You owe me another round!"

His friend didn't, but Orsin was willing to bet that *he* wouldn't remember that, and if there was anything Torben liked more than flirting and bragging about himself, it was drinking.

"I heard there was some three-honey mead over by Bjornnen's fire," Orsin said, trying to tempt his friend away before he made an even bigger fool of himself.

"I will slay three barons single-handedly on my Trial, like the great—no! Four! *Four* barons. And—"

"Yes, yes," Orsin said. 'And I'll bag myself a Herd Prince while you're doing all that."

"What! No! I will be the first to slay a Herd Prince. No one before had ever done such a thing—"

Because it was suicide. Herd Princes and the Queen they served were titans of the species. They were deadly beyond belief. But before anyone could laugh at the audacity of the very idea, Torben's head finally caught up with what his ears had heard.

"Three-honey mead? Let's go!" Torben grinned manically.

Torben took off, yanking Orsin along behind him. Orsin sent the two she-Fursja an apologetic smile as he was hauled off. They smiled and giggled at him.

Maybe not a total loss then!

"Three-honey mead, three-honey mead, a proper warrior drink to give us fuel before the Trial." Torben's nose was quivering. "Where is it?"

Orsin was saved from having to answer that by a shout from his vador, of all people. It carried over the crowd and drew attention—including Torben's—to the older Fursja.

Time for a tale. Orsin recognised the signs. He smiled.

"Gather round, cubs, and I'll tell you the tale of the fearsome *enrij*!" Ljorn roared out.

Many of the cubs had already fallen asleep, but those who had not, as well as the vast majority of Orsin's friends, all gathered around his father. While the older Fursja was a respected warrior, his mother always said that he very nearly became a skald, for he had the talent. Weihlaris had other ideas though, it seemed.

Orsin and Torben drew closer, though they stuck to the edges of the crowd. It wouldn't do for them to be seen to be too interested in their vador's stories. They were very nearly blooded warriors after all.

"All the girls are here listening anyway," Torben muttered, all thoughts of three-honey mead suddenly gone from his head.

Orsin smiled at the justification but didn't say anything. He didn't dare. Ljorn had already begin to speak.

"The enrij are fearsome beasts, for all that they begin life as simple goats. For you see, there were once a tribe of Fursja that lived in the mountains to west, and they raised mighty rams and ewes, so large that they could carry their masters into battle! Their horns were often shod with iron, and the largest of them could batter down the gates of a human castle with one blow!"

The smaller cubs oohed and aahed appreciatively.

"But then the Herd came," Ljorn's voice became dark and serious. "The Fursja of the mountains, not knowing the danger they faced, went into battle but did not know to prepare the special herbs that stave off infection. They did not know to apply them even to their prized goats. And what do you think happened then?"

"They beat back the Herd monsters and saved their villages!" one hopeful cub shouted.

"No," Ljorn shook his head sadly. "No, if only that were true. Though they were mighty, and they slew many Herd beasts, some of the goats were wounded, and the infection quickly took root amongst the goats. Their magnificent white coats began to blacken and turn green with a slimy pus, and their horns began to rot and ooze. When the Fursja went to tend to their goats, the goats went mad and attacked them, but the Fursja, well, these goats were their friends! Their steeds and their source of food. The Fursja, instead of slaughtering every last goat, tried to tackle them, to pull them down to the earth and tie them in place until they could find a cure."

"But there wasn't one, was there?" An older cub spoke up this time, nodding her head as if she were an ancient sage.

"No. We know of no cure for the Herd infection. Only the herbs that keep it away." Ljorn looked on the cub with approval. "So the infection spread from goat to Fursja, twisting not only flesh but also their spirit! The infected Fursja released their goats, mounting them once again, but this time their flesh began to melt and fuse, until you could not tell where one ended and the next began! They became the terrible enrij, and you can still see a very few of them roaming the Herd lands this very day. And one never knows when they are out there, when an enrij might come charging around a hill and—"

Ljorn suddenly leapt at the audience, making a great bleating noise like some kind of maddened demon goat. Everyone screamed and jumped back, even those who had heard this tale time and time again. Such was Ljorn's skill.

Screams quickly gave way to laughter, however, for the fear was far away and the firelight was very close.

"Now," Ljorn demanded, "tell me what you know of the Herd infection! How does it spread? What do you do if you find someone you think is sick with the disease? What should you always carry on you?"

"Fangs and claws!" One cub shouted. "If you have even a scratch you need to treat the wound."

"If you find someone sick you go to the shamans, if you can. Do not let them within the walls." Another added.

"You can treat them, if they are not too far gone," an older cub said sombrely. "And if you have enough *valendjahr* for both yourself and the infected. But only if you have enough for both."

Valendjahr was a mixture of herbs, grown and infused with magic by the shamans of Weihlaris. Every Fursja in Svanhalor carried a pouch thick with the stuff. Usually, it was worn around the neck on a thick leather thong. Every Fursja in Svanhalor knew the look of the herbs and where to find them in the wild, as well as the prayers to Weihlaris that blessed them, though those herbs prepared by the shamans were much more potent, and were needed if one was infected by one of the stronger herd beasts.

"Well done," Ljorn said, nodding. "You have learned your lessons and it may very well save your life or that of another Fursja, someday."

Orsin and Torben, further from the fire, deeper in the shadows, were not so quick as the others to throw off the frisson of danger evoked by their father's words. They were closer to their Trial than anyone else around that fire. They knew that they faced the very real possibility of facing an enrij in the near future, and they would have to do so alone, with no aid other than the weapon they had forged themselves, with their own hands. Even though they would each be out there, on the tundra, neither would be able to come to the other's aid. To interfere directly with the Trial of another was to fail, and face censure in the eyes of the gods.

The Trial demanded no less. It was a proving ground in every sense of the word. To fail was to die, usually horribly at the hands or pincers or tentacles of some Herd abomination.

But to succeed was to win a place of honor and glory, to become a berserker, and to be touched by the hand of Weihlaris himself!

Torben shook himself, as if emerging from a deep pool. A moment later his usual grin was back in place. Orsin could not help but smile in return and he felt the chill hand of the looming Trial release his guts.

"Ghost stories," Torben said dismissively. "Good for warming the blood on a winter night. Nothing more."

"Nothing more," Orsin echoed, though he knew it was far more than just a story. Still, he shook off the chill and leaned into the smile that had infected him. "But you know what else is good for warming the blood?"

Torben grinned back at him and hefted his mug, slamming it into Orsin's.

Then as one they shouted, "drink!"

CHAPTER 3

Clang! Clang! The forge rang out with the sound of hammers and the feel of steel hitting steel shuddered through Orsin's bones. The fires around him roared, turning the air into a scorching vise that threatened to crush the air from his lungs in order to feed its own burning hatred. Still, he leaned into it and redoubled his efforts, his vast muscles straining as he pumped the bellows, forcing the fire hotter and hotter beneath the forge as Torben worked the ingots that would become his massive, double-headed hammer.

Orsin winced. The worst was the sound though, definitely. Each ringing blast sent knives of pain through his ears and eyes, down to his stomach where the vibrations rumbled his breakfast and threatened to evacuate it back up his throat and out over the anvil.

His mother had just smirked at him when he stumbled in for breakfast, Torben half-dragging behind him. His father, thankfully, did not, instead proclaiming that their hangovers looked worthy of great warriors.

Both their parents quickly shooed them out and sent them to the forge, however. This was an almost holy day, the day when they would stand within the sacred forge that burned at the heart of the Fursja nation. No other people of the world had such skill in crafting armour and weapons, and many nations traded precious goods to the Fursja for aid in arming themselves. It was one of the great points of pride for all Fursja, and today was the day that Orsin and Torben would stand in the great forge and craft the weapons that would see them through the Trial. Today was perhaps the most crucial of all preparatory days.

You can forage for food if you run out of rations. You can thaw snow for water, and construct shelter from materials found in the wild. But without a weapon, solidly forged and finely honed, you will struggle to meet the oncoming hordes of the Herd and stand toe-to-toe with the most dangerous beasts.

And it was more than that as well. A weapon, forged by your own hand, in the waning days before the Trial set by Weihlaris himself? That was a thing of legend. A connection was forged between warrior and weapon, as much as the iron and blackrock which combined into steel.

No hand but your own could forge such a weapon. No hand but your own could wield the hammer and shape the metal. It was a sacred, personal thing, open only to the closest of friends and family, and even then they were only permitted to assist in such things as pumping the bellows or fetching fresh oil for the quenching.

Hence why Orsin was heaving at the bellows while Torben worked the metal.

"Give me your paw," Torben shouted in between blows as he heated the lump of metal that would become the hammer's head and then brought it to the anvil.

"What? Why? I can't— "

"You won't be. Just give it here."

When Orsin drew near enough, Torben reached out and grabbed his paw, flipping it over and driving one of his claws deep into the fleshy part on the side. Orsin growled and tried to jerk his paw away but Torben held fast, squeezing until three bright red drops of blood welled up and fell onto the cherry glow of the metal.

They sizzled and hissed as they hit, water boiling away and the rest becoming one with the iron.

Torben released Orsin's paw and immediately began hammering and folding the metal, incorporating the drops of blood into the heart of the hammer.

"I don't think—" Orsin began.

"There is nothing against it," Torben said, anticipating him. "I checked with the shamans. No paw other than mine will forge this weapon, no paw other than mine will shape it or quench it. This is no more a violation of that than you working the bellows."

Orsin didn't know what to say so instead he stuck his paw in his mouth and nursed the wound left by Torben's claw. This was not a side of Torben he saw often. It was, he reflected, nice.

"Besides," Torben added, "this way a bit of each of us with be with the other throughout our Trial. When I am alone and I need courage, all I need do is look to Hjarsurung here and I will know you are with me. What more courage could I need than to know my brother is by my side?"

"I'll be claiming three drops of blood for my own weapon, when we're done here," Orsin replied, taking his paw out of his mouth.

What could he do except echo the sentiment? Though Torben had been adopted by Orsin's parents after his own were killed, Orsin thought of him in all ways the brother of his blood. He knew his parents thought of him as their own child. This way, the exchange of blood, it would be even more of a bond between them. They could carry a part of one another through life, as all families did.

For better or worse.

"Of course! Now get back to working those bellows! The fire is fading and it needs to be hot as dragon's breath if I'm to have a hammer worthy of my might!"

Torben roared with laughter and raised the forge hammer high above his head. Orsin leaned into the bellows and heat spiked around them once again. Torben began to pant in the heat, his tongue lolling out of his mouth in a wide pink river, until it was too much and he reached up to the chain hanging near his shoulder and yanked on it.

The chain clanked and a mechanism in the ceiling rotated. A small sluice gate opened and a stream of water, chilled near to freezing in the cisterns above the forge, poured down to cool the smith as he worked. Torben's brown fur darkened to black where the water struck him, clumping and coiling about itself. The heat of the forge quickly evaporated it, however, returning the rich chestnut shades to the fore as his mighty muscles stretched and heaved, working the hammer that pounded his will into the waiting metal before him.

Again and again he worked the metal, until he was satisfied with the core shape of it. Then he began the finer work, the flourishes and runic markings that were a part of the secret to forging a weapon strong enough to withstand the Trial, linking it irrevocably to Torben's will. As long as the warrior's will endured, so would the weapon. It would never dull, never break.

Not unless its wielder broke *first*.

Finally, Torben was finished. He took his weapon from the forge, still glimmering from being quenched, and carefully set it aside in the place that had been prepared for it. Torben leant in close and whispered the weapon's name to it.

Orsin fancied he saw a shimmer go across the metal in that moment.

Then he took Torben's place before the forge. If his best friend and brother thought that he would pull out the design that he had agonised over for months and pour over it one final time, he was mistaken. Every line and curve of Orsin's weapon was etched behind his eyes and upon his heart. He could forge this axe with his eyes closed and one paw tied behind his back. He knew it that well.

The forge flared, a blast of heat slamming into his face as Torben pumped the bellows enthusiastically. Orsin felt a smile stretch itself across his face and he began to heat the ore. Soon they glowed ready.

The hammer fell, ringing blows that echoed through to Orsin's bones. When the time came, he claimed three drops of Torben's blood and folded it into the metal, working it until there was no division between the two.

The axe grew from the glowing metal, two graceful and deadly arcs sprouting up like flowers to either side of the haft. Orsin called the shape forth with the strength of his arm and the purity of his vision. This would be an axe to be proud of! An axe worthy of legendary feats.

An axe strong enough and sharp enough to bring him home. To bring him home to his family.

The form was set. Orsin's claws danced across the metal, etching runic markings and flourishes representing his life and his family traditions. It was a weapon of war yes, something made to kill, but it was also a symbol of defense, of protection for all those things that the Fursja valued and the Herd threatened. Yes, the Trial was about proving himself to his people and to his god, but the wider missions as about saving the Fursja from their ancient enemy and protecting the entire world from the depredation of those abominations.

Almost before he realised it, Orsin was finished. He blinked and settled back on his haunches. His body was shaking, quivering with the effort he had expended in forging his weapon, this external part of his soul, but he had not noticed the pain or the strain until now, when the physical part of his task was complete.

The axe glowed in the light of the forge, still wet from its final quenching.

Orsin lifted it recently from its place on the anvil and transferred it to the nearby table that awaited it, marked with runes and blessed by the shamans of Velegard. The world seemed slightly fuzzy, as if he was wrapped in a snowstorm of warm motes of light. His eyes, the deep emerald green of drasil leaves, his mudor always told him, stared back at him from his reflection.

The eyes in his reflection slowly blinked at him.

Muinnajhr.

The axe whispered its name to him. Orsin took up the word and whispered it back, echoing it in the real world even as it was spoken in the spirit world.

"It is a good name," Torben said, nodding.

Orsin blinked. He had forgotten his brother was there. Slowly, he mirrored Torben's motion.

"Yes. A good name."

"And yet you look troubled." Torben reached out and punched Orsin in the arm. "Why? We have finished our weapons! We're so close to embarking on the Trial! There will be blood and glory enough to glut an army of Fursja warriors, I just know it!"

"So long as we do not each need to be an army embodied all in one person to survive," Orsin replied.

He ran his claws lightly over the haft of his axe. The feel of it was reassuring, yet he still wished to have it in his hand, firm in his grip. Something about the coming Trial, some chill of ill-omen was settling into his gut.

"Bah! Of course the Trial is dangerous. It would not be a test worthy of Weihlaris if it were not! But you have nothing to worry about. Your skill is amongst the greatest of our cohort, and no one is as careful in their preparations as you." Torben snorted. "Mudor told me you've had everything assembled and packed for days. Double-checked and hidden in the storeroom."

"It's not just myself I worry about," Orsin said suddenly, fixing his gaze on Torben. "I worry about all of our people. I worry how many of us will not return. I worry about—you." Orsin growled quietly. "I do not think you understand quite how much I would miss you, if you—or I—were to fall out there on the Tundra. I wish to live a long, long life, with you as my brother and as my brother-in-arms. The thought of losing that— "

Orsin shook his head. He couldn't finish the thought. To speak it would give it too much power.

"You worry too much!" Torben's words were brash but his eyes were soft.

For a moment, at least. Then the brassy, bold bear was back.

"Besides, nothing could kill me! You may be good, but I'm better. You may be strong, but I am stronger. I am the mightiest of our cohort, and everyone knows it." Torben smirked.

Orsin grinned and resisted the urge to add *everyone except Mathjara.*

"And do not forget," Torben added, "we will have *these.*"

Their weapons, hammer and axe, gleamed red in the forge light, thirsty for blood and glory.

# Chapter 4

The twilight skies were quiet as Orsin rose, stretching. Today was a day of final preparations, of gathering his supplies and checking that he—and Torben—were properly outfitted for the coming Trial. It was a test of survival, and of self-reliance. And while a fully grown Fursja was mighty and could carry a great deal, it was impossible to pack vast stores of food and water. To survive the Trial you needed to be smart, and prepared, as well as self reliant.

Could he survive for a good long while off his fat stores? Yes. But he would be weeks if not months out on the Tundra, hunting Herd beasts until he had accumulated sufficient glory in the eyes of Weihlaris.

Breakfast was a quiet, unhurried affair, if only because the rest of his family, like Orsin, was unable to sleep easily knowing he would depart today. Torben blinked blearily as Grunin moved around the table serving the food.

It was quiet. There was a hint of expectation in the air but Orsin fought it off, choosing instead to store up this moment of peace and togetherness with his family. It would carry him through the cold days of his Trial, and feed the flame of his determination, reminding him what he was fighting for.

What all Fursja fought for.

"Eat up," Grunin said quietly. "This is the best meal you'll have in a long while."

"Indeed," Ljorn chimed in. "So show some appreciation."

"Thank you mudor," they chorused.

"How long is the journey to the wall again?" Torben asked, perking up a bit more as he ate.

"Two days," Ljorn answered. "You can get there faster moving at speed, but the caravan with your cohort will move at a more sedate pace. You'll need to conserve your strength, after all." The older Fursja smiled, and if it was a bit forced, none of his family dared to mention it. "You want to be at your best when you do to face the Herd."

"We will be," Orsin said firmly.

Torben glanced at him, eyes widening just a bit in surprise. Orsin wasn't usually quite so vocal in his certainties. But Orsin knew what their parents needed to hear, and he said it. He said it firmly enough, and strongly enough, that they had to believe it.

"Indeed," Grunin said firmly. "Now, finish up, all of you. We should begin walking towards the caravan staging grounds now."

Orsin and Torben nodded, rising to fetch their packs and gear while Grunin cleaned up the remains of breakfast. There weren't many. Orsin and Torben knew the value of storing up a good meal before lean times.

Then they left. Orsin turned back and looked once more at the tall, blue granite longhouse that had been his home as long as he could remember. Cheery yellow light glowed from the windows. Most houses kept small lights glowing throughout the grey season, to chase away the gloom.

Orsin smiled. It was a good sight. Then he turned to follow Torben and their parents, already striding away toward their destination.

Grunin and Ljorn accompanied them, walking in front of them chatting amiably, of simple, mundane things. Orsin and Torben followed quietly, listening. In the blink of an eye they had passed through Velegard to the assembly point where Orsin and Torben's cohort were gathering. Friends and family gathered all around, and a sombre closeness dominated the assembly.

There was joy here, but it was fierce and guarded. Everyone knew this may be the last time they saw their loved ones. And yet there was honor in the battle, and glory in the service to Weihlaris and to the world, so there was little sadness.

An honor guard of seasoned Fursja warriors was assembled to escort them. These older warriors were beyond regular active duty, but there was still might within their arms and determination showed in the grey of their muzzles.

"Form up!" The captain of the honor guard called out. "Prepare to depart!"

A swirl of activity followed those words as caravaners quickly checked the security of their goods and the readiness of their beasts. Families flurried into a final blizzard of farewells and whispered words. Orsin's family was no different.

"It's time. Goodbye my loves. Return safely to me." Grunin smiled and kissed each of them on the cheek.

"Weihlaris watch over you," Ljorn said.

Orsin said his farewells quickly, quicker even than Torben, which surprised him. His adoptive brother had talked of little else for months, yet now that it came time to depart he lingered with their mudor and vador, storing up the moment like it was fat for the lean season.

"We shall be back," he said firmly. "We will make you proud and bring glory to the family. Praise Weihlaris."

"Praise Weihlaris," Torben echoed, paw still clasped with that of Grunin's.

The family shared one more small smile amongst them and then parted.

Orsin shouldered his pack and made sure *Muinnajhr* was secured at his side. Everything was in place, including his pouches of valendjahr (the one he always carried, the one his mudor had given him, and the spare his vador had prepared). He'd checked and double checked. There was nothing left to do.

The caravan was beginning to shift and move. Torben was at his side. It was time to go.

Orsin stood next to Torben, the two of them shifting slightly in the line of assembled warriors-in-training who would undertake the Trial this year. They stood assembled before the Bloody Gate, which had held back the might of the Herd for centuries without ever once having been breached. It rose high above them, several times the height of the tallest Fursja warrior. It was said that in days of old the Fursja counted giants amongst their allies, and that was one reason that Vaeggdor was so large, that giants had helped build it.

The journey to this place had been, if not easy, not at all arduous. Those who guided the hopefuls to the Trial knew the importance of conserving their strength. There would be little enough time for rest beyond the wall, and every moment that could be granted to prepare the young Fursja for what awaited them was given.

Orsin had hated the pace. His fur itched constantly with the need to be somewhere, to be doing something. But the journey was slow and uneventful and he was left with only his thoughts for company. That and Torben's and Bijask's abysmal jokes.

After they had arrived, Orsin had checked his gear. Then he had checked over Torben's gear. Then he had checked his once more.

Everything had been in order.

The cohort had been given the chance to sleep, but Orsin had been unable to. And judging by the muttering coming from the bedroll next to him, Torben hadn't been able to either. Orsin suspected none of his fellows had.

Now they stood assembled before the wall. It was a massive stone construction, rising meter upon meter into the air, and Orsin knew it was incredibly thick as well. Only a very few gates—like the one in front of him—pierced the might of Vaeggdor. They were titanic things, forged of the strongest metals known to the Fursja and reinforced with ingenuity and every blessing and spell the shamans could conjure. Runes all but burned into his eyes from the metal of the gates.

"Impressive," rumbled Sengetiid, the sight drawing an unusual number of syllables from the usually taciturn Fursja.

Orsin was more focused on what would happen next. Soon those gates would open and he, Torben, and the rest of the cohort would pass through in the lands of the Herd and the Trial would begin. Well, it would begin properly once they had journeyed for a day from the gate itself. Herd territory did not truly begin this close to the gate. The Fursja defended it too ferociously. It would not be a Trial this close to their might.

"Warriors of Weihlaris," Warlord Ursahre roared from the battlements above the gate, interrupting Orsin's thoughts. His voice, vast and rough, echoed easily down to their ears in spite of the vast distance and rolled across the tundra in all directions.

"For that is what you are. Warriors," he continued. "To simply stand here in the face of death, to defy the abominations the Herd had created, has made a part of itself, that requires the heart of a true warrior."

Ursahre began to pace back and forth, a short span along the battlements, never quite moving past the edges of the gate that loomed before them.

"Yet even with a heart filled with the Fury of Weihlaris himself, warriors fall. Some of you will fall, out beyond these gates. For our foe is a mighty one, and a cunning one."

A murmur sprang up amongst the assembled Fursja youth. That almost sounded like praise for the enemy. It was not something they had heard spoken before, not in the reaches of Svanhalor further from the great barrier wall, Vaeggdor.

"Yes," Ursahre answered the question no one dared shout to him. "I do respect the enemy. To disrespect a foe is to risk underestimating them. To risk overestimating them. Either course of action can get you killed. I say this not to fill your hearts with fear but to gird you with knowledge. The knowledge that may very well save your life, beyond these gates. And you know what lies beyond these gates! You have seen it, now. Heard the things that cry in the gloaming, hungry for fresh flesh."

They had. When the caravan had arrived yesterday they had been taken to the top of the battlements and allowed to gaze out into the wilds controlled by the Herd, the territory beyond the wall. Misshapen forms roamed the land, in large solitary strides and in quick, deadly packs. It was like they were just waiting beyond the gate, hungry for Fursja and somehow knowing that very soon those gates would open and the Herd beasts would have their chance for blood, fresh and hot and spurting from the vein if they could claim it.

"But know this also!" Ursahre's voice roared out, louder even than before, the purple mark of Weihlaris—the mark of a berserker—pulsing across his fur. "You are warriors of Weihlaris, questing for the favour of the god himself! You are a force to be reckoned with and you are a match for the horrors beyond this wall. The Fursja are the shield upon which the world has rested for centuries. Our blood and our sacrifice keep the other nations and peoples of this world safe, and happy, and living free. This is our duty and our honor. You are the latest in a long line of warriors to take up this standard, but you are not the least, and you shall not be the last!"

This time a roar burst form the mouths of the assembled Fursja. Orsin's fur danced and he felt like sparks were zipping from strand to strand. His heart pounded in his chest and he tasted sweet copper on his tongue. Beside him, Torben roared a battle cry and raised his war hammer high above his head. Several other Fursja in the line echoed the movement.

Above them, on the battlements, the grizzled veterans who defended the wall began to beat their weapons against shields, water barrels, weather shelters—whatever they could find nearby. A deep, pounding rhythm sprung up and tension began to mount as it pushed forward, demanding release.

"Warriors," Ursarhe roared, "are you ready to face your foe? Are you ready to seize glory before the eyes of Weihlaris? Are you ready to cull the Herd?"

Orsin and his assembled cohort roared their assent. Someone, he couldn't see who, suddenly broke and began running toward the gate. Quickly, the rest of the assembled Fursja began charging after the leader.

"To battle! Blood and glory!" Warlord Ursahre cried, raising Valaharion defiantly to the sky.

The gates were flung open wide as the assembled Fursja roared their defiance to the death which waited outside their walls.

 CHAPTER 5

Orsin charged forward, his brethren around him. If there had been more light in the wintry gloom, it would have flashed off their weapons, all fresh and newly forged, sharp and eager for their first taste of blood. Sharp, cold air bit at the back of his throat, crisp and fresh, though soon enough the tang of copper and the cloying sweetness of Herd rot would surround them.

The tundra beneath their paws was slick with frost. Were the Fursja not so well suited to their arctic home it might have made the terrain treacherous. But the heat of battle was more than a match for any nibble of frost that might try to make its way past the innate Fursja resistance to cold.

Torben was charging forward next to him. They moved, shoulder-to-shoulder almost, hammer in Torben's hand, axe in Orsin's. As one they roared defiance to the Herd.

And the Herd answered. Beasts of all kinds boiled out of the low hills beyond the wall. Lesser Herd beasts, all of them, but they were no less dangerous for that fact.

And what Baron would be this close to Vaeggdor, let alone something like a Prince? If there had been one of those monstrosities so near to their lands it would be the full Fursja army charging across the tundra, not Orsin and his cohort.

Orsin's eyes were quick and the lessons his father, the might-have-been skald, drilled into him with many many tales beside the firelight over the winter nights of the past several years allowed him to quickly pick out his foes. While no two Herd beasts were the same, the disease that created them mutating them all in strange and different ways, certain patterns repeated. There was a ruthless efficiency to the things, and successful changes—deadly mutations—persisted.

The larger beasts were easier to pick out first. Orsin spotted several *streidnirs*, massive beasts twice as tall as the average Fursja, with eight legs that gave them a scuttling movement and almost impossibly fast reflexes. They had massive horse-like heads filled with razor-sharp fangs and faceted growths for eyes that made it impossible to sneak up on them as they could see in all directions.

There were also lanky, sleek things like giant cats with hyper-extended legs. They could cover vast distances and their persistent roaming had earned them the name *rangers*. They were relentless and cunning, and their natural colouring shifted, allowing them to become almost invisible as they stalked their favorite prey: Fursja.

Between the larger beast, smaller packs of things roamed. The remains of what once had been loyal pets such as hunting hounds and wild canines like wolves and foxes. Their similar mutations brought them together into a hive mind that allowed them to cut down foes with ferocious efficiency. Great patches of fur fell from these, replaced with a pulsating, roiling mess of boils and sores that leaked a virulent green pus, highly infectious to the touch. The rotten fangs in their mouths were sharp, and could drive deep into Fursja skin where they would break off and slowly dig themselves deeper into the flesh of their own volition, seeking a vital organ to puncture and infect.

Orsin and his cohort began the battle as a tight formation, charging forward and cutting into a pack of the smaller Herd beasts and sliding through them like a hot knife through butter.

Bladed and blunt weapons flashed and Herd beasts keened in agony. Fur and flesh parted and gouts of black ichor stained the white tundra all around them. Against the assembled might of the cohort, a single pack stood not a chance.

Orsin spotted Bijask and Sengetiid fighting together with Tharsuld, another young Fursja Orsin had met only briefly the night before. Together the trio methodically dismantled a group of herd-twisted wolf-things, though the pack was so mangy and rotted it would have scarce been a threat to a single one of the warriors. Still, they worked well together, an efficient machine of death.

But Orsin had an ally of his own to fight with. Torben fell into an easy rhythm with him. His hammer fell with ringing blows, stunning those it did not crush outright. Only the largest of the pack beasts could withstand even a glancing blow from Torben;'s mighty arm.

Orsin's axe glimmered and flashed, slicing with lethal efficiency into the opening left by Torben's slower blows. The metal of the axe head cleaved through the spine of one of the smaller fox-like creatures, sending long streams of entrails spiralling out into the frosty air. Black ichor splattered across Orsin's fur and the ground beneath their feet became increasing dark with spilled vital fluids.

They charged forward before the battlefield could become mire, however. There were more and more Herd beasts pouring out of the nearby hills, drawn by the sound and scent of battle. Mindless, they threw themselves at the Fursja.

The cohort began to draw apart, individual Fursja chasing choice targets and generally following the call of the Trial, which demanded they separate and stand on their own for battle. Small clumps remained, however. Close friends, family members, those used to working together as a cohesive unit, all of these remained, gathering kills with greater speed and efficiency. There was no need to sprint off alone immediately. The Trial would not begin properly for a given Fursja until they were a day's journey away from the wall.

Torben and Orsin remained together, though they had struck out further to the northwest than the rest of the cohort. They had just dispatched the last of a pack, Torben's hammer caving in its skull sending grey-and-black brain matter spraying across the frozen ground. In that moment, when they were catching their breath, the streidnir struck.

A long, clawed leg lashed out as the thing galloped past, drawing a thin line of blood across Orsin's shoulder. He roared in rage and pain, lashing out with his axe, but the damned thing was too fast and evaded his blow.

Torben roared a challenge and the thing answered with a shrieking neigh-like sound. The Fursja warrior whirled his hammer to fling the last of the brain and viscera from it. Orsin grimaced at the stinging fire from the wound in his shoulder and gripped the haft of his axe more firmly.

When it charged again he would be ready.

Charge it did, leaping into the air and dashing down the hill to strike at the two Fursja again. But this time they were ready. Orsin's axe flashed, and when the streidnir leapt aside to avoid it Torben's hammer struck, slamming into the knee of its left foreleg with a solid crunch and sending the thing tumbling head over claws across the frost. Roaring in fury, Torben's other paw lashed out and seized the ankle of the wounded leg and with a mighty twist and heave, tore the foreleg free from the crushed knee and sending a glimmering arc of black ichor cascading through the air.

The streidnir screamed in fury and rose to its legs once more. It had seven remaining. The loss of one would slow it, but came nowhere near to incapacitating it.

Orsin didn't wait for it to move again. He was already charging, Torben close behind. Orsin slashed at the thing, forcing it to scramble back, and Torben followed, wild swings of his hammer making the thing flinch back in an attempt to protect its remaining limbs. It was cunning enough to know that Torben had hurt it, that he was a threat.

That meant it underestimated Orsin. The streidnir was so busy keeping its legs away from Torben that it forgot to guard its belly. Orsin watched, and as soon as he saw his chance he seized it, his axe flashing into the gap left by those scrambling legs and slicing a long deep line across the thing's abdomen.

A great steaming pile of entrails erupted from the beast's belly, almost seeming to smoke in the frigid arctic air. The streidnir neighed in fury, mad with bloodlust and hate. It scrambled to throw itself at them once more, it's seven remaining legs clawing at and becoming entangled in its own guts, ripping further and further lengths of them from its body.

Torben's hammer swung, a roundhouse blow that took the thing in the temple and knocked its head to one side. Orsin was ready, and when the neck was exposed he lashed out with Muinnajhr. The axe slid easily into the beast's throat, parting the flesh and sending vast gouts of black blood pumping from its jugular. The axe slid so deep within the neck of the beast that flashes of white from the bone of the streidneir's spine was visible.

The head flopped back, hanging loose and a wheezing gurgle issued forth from the gap as the thing tried to loose a death cry. Wet bubbles of blood burst in the gaping hole as its legs spasmed and split the entrails entrapping them.

Orsin didn't wait. He stepped close and brought his axe down again, fully severing the head from the body. Torben stepped up next to it and pulverised it for good measure. You could never be too careful with Herd beasts. Some had strange mutations which gave them horrifying abilities, even in seeming death.

"Tend that wound," Torben said. "I'll stand guard. Better to catch it early, whatever it is."

Orsin glanced around them to make sure there were no other nearby enemies before nodding and retrieving his pouch of valendjahr and crushing a small pinch of the herbs and massaging them into the wound. That should stop any potential herd infection.

After stowing the pouch safely once again, Orsin glanced around. There were few herd beasts in their immediate area, and most of the nearby trash had been soundly dealt with by the rest of his cohort. Now, the Fursja were drifting away, some faster than others. Orsin spotted some minor injuries, but no dead or fallen.

A good start, he thought.

"Time to head out," Torben said, his voice reaching out and snagging Orsin's attention. "Be well, brother."

"Be well," Orsin answered. "Weihlaris guide your hand in battle."

"I'll see you when we're both standing at home, covered in glory." Torben grinned and then began to carefully clean his hammer.

"See you." Orsin clapped his brother on the shoulder and squeezed tight, saying with that single gesture all the things his tongue was not nimble enough to speak right now.

Torben reached up and squeezed his paw in return. They stood there for a long moment, connected and communicating wordlessly, before Orsin's paw returned to his side and Torben went back to meticulously cleaning his hammer.

Orsin took one last look over his shoulder at the vast expanse of the wall that was Vaeggdor, behind which his people lived and prospered. The vast gate he had charged through was shut once more. Now, it was his turn to be that wall, to be the shield behind which his people sheltered.

The wilderness called and Orsin answered, not looking back again.

Torben watched as his brother disappeared behind a small rise. He waited three more breaths and then judged it was safe enough to follow. It was easy enough. Orsin wasn't bothering to hide his tracks yet.

There were many restrictions placed upon those who underwent the Trial. First and foremost, of these was that they complete it on their own. It was a test of self-reliance and a measure of strength in the eyes of Weihlaris. A hopeful berserker must fight alone to be properly judged.

But there was a lot of room in the margins, there. Torben had spoken with the shamans. He had spoken with them a great deal about the rules of the Trial, and the will of Weihlaris, of what was expected and allowed and what was not. The shamans took it for piety, and for preparedness.

And it was, to a degree. But it was also Torben looking for any ways in which he could do everything he could to ensure his brother came home, safe and whole, without spoiling his hopes of becoming a berserker and gaining Weihlaris's blessing.

Torben wouldn't interfere with the Trial. He would never cross the will of Weihlaris like that. But he could still aid his brother from the fringes, could watch over him from a distance as he slept and pick off any Herd curs that might nip at his heels.

So long as he didn't get too close.

Chapter 6

Small tendrils of vapour rose from Orsin's nostrils as he took deep breaths in and out. The tundra air around him was sharp with the cold, and fresh. Well, mostly fresh. He was encroaching on Herd territory and the sickly-sweet scent of rot was beginning to grow.

Orsin had been taught to recognise the scent, in many of its variations. There had been excursions to the wall as part of his training, to remote and desolate bits of tundra where pieces of defeated Herd beasts could be brought and held without fear of the infection held within them spreading. His nose was tuned to the cut-grass and copper smell of the whinging little canines and to the honey and vomit scent of the larger, cat-like rangers. There were many others, of course, though it was impossible to bring back specimens of every kind of Herd beast. Not only was there an infinite variation in their gross and aberrant mutations, but some of them were too dangerous to bring even that near to Fursja civilisation. Anything of Baron rank or above was far to virulent to risk bringing near, even for purposes of training.

Those scents—Baron, Prince, and Queen, the rest of the Herd nobility—those he knew only by description. He simply had to hope that he recognised them in time. Though if his instructors were correct, he would know simply by the sheer *intensity* of the smell. If he was gagging from the strength of it, he'd know he faced a foe truly worthy of respect.

Orsin didn't expect to encounter such a foe this far from the depths of Herd territory, however. They rarely ranged so far outside of their stronghold, unless they were up to something or they were making a concerted attempt at felling the wall. Such an event had not occurred in Orsin's lifetime, however.

The only flecks of green in the wide expanse of the scrubby, frosted tundra was Orsin's eyes. His gaze ranged across the horizon, seeking any hint of movement. For a moment the thought he saw a faint flicker of something, trailing along behind in the direction he had travelled from the wall, but Orsin dismissed that as a threat. The territory nearby to the Vaeggdor had been largely cleansed by his cohort. If there was something back there it was likely a reindeer or other large animal simply foraging for food now that the dominant predators had cleared the area. For a few days at least.

Orsin took another deep breath. The scent of rot was stronger from ahead, and he continued on that direction, working further north and west from the place he had come through the wall. Herd territory was largely in that direction, he knew. He and his cohort would travel closer, and deeper, as they sought blood and glory.

As he went he foraged, as he had been taught. The tundra held a few resources for the canny, and to make his supplies stretch as far as possible, Orsin took advantage of every one he could find. He scraped two pawfulls of lichen off the side of a stone. It tasted of petrichor and bitter herbs. A couple hours later he spotted slim grey spears of vegetation rising in a small patch. Digging, he found a small grouping of tender bulbs. They crunched between his fangs as he gobbled them down and made his tongue burn with the icy heat of them. He enjoyed sucking in breast breaths and feeling the cold take fire on his tongue.

But the real treasure was found when he was rooting beneath several large, loose stones for small insects or grubs. Instead, he found a rare delicacy. As he lifted the rock, a sharp, citrusy odor rose to meet his nostrils. There! A large glob of glutinous orange substance was growing in a small pocket of earth. He reached out with his claws and delicately lifted it up. It came away in long, stringy tendrils and when he placed it on his tongue it fizzled with a pleasant and astringent flavour. Djintonn fungus. Delicious.

Orsin licked his jowls as he continued on feeling very well fed and pleased not to have broken into his supplies yet. Food would get more and more scarce the closer he came to Herd territory, so the longer he could put off digging into what he had brought with him, the better. Once that was gone all he would be able to rely on would be the large layer of fat he'd built up as part of his preparations for the Trial and what little he could find in Herd territory that might be untainted.

A flicker of movement caught his attention from ahead, in the small crevice between two slight rises in the landscape. Orsin immediately froze and sniffed deeply. The wind was at his back, however. Whatever lurked ahead was well concealed from his nose.

Excitement flared through Orsin; it felt like small spikes were driving themselves into his jaw and the knuckles of his paws. His grip tightened around the haft of his axe and he moved forward again, senses tuned to the environment around him.

He was a Fursja in the first flush of his prime, ready to prove himself. He had whetted his appetite for battle the day before when crossing through the gate and now he was ready—eager, even—to delve into the Trial and prove himself.

He had trophies to collect!

The rises drew nearer. There was a shadowed gap between the two, what looked to be a well worn path that reindeer or other tundra herbivores used regularly.

There might even be a stream nearby. Orsin took a slow deep breath and scented water on the air. Good. He'd be able to slake his thirst and clean himself after he slaughtered whatever Herd beast was lurking nearby.

Because it was definitely a Herd beast. He could smell it. The scent of rot. Not the small canines. Something larger, he thought.

Orsin crept forward, deceptively quick and quiet in spite of his massive frame. He kept his breaths deep and steady, only two small tendrils of vapour steaming in the cold air to betray the fact that he was breathing. The haft of his axe was firm in his paw.

As he drew nearer to the trail that cut between the two small rises, more flickers of movement became visible. It was a reindeer. Orsin could see the tawny hide and caught flashes of antler. Now that he was closer, the coppery scent of blood was evident, in spite of the wind being against his back.

The smell of rot was still there as well. Growing? Orsin squinted. Something had savaged the reindeer's left foreleg. It was hobbling along, moving slowly. Greenish-black foam bubbled at its mouth and there was a mad glint in its eyes.

Some other herd-tainted creature had clearly attacked it. Judging by the wounds—long, rent-like slashes in the hide of the leg—it wasn't anything that started out as a canine. Maybe it had been one of the felinoid rangers.

The reindeer let out a groaning, guttural moan and staggered to one side. It's infected leg could no longer support its weight, liquifying and sloughing off as it was from the virulent disease consuming its flesh. As Orsin watched, skin and flesh slid away, leaving only a small, whipcord wrapping of muscle around bare white bone. Twisting, spiralling growths began to force their way out of the bone, spars of off-white clear even in the pale grey light of the season. Orsin suspected they would be razor-sharp if he were unfortunate enough to end up on the receiving end of a blow.

The reindeer's breathing was laboured now, and the green-black pus off the infection was beginning to show on the antlers. Soon they too would start sprouting spikes and thorns of bone.

Orsin's had tightened on the haft of his axe. It wasn't worthy enough a foe to be a trophy, but he might as well put the beast out of its misery, spare it of an interminable, tortured existence as a member of the Herd.

He braced, then sprinted forward. His powerful legs closing the distance between himself and his target in mere moments. The reindeer, caught up in the torment of the infection, didn't notice him coming and didn't even react as Orsin's axe swept down and neatly parted its head from its neck. A second blow severed the most infected leg, followed by a series of brutal and efficient strokes that neatly butchered the infected deer and reduced it to its component parts. Orsin didn't stop until he'd cracked the rib cage and made certain the heart was cut out.

It didn't seem to be infected, but even so Orsin tossed it aside. He was not so desperate now that he would risk eating tainted meat. He'd taken no wounds; he'd moved too fast to. He'd clean up in the spring and then—

Suddenly three parallel lines of pain exploded across his back. A lithe form flickered in and out of his peripheral vision. A ranger! Orsin had been so intent on the suffering of the reindeer that he hadn't checked carefully enough to find the predator that had initially inflicted to the wound!

Orsin roared a challenge to the beast and whirled his axe around in a defensive pattern. The thing was fast, he needed to try and deter it.

The ranger yowled, a deep rough noise that echoed form the back of its throat. It darted to the left, but was forced to dodge away from Orsin's blade. When it tried the right next time it met the same resistance.

The thing hissed at him and its barbed tail lashed in displeasure.

Orsin charged, bellowing a war cry. The thing scrambled back, easily darting out of the way of the powerful blows of his axe. Orsin grunted angrily.

He needed to slow it down. But he couldn't land a blow. This ranger was young and smart, meaning it was fast and cautious. Well, if it wouldn't come within arms reach, there were other options.

The tundra was scattered with rocks, many of them broken and sharp-edged enough to be weapons in their own right if used properly. He leaned down and grasped a moderate sized stone with his paw. The ranger eyed him suspiciously, but continued to stalk around him, looking for an opening.

Orsin watched carefully, then, when he was sure of the thing's path, whipped the rock as hard as he could at it. The stone whirred through the air and collided with the ranger's shoulder with a dull crack.

The ranger screamed in rage and pain, stumbling backward. Orsin didn't give it a chance to flee. He charged forward swinging his axe in a vast overhead blow, trusting the pain and confusion to stall his opponent long enough for his axe to land.

It did. The head of Orsin's weapon buried itself deep in the rangers skulls. The cat-like beast spasmed, lashing out wildly with its claws and forcing Orsin to leap back or be disemboweled. There was no way he was risking being without his weapon, however, so he pulled it free with a vicious tug, sending grey matter flying through the air.

Large globs of the stuff landed with a wet plop on the frosty tundra and began to smoke in the chill.

Quiet fell once more. This time Orsin carefully checked for more enemies before relaxing. When he was sure he was safe, he gently lowered his axe.

His body screamed at him in pain.

Orsin grimaced and reached around behind himself to apply the herbs to the wounds on his back. He wasn't certain he managed to coat the whole of each slash, having no way to see his own back, but he was confident in the potency of the herbs to stave off infection. For good measure he offered a prayer to Weihlaris and consigned what would have been his trophy to claim to a small shrine he erected. There would always be more glory to be had, so long as he survived. He could afford to forgo this in favour of some divine goodwill.

Besides, a ranger—dangerous as it was—well well known. A moderate threat at most.

He was after larger prey.

Chapter 7

Orsin growled and massaged the deep tissue of his thigh. That last battle had been rough. He'd escaped without any cuts or loss of blood, but his whole body felt deeply bruised. Whatever that thing had been before the Herd took it over, it had been monstrous when warped by mutation. It stood on two legs like a Fursja, but was two metres higher and even more heavily muscled. Grotesquely so. It had slammed Orsin into rock after rock before the Fursja warrior had finally managed to drive his axe deep enough into the thing's neck to kill it.

That had been two days ago. By Orsin's estimation, at least two weeks had passed since he moved through the gate and into the tundra beyond the wall, beyond the lands the Fursja controlled. In that time he'd not seen a single other of his kind. It was strange, but it was also peaceful, in a way. There was no one else to rely on out here save for himself. It was simultaneously both sobering and freeing. Orsin felt a fierce exultation at the thought. This was his Trial! He would prove himself before his people and before their god.

He had certainly made a good start of it. After he and Torben had parted ways, he'd faced an increasing stream of smaller Herd beasts and the occasional big bruiser, like the one that had thrown him around so energetically a couple of days ago. He had trophies to prove it, as well.

There was the growing network of small scars mapping the course of his Trial across his body. Many of his wounds were small, and would easily have been lost in his fur had the special herbs he carried, the work of the shamans, and the hand of Weihlaris not left a mark where they had been used. In each place he applied them, disinfecting the wounds and driving the threat of Herd infection from him, his wounds gave way before fresh, supple skin and sinew while also changing the color of his fur, so that any who looked upon him could see how he had fought.

And were that not enough proof, Orsin also carried a small collection of trophies harvested from the worthy Herd beasts he defeated. They were dusted carefully with herbs to kill any lingering infection and rolled tightly in his pack so there was no risk he might prick his paw on them and unknowingly infect himself.

Orsin's mind drifted back over the bootable battles of the past days. He carried five ranger claws with him now, one from each of the beasts he had slain. There was the large incisor of the bruiser he'd defeated two days ago. Two pointed fragments of horn or thorn from mutated reindeer, the barbed tail of a beast with too many legs and a mane of spines around its neck—why was almost everything warped by the herd so *sharp*?

Still, it was a good start. Orsin couldn't help but feel a bit of dissatisfaction, however. While the foes he had faced so far had been worthy ones, none were truly worthy of a good tale. Did that make them less worthy in the eyes of Weihlaris? The shamans would say any victory over the herd was worthy and would contribute to passing his Trial, but did Orsin simply wish to pass? Or did he want to seize a massive pawful of glory? To truly win the approbation of his god and the admiration of his fellow Fursja?

The wind rose around him, sharp and biting, like the breath of his god, but it carried no answers upon it. Orsin squinted and drove himself forward on powerful legs, heading deeper into Herd territory. There was more killing to be done, more glory to be won.

The landscape was still mostly flat, with gentle rises here and there. He was far from the mountains that bordered the southern reaches of Herd territory, and not yet deep enough to encounter some of the weirder constructions the beasts had erected. Or so the tales said.

This had been Fursja land, once. There had been villages, even cities, that existed and prospered out here on the plains, before the coming of the Herd. Orsin kept his eyes peeled for any he might come across. While this close to Fursja territory they had likely already been stripped clean by previous Trial cohorts or regular Fursja patrols ranging out to suppress the beasts, there might still be something to reclaim.

Orsin liked the idea of bringing back something that the Herd had taken, and restoring it to Fursja paws. Someday, they would take back the entirety of this land from those abominations, and drive them fully from the earth. His grip tightened on the haft of his axe and Orsin felt his pace increase, as if his body itself hungered for battle and could not wait for him to direct it.

Something caught his eye, a dark smudge against the otherwise pale expanse of white and grey and green. It was slightly further north of his present course, so Orsin adjusted, moving toward it while also keeping a slight rise between himself and whatever lurked there.

He reached the rise in no time and reined in his body. Charging in had its place but he was still a lone Fursja and the Herd bred terrible beasts. Heedless, reckless warriors were often dead warriors. Taking deep breaths offered no hint as to what was ahead, aside from the sickly-sweet scent of rot, fresh but growing more putrescent.

Something of the Herd had definitely been here recently, if it was not still lurking just the other side of the small hill.

Orsin moved on soft paws, quick and sure, cresting the rise cautiously until he could peer down and get a proper look at the thing which had caught his attention. He quickly countered eight limbs, all askew, and adrenaline spiked remembering the massive horse-like beast he and Torben had fought near the gate of Vaeggdor.

But the thing didn't move. And Orsin's mind caught up with what his eyes were seeing. It wasn't one creature with eight limbs, it was two with four apiece. Was was a herd beast, yes, a ranger, but the other form was Fursja! The two were locked together in a death-grip.

Neither moved. Though there was something chillingly familiar in the shape of the fallen Fursja. He shifted slowly around to try and get a better view, axe held close in case it was all part of some Herd ruse.

Then he got the view he was looking for.

Orsin went still. He knew that form. He'd seen that face before, so many times.

It was Bijask. Rumbling, jovial Bijask who had stolen a sip of three-honey mead but given it to his father instead of keeping it for himself. Cunning, punning Bijask, who told the raunchiest jokes with the most innocent and sweetest of faces, which just made them all the funnier. Bijask, who he had known since they were both cubs.

Bijask, whose eyes not stared glassy and unseeing towards the sky above.

Orsin drew nearer, slowly, his guts churning. Part of him wanted to rush forward, to see if there was anything he could do tho save his friend. Another, wiser and sadder, part of him knew there was nothing to be done, and that he needed to be cautious. Many were the tales of reckless Fursja, caught in the powerful grip of grief, who had rushed to a fallen comrade only to find that it was only a husk, the insides consumed by a lurking Herd beast that had already feasted and grown fat on the innards.

The thought that one of those abominations could burst out of the remains of happy, hopeful Bijask loomed over him, but as he approached nothing happened. There was a rich green foam around Bijask's snout and Orsin scented the pure, sharp scent of shamanistic herbs.

The fallen Fursja must have started stuffing them down his mouth even as he died in hopes of staving off a fate worse than death: becoming a host for the Herd disease.

Orsin sent a prayer winging to Weihlaris even as he began systematically disassembling the body. There was no pyre, here. No way to be completely certain some bit of Herd infection wouldn't persist and eventually warp the remains of his friend into something dreadful.

No.

Orsin's paw tightened around the haft of his axe. No. He would not allow that.

With reverent efficiency he dismembered the corpse, and carried each piece away in a different direction, erecting a small cairn of stones over them after digging shallow graves for each. Though the soil here was warmer, it was still too cold and hard to dig deeply. Hopefully the stones and the earth would trap anything that might arise from the corpse, keep it pinned and close until it died, painfully starving from within from a lack of sustenance.

It was a pitiful, petty revenge, but it was the best Orsin could hope for, if any of the disease did still linger within the remains of Bijask.

The head he carrried to the top of a small rise to bury, hauling the largest stone he could find with him. He turned it to face southeast, back towards home, and etched the rune for peace upon the stone after he set it in place.

It was all the rest he could offer.

He stood for a moment, looking back in the direction of home. Bijask would not see it again. The other Fursja had failed the Trial and been deemed unworthy of the Mark of Weihlaris. That did not make him an unworthy warrior, though. That did not make him an unworthy Fursja. He had given his life in the hopes of protecting the world. It was a noble death.

It was a noble death, Orsin repeated to himself.

Bijask should be alive. He should be home, warm near a raging fire, drinking ale and telling the worst jokes in the best way. Orsin would never again hear that great, braying laugh. He would never again stagger under the weight of the other Fursja, as they walked home after a night of revelry.

Bijask always ate too much and drank too much. At least his life was well lived, if it was to end so soon.

So unjustly.

Orsin felt a deep, rumbling fury spark to life in the pit of his stomach. He turned his back to the view towards home and looked deeper into Herd territory. The terrain was becoming more broken, harder to navigate. Small tufts of unnatural greenery appeared, like oases in a desert, across the white and grey expanse of the natural tundra.

The abominations warped the very earth around them. It was not enough to twist flesh and subdue the spirit, no, they had to prone the very earth itself. The earth that now embraced the cold remains of Bijask.

The spark of fury in his stomach flared into a fire. It felt as if every strand of fur on his body suddenly shivered and went sharp.

The enemy was out there. Right in front of him, even if they were currently hidden away.

He would find them. He would root out the abominations and rip them to shreds so small they could never again rise to hurt anyone or anything he loved.

Orsin's feet began to move beneath him without his consciously willing it. His legs ate up the ground at a terrifying pace, driven forward by the blast furnace of rage in his heart. He moved in a straight line, heading for the nearest patch of unnatural greenery. Where the landscape was so warped there had to be Herd beasts. There had to be prey.

And there was. As Orsin neared the small stand of twisted evergreens that were clawing their way up from the frozen ground like dead fingers clawing out of a grave, a small pack of arctic foxes, irrevocably twisted by the Herd disease, spilled out from amongst the wizened trunks and darted toward him, yipping and howling.

The foe had presented itself!

Orsin roared in fury and charged forward. His fallen brethren would be avenged! The herd would pay and pay dearly for this!

CHAPTER 8

Orsin huffed, sending a great plume a vapour out into the chilly air. What was disconcerting was that it was not nearly so chilly as it should be. It was cold, yes, but also dank and wet in a way that felt alien to his skin. Moisture crawled along his fur, the thick fog all around dewing him with droplets of water. Slowly, the droplets froze and his fur constantly cracked and crackled with breaking and falling ice.

He had tracked the pack of arctic foxes across the tundra, picking off stragglers as they ran. Relentlessly he pursued them, fury hot and bitter in his mouth. They were small foes, Herd beasts hardly worth the effort of hunting them down, barely worth a spit of glory.

Orsin didn't care. Bijask's dead eyes stared at him whenever he closed his own. His friend deserved blood in recompense for his death. And Orsin would make sure the Herd paid it.

He'd followed them close, senses primed like swooping hawks to catch and exploit any sign of weakness, to stop any hope of escape. The mutated fox-beasts fled before him, yipping and howling in distress. Blood and gobbets of flesh stained his fur but he had taken no wounds so Orsin did not bother to slow and clean himself, nor to apply the warding herbs he carried.

The fog had made things more difficult. It rose up from the ground as the heat increased, fat, coiling tendrils of the stuff clinging to him as he moved through it. Small eddies and whorls betrayed the dashing movements of the foxes, enough for him to continue the hunt, though the rate at which he killed the vile things slowed.

His fury did not abate, however. It was hot and coppery on his tongue. So Orsin kept going.

When the first tree suddenly loomed out of the fog—which had by then risen above Orsin's head— his head nearly slammed into it, reducing it to splinters. His warrior's instincts were on high alert, however, so Orsin nimbly dodged the vegetative assassin.

But it was enough to snap him out of the red haze he had been running in. Trees? Here on the tundra? That was unnatural, and if it was unnatural it meant there was a Herd connection.

Orsin lashed out with his axe, the metal of his weapon slicing neatly into the back and driving deep into the woody flesh beneath. Thick, black ichor began to ooze from the wound and Orsin swore he could almost hear the thing shriek in pain and hatred. The branches above his head quivered and suddenly sprouted a length of thorns along them, the stiletto-sized things exploding into view with concussive force.

A wave of heat washed over him. The trees! They were the source. Somehow the Herd virus had infected them and turned them into, what? A heat source? Traps? Weapons? They weren't mobile like the herd beasts. Was this some kind of defense?

Orsin had heard tales of strange clubs of vegetation. He knew they grew bigger, wilder, and more frequent the further one pressed into Herd territory, and that many dangerous creatures used them for shelter and food, but he'd not heard of this before.

Was there some link between the twisted vegetation and the way the land changed? Could there be? The thought that the Herd was capable of exerting so much control over the land itself—land that once was entrusted to the Fursja to protect—sickened him.

He felt a deep growl rise up from within his chest. His axe lashed out again. Once. Twice. Thrice. Then he sheared completely through the trunk of the mutated tree and it fell crashing to the ground, black ichor spouting like a fountain from the ragged trunk where it had once stood.

The howls and yips of the fox pack he had been pursuing seemed to mock at his ears. Orsin whirled around, squinting through the fog to try and pinpoint his enemies. After a moment his eyes adjusted enough to make out the ghostly boles of several more trees. It looked like he was near the edge of a whole copse of the things.

But the fog still clouded much of his vision. He sniffed deeply, hoping his other senses might compensate. Then a chill clawed its way up his spine.

There was something else here in the trees.

Orsin paused. Those hadn't been howls of distress. Those had been howls of warning. Or calling.

A branch snapped with a sharp retort. Orsin flexed. That was no fox. Something large was moving through the trees. He glanced around him, trying to find the source of the sound. The fog made it difficult. But eventually he caught a glimpse of something moving, something large and sinuous.

A feral grin shoved its way to the forefront of Orsin's face. This was the biggest herd beast he'd seen yet. A worthy challenge for his skills, a worthy blood-price for poor, broken Bijask.

Orsin muttered a brief prayer and began creeping through the trees, attempting to stalk whatever it was that hid from him in the fog.

Sharp, yipping voices broke the silence. Orsin resisted the urge to growl. He had a sneaking feeling that the foxes were communicating his location to the larger thing. Too bad he hadn't slaughtered them all before getting to this place.

Carefully, he picked his way over the roots. It wouldn't do to trip and fall, exposing himself to attack. So he went carefully, his senses tuned all around him, seeking anything out of the ordinary.

Out of the ordinary. It took him a moment, but eventually Orsin's mind drew his attention back to the roots. They were growing in an unnaturally grid-like pattern. Something about it tugged at him, strangely familiar.

It looked like the paving stone pattern the Fursja used for their streets. The sight of that pattern, choked and warped by creeping Herd-growths, stopped him in his tracks, nausea surging up from his guts.

It was in that moment that the monster struck.

The beast lunged out of the woods to Orsin's left, jaws wide and tearing. It went straight for his hamstring and only Orsin's training and razor-sharp reflexes saved him from that crippling strike. He deflected the teeth with his axe but the metal rang as if striking stone and the edge of his weapon found no purchase and drew no blood.

Yipping, mocking barks echoed out of the fog and the trees.

Orsin could see his opponent now. It had the shape and the bearing of an arctic fox, all mockery and toothed grin, but it stood taller at the shoulder than Orsin did stretched to his full height, and had several large tails in place of the regular one. There were too many teeth, too sharp and took long in its elongated snout, and its claws were a deep and wicked red.

But the worse of it all were the eyes. They were deep and limpid pools, with a cunning and cruel intelligence sparkling within them. Those eyes beheld him and, Orsin felt, instantly knew far too much about him.

It was a Baron of the Herd. It had to be. It's size and speed, its strength and the look of intelligence in those eyes—all of these things combined to say that here was a ranking officer in the army of the enemy.

Orsin lashed out with his axe, great arcing blows that sped as fast as his muscles could propel them toward the beast. It grinned at him even as it dodged easily. Orsin roared a battle cry and redoubled his efforts.

How dare that thing mock him? It was like the grin in front of him was laughing at not only him, but also the cold and lonely body of Bijask, at the nation of the Fursja, crouched weak and afraid behind their silly wall. It was as if—Orsin shook his head.

Where were these thoughts coming from? They didn't feel like his own.

A yipping laugh, deep and resonant and full, careened off the trees around him as the Baron made a sound for the first time. Its tongue lolled out of its mouth and it watched as Orsin charged, only to nimbly dodge aside and drive a set of fangs like daggers into the Fursja's leg as he passed.

The wounds immediately began to burn and steam with the hissing acid of the venom on those fangs. Orsin's eyes bulged. He had thought he'd been inured to the touch of Herd venom, but this was orders of magnitude worse. His flesh immediately began to burn with a sick heat.

But he did not take a wound for nothing. As the thing slipped its fangs out of him, Orsin's axe whirled around, catching the giant fox on the shoulder and drawing a long line of black ichor.

The thing growled and fell back. The smaller arctic foxes around it suddenly began to whine and shriek and Orsin saw why in just a moment. The monster lashed out, catching one of the smaller foxes in its jaws and gulped it down with a great crunching of bones and spurting of vital fluids.

Black ichor painted its jowls as it smiled at him again. Orsin watched in horror as the wound he had inflicted on the thing's shoulder began to visibly writhe and knit itself closed. It was healing itself by consuming the lesser herd beasts!

Then it moved again, faster this time. Maybe consuming one of its own gave it a burst of energy, or it had been playing with him all this time, but those deadly fangs closed around Orsin again and again, catching both of his legs and his free arm at different points as the Fursja furiously scrambled to land some kind of killing or at least debilitating blow.

Even then, facing those odds, and that fight, Orsin's spirit was unbroken. He roared defiance in the face of the monstrosity and his axe whirled about him, a glittering arc of death which soon dripped black with the ichor of his foe.

But each time he came close to seriously wounding it, the Baron would dash off and gulp down another of the smaller foxes, restoring itself. Orsin felt himself tiring. The flame of his anger still burned but eventually the fuel would run out. If he had to face the Baron at less than peak condition, he wasn't certain he could prevail.

"Ff-ff-unnn. Ff-ff-urrrr-skaaa ff-un."

Orsin's blood froze in his veins as the Baron locked eyes with him and spoke, the words bitten off by those knife-like fangs. In all the tales he had heard, in all the advice given by the shamans and by older warriors, none had said anything about a Herd beast that could speak.

This was something new. Something dangerous. Orsin should kill it.

But his wounds were stinging. He was coming to the end of his endurance. Orsin could feel it. Exhaustion was starting to weigh down his limbs like leaden shackles.

But should he stay and fight or flee for now and return better prepared? It was an easy question. The Trial required he defeat as many Herd beasts as he could and to do that he needed to survive. He needed to escape, track this monster, figure out why and how it was like this, *then* kill it and make sure he lived long enough to return and warn his people that something new was brewing here in the Herdlands.

It was his duty.

Decision made, he wasted no time in looking for a safe avenue of retreat. He'd kill the beast if an opportunity presented itself, but that did not seem likely. There were still far too many of the little foxes.

Fortunately, he was not entirely on alien ground. Orsin's eyes raked across the paving stones. If this was truly once a Fursja settlement, and these stones laid by his ancestors, then—there! His eyes caught what they were hunting, a large, hexagonal stone set at what must have once been a crossroads.

He dashed for it, wounds steaming viridian in the fog. He didn't have time to waste, and he didn't have the energy to fight. So he ran for the stone.

Mocking laughter followed him.

"Rrrun, rrrun, furrr-skaaa! Rrrun ff-ff-ffun!"

The puncture wounds on his left leg screamed at him as he slid into place next to the stone, and his claws threatened to pull out of his paws entirely as he rammed them into the crevices, choked with centuries worth of dust and frost. He roared in anger and pain and his muscles bunched.

Nothing.

Orsin tried again. This was his only chance. His arms screamed in pain but the stone was more yielding than Orsin's will.

It shifted.

Orsin immediately dug his claws in deeper and hauled it away from the hole it was concealing. Immediately he dropped down into the ruins of what once had been the sewer beneath the town, yanking the stone back into place as he did. Mocking yips followed him as he stumbled quickly away down the tunnel.

His vision began to blur as his wounds stung, the pain of them lancing more and more deeply into his flesh as he walked. Orsin imagined he could feel the Herd venom gleefully eating its way into him. He had to deal with it, and soon.

A small alcove was the best he managed. He hauled himself into it, so at least nothing could sneak up behind him. He'd have to hope if danger came from one direction down the tunnel he could flee toward the other.

Orsin pulled out his pouch of herbs and began applying them to his wounds, spitting on the things and crushing them between his paws to make small pellets to shove wholesale into the punctures that dotted his legs and arm. Hopefully he found all of them.

There. That was the best he could do. Orsin's arms dropped to his sides, exhaustion and pain warring throughout his body. It was in Weihlaris's hands now. His eyelids drooped, and fitful, feverish slumber claimed him.

CHAPTER 9

"Wake up sleepyhead."

That was his mother's voice. Orsin opened his eyes, only to find himself at home, the longhouse rising warm and strong around him. Firelight flickered from the hearth but everyone else was asleep. His mother stood at her customary place, but shadows covered her. Orsin couldn't make out her face. It was her voice though, and it spoke again.

"It's time. Your Trial is at hand. You must hurry. Our masters are hungry."

Hungry? Masters?

Orsin pushed himself up from his bed. The room began to spin around him, a nauseating whirl that left streaks of color weeping at the edges of his vision. The shadowy form of his mother remained, however, a fixed point that drew closer to him even as everything else fell away.

Then she stepped into the light and Orsin felt his gorge rise. The thing wore his mother's face, yes, but it was a Herd monstrosity! Great gaping maws yawned where his mother's eyes once sparkled, and green venom hissed in the pits that had replaced them.

The thing that wore his mother's face reached for him, claws black with congealed blood and fresh ichor, but Orsin bellowed a denial and suddenly his axe was in his paw, swiping through the monstrosity.

The thing exploded into viridian mist, it's howling, hungry voice calling once more after him.

"Your masters are hungry..."

The fog cleared and Orsin found himself on the tundra once more, but everything was off. The perspective was all wrong. No. He realised. He was all wrong. He was seeing everything from the sight line of a cub! The tundra hadn't changed. He had.

Fear spiked within him. No cub was a match even for the beasts that ruled this place! He began to run, stifling the urge to cry for help. His little legs could not cover much ground however, and he quickly grew tired.

Shadows loped after him, long, dark things that changed their shape every time he so much as glanced at them. He tired, again and again, but each time some new horror would rise behind him and the fear would drive him on again. He couldn't think for the stench of it.

There was something behind him. He just knew it. For every step he took he heard another crunch the frosted ground behind him. If he sped up, it sped up. If he stopped, it stopped.

Finally, unable to stand it any longer, the cub that was also Orsin suddenly stopped and whirled around, eyes glinting, ready to face death like a Fursja warrior.

He blinked.

"Why were you running?" Torben asked him.

It was Torben as he had been as a cub. Chubby face and devilish eyes. There was honey stuck to the ends of his claws and he absently sucked on one as he looked at Orsin with confusion.

"I was trying to keep up with you, but you just kept running. You're going to leave me behind." Torben's voice was immeasurably sad.

It made Orsin think of the sea for some reason.

"No," he said, stammering, "no, I'd never leave you behind."

"You will." Giant tears welled up in Torben's eyes. "You'll leave me!"

"Never!" Orsin insisted.

He reached out to take his friend's paw, to reassure him that things would not change, that he would not leave him behind. He'd let Torben follow him to the end of Herd territory and beyond.

But when he took Torben's paw he was no longer Torben. The massive corpse of Bijask loomed over him, putrid and rotting, its various limbs somehow pulling themselves together with writhing tendrils of sentient disease, green and black and dripping.

Orsin stumbled back. His arms caught him, strong and full-grown once more. But his axe was not in his paw. It was buried in Bijask's chest, sinking into the cavity it had cracked open, pulled away from him by those tentacles of filth. They wrapped around the haft and pulled it inward, even as the edge of the blade split them again and again.

A deep, gurgling growl issued forth from the ragged stump that was Bijask's neck. Ponderously, one mangy arm rose to point behind Orsin. The claw at the end of his paw wiggled and fell off, a green maggot writhing at the end of the stump.

Orsin didn't look. He didn't want to look. As soon as he turned his back that thing might attack him.

But there was something in the hollows where Bijask's eyes used to dance. Orsin felt no sense of malice from the bones of his friend. And while the disease coursed through him, consuming what was left of him, he knew, instinctively, that the ghost of Bijask was whole, uncorrupted.

So Orsin turned.

The tundra stretched before him. A grey expanse of land rolled out before him, mirrored by a leaden sky above. At first that was all Orsin could see, but then small flecks of green began to grow.

They were nothing more than dots at first, so tiny he might have imagined them. But before his eyes they grew. Or perhaps he was flying and somehow drawing nearer and nearer to them and their growth was only the illusion of his motion.

The patches of green grew to small copses of trees and pockets of bog. Areas of denser and denser vegetation, thick with Herd corruption. Orsin felt the cold shiver, then break, a casualty to the monstrous, aberrant heat the Herd-infected plants pumped out into the nearby environment.

It was some kind of dome.

Orsin's eye hungrily took in every detail of the unnatural structure. If the proportions were correct, judging by how it rose above the trees it was a massive structure. It almost seemed more a natural mountain, low and rounded, than something that could have been created by any hands other than those of the gods. It's surface was faceted, like some kind of rough-cut gem still waiting the hand of a master to finish it into smooth planes. Along the edges, Herd-tainted greenery grew.

Perhaps that was how the Herd managed to construct it?

Orsin knew instinctively the Herd had created it. In fact, something deep within him whispered that it was home. That it would be his grave and his destiny.

He felt his veins burn with green fire, for a moment, and his heart stuttered under the strain.

The dome grew in front of his eyes. He drew nearer, the trees near to the dome rushing past and around him as he did so. Vast Herd beasts, all manner and kind, prowled around. Beasts he had never seen, nor imagined, things not spoken of in shaman's tales or even around the fire by the oldest of warriors.

No Fursja in living memory had gotten this close to the heart of Herd territory.

There was a sense of reverence within him for this place. Something deep in his guts writhed in obeisance to the royal presences he sensed within the dome.

This must be the place of the Herd Queen and the Princes that served her!

Orsin's stomach spasmed again and he coughed up a great gout of green blood. It stained his paws and he stared at them dumbly. The scent of Herd rot was strong.

Too strong.

He clenched his paws. No. He would not surrender to this thing. Not even here, in what he suddenly knew to be a dream. The Herd would not claim him.

The feeling of reverence shivered and withdrew, slightly, before coming roaring back. It screamed at him from inside his own mind. It demanded that he submit. His own flesh rippled and his vision went over green, as if he stared through a summer's puddle thick with scum.

No!

Orsin pushed back with all of his will. The image of the dome ahead of him shivered, then cracked. A great wailing shuddered up from his guts to the tip of his nose. His breath came hot and fast and his vision warred between the green-tinted sight that had been forced upon him and the blackness of oblivion.

"Come now, are you a cub or are you a Fursja warrior undergoing his Trial?"

It was his mother's voice again, but this time the apparition that appeared with it was whole, and exactly as he remembered her on that final day he had left home and family behind to embark upon the Trial.

"I am a warrior," he ground out, panting with the effort.

"Good. Then fight. Is it really that different? Whether the battlefield is in front of you or within you, it is still a battlefield and you are a warrior. You are far from helpless. You have more weapons at your beck and call then you can know."

Orsin gritted his teeth and envisioned the cleansing light of Weihlaris pumping through his veins, as hot as the fury of a god and strong as the foundations of the world.

He had to be dreaming. It was the most painful thing he could imagine. If it was real life the pain would definitely have been worse.

But he pressed on. Green vapor began to steam out his nostrils and he coughed again, more green. He redoubled his efforts. The results were the same.

He took one last deep breath and tried again. This time the green was chased with red. His body was expelling the infection!

The image of his mother gave him a proud look.

"We are Fursja, my son. We do not fall lightly. We fight the corruption with every breath in our bodies. *Now wake up!*"

Orsin's eyes snapped open. A layer of ice cracked and fell from his face. He must have panted greatly in his fevered sleep, the moisture from his units freezing to his fur. But now he felt fine. Stronger than ever, in fact.

He carefully checked the wounds left to him by the Baron. Every one he could find had healed over, marking his fur with a pattern of spots from all the punctures those teeth had left him with. Orsin growled. Each and every one of these wounds would be paid for. He'd take the cost out, with interest, from the hide of that beast, dangerous smart and capable of speech or no.

It was time to go hunting.

CHAPTER 10

The sharp edge of a stone, cold and unyielding, dug into Orsin's belly. The warrior would like little more than to shift and remove it, but he didn't dare. As soon as he did so the movement would give away his position to the group of Herd beasts below. And he wasn't ready for that.

No. Orsin had awoken from his fever with the conviction that something strange was going on out here. There was something he needed to understand so he could report back to his people. And to find out as much as he could, he was going to have to hunt these beasts, study their habits and understand what drove them. Because after the encounter with the fox-baron, it was clear that their behaviours were more than he had been led to believe.

Or the behaviours, like the bodies of the infected beasts themselves, were mutating into the most dangerous form they could find.

Which was why he watched the Herd beasts below for now, rather than charging directly at them. It looked like they had once been reindeer. They had the general shape, and the antlers replaced with thorns he had encountered before, but these specimens were absolutely massive. Each was easily three- or four-times the size of a normal reindeer.

They moved and hunted more like a pack of wolves, though. Orsin had been following them for hours, now. Up to this point, most of the Herd beasts he had encountered (except for the Baron) had seemed almost mindless, driven only by the nameless hunger that gnawed at the core of all of them. They were dangerous beasts, but they were still only beasts. It made them easier to fight.

These reindeer-things, however, they moved with purpose. It was almost as if they were looking for something specific. It was sleek, predatory behaviour, and came across all the more unnatural for seeing it in grazing animals.

Orsin had seen them tear into several animals, untainted by the Herd virus, and consume them whole. That had been strange. He had expected them to leave a few behind, infected with the Herd disease, to mutate and add to their numbers. But they never did. They simply consumed them and moved on, following tracks and signs that Orsin either could not see or dared not get close enough to inspect for himself.

Plumes of breath, faintly green against the grey backdrop of the tundra and sky, flowed from their nostrils, moving eerily against the wind. It was like their breath had a mind of its own and was ranging away from them like a hunting hound.

Orsin had yet to see any of the breath return, but his mind would not stop whispering that it would, as soon as it found whatever prey these beasts were after.

He was tempted to follow them until they found what they were looking for, but he had no idea how long that would take. No. This was still a Trial by battle. He would watch until he found a weakness, gained some understanding, then he would slaughter the herd for the glory of Weihlaris and move on to the next monstrosity.

There were so many to catalogue, and understand. Orsin thanked his father's early training as a skald. The mnemonic devices he had inherited from him were coming in very useful in recording the things he discovered.

He had begun by seeking out more of the canine packs that roamed throughout Herd territory, hoping to find one that might lead him back to the Baron he had encountered. And packs he found, but none led him to the Baron. Though after some careful observation, Orsin began to understand how they communicated and how they fought. That knowledge brought him more victories, and faster ones.

It was a pity it did not also bring greater trophies and more glory.

It would come, he had told himself. He would seek throughout Herd lands, and discover the secrets of the enemy. He'd find the Baron and this time he would cut it off from the yipping bastards that it so gleefully consumed to heal itself and cut it to ribbons.

Those fox fangs would make a glorious trophy and the tails a worthy offering to Weihlaris.

But until he could find the Baron, he would content himself with gathering other trophies and learning what he could. This herd of thorn-deer was promising. They were large and they were intelligent.

Orsin had first thought that larger beasts tended to be more intelligent, but after observing several different kinds of beasts over the past several days he had come to the inescapable conclusion that the more deadly a beast was the more intelligent it was. Generally, that also came with a great increase in size, as with the fox-baron and the thorn-deer beneath him, but not always.

Just two days ago he had encountered a vast nightmare of an aberration that was not nearly so smart as it should be, if larger size always meant greater intelligence in Herd beasts.

Orsin had thought it just another large boulder, scarred and rough. He'd crested the small rise and blinked in the unexpected warmth. He didn't see any of the unnatural greenery he had come to associate with the feeling, but the source revealed itself soon enough.

The rock moved, uncoiling into the form of a massive serpent with not one but two heads!

Orsin had narrowly dodged its first attack, and deflected the second with the flat side of his axe. The force of the blow sent him tumbling head over paws down the rise. He'd managed to roll to his feet at the base of the slope, just in time to brace for another attack.

The snake-thing was fast. A *fjorkniir*, his mind told him, pulling the description from an old tale of his father's. Two heads, incredibly venomous, but vulnerable to confusion if a clever warrior could force the heads into conflict.

Orsin had hoped the thing was less intelligent than the fox-baron and charged around the rise to the right. The serpent coiled, its two heads lashing back and forth as the thing had traced his movements. That had been fine by Orsin. He'd wanted to get to its tail and the caution of his foe allowed him to do that.

He was no weakling, no cub. As soon as he had gotten close enough, Orsin reached out and seized the thing by the tail. A shiver of hate and shuddered through the snake-thing and nearly thrown him, but Orsin had held his ground.

He had stopped moving, exactly what the fjorkniir had been waiting for.

It had struck with both heads, infuriated that this little thing dared lay hands upon it. Orsin had been hoping for just that. At the last moment he had thrown himself out of the way, yanking the tail up and into the air as he did so.

The fjorkniir's jaws had snapped closed reflexively on its own tail and the thing had pumped itself full of a double dose of its lethal venom. The stuff was so deadly that it began to eat away at the fjorkniir's flesh immediately. Orsin had taken advantage of the distraction to charge in and sever first one, then the second, of the heads.

Victory was his, but at a cost. He had lost the fox pack he was hunting, and the fangs of the beast were too venomous to even claim as trophies. He had had to settle for a large scale pried carefully from the tail of the still thrashing fjorkniir.

All was not lost, however, because the battle had brought him to these beasts, the savage reindeer with antlers like a thicket of thorns. They had appeared to snuffle the remains of the battlefield where he defeated the fjorkniir. They ranged over the entire site of the conflict, huffing and licking and bellowing back and forth to one another, almost as if they were talking amongst themselves.

It was deeply unnatural behavior and Orsin felt a strange compulsion to try and understand it. If he could understand it, he could predict what his enemy would do, and he would stand a much better chance at felling the whole herd of abominations.

When they left, clearly not finding whatever it was they sought, he followed. It was like they were looking for something. Hunting something.

Maybe it was even him.

But why?

❇ ❇ ❇

What was his friend doing?

Torben had trailed Orsin for days. He had carefully inspected the site of every battle, trying to assess how well his brother had fought. It was pleasing to see that Orsin was more than holding his own. He had achieved some glorious victories.

That giant fox-thing! Torben didn't know what it was, but he'd passed close enough to catch a glimpse of it fleeing the copse of trees he'd seen Orsin enter right before the fog cut off all visibility. He'd carefully studied the ground and got some sense of the fight, and been relieved when he saw where Orsin had hidden himself.

Fursja ruins! Torben felt a moment of pride that even in death their people had managed to extend some small aid to his brother.

And his own Trial was proceeding as well. Torben travelled close to Orsin, but not so near that there were not plenty of Herd beasts for him to fight and slay on his own.

Torben liked to think he had spared Orsin some trouble as well, by eliminating larger Herd beasts that might otherwise have scented the other Fursja and stumbled across him at an inopportune moment.

But then he'd noticed Orsin's path change. Before, his brother had been moving more or less in a straight line deeper into Herd territory. But not long ago that had changed. Orsin had begun wandering erratically. Torben had had to pay a great deal more attention not to lose his brother's trail or stumble too close to him, endangering the Trial for both of them.

"What are you doing?" He muttered to himself as he watched Orsin from behind cover of a large pile of rocks topping a small rise.

Orsin—a tiny speck at this distance—was just watching a group of Herd beasts—themselves slightly larger specks. Why wasn't he charging them, letting that axe of his lead the way and split them skull from spine? Was it a sign of early Herd infection? Some madness or fascination?

Or did Orsin, his clever brother, have a reason for watching instead of fighting?

He could wait and see, for now, Torben decided.

Though the itch of curiosity was going to be damned uncomfortable the whole while!

Chapter 11

Orsin squinted against the wind as it ruffled the fur on his face and drew lines like razors across his scars, the only places on his body not protected by the thick hair that covered him. The day had been sharp but clear, so the Fursja had decided to take advantage of the weather and hunt to fill out his store of provisions. It would also be a good outlet for his frustrations. The herd beasts he had attempted to follow vanished before they could lead him to anything useful, and though he had searched and searched, he had found no sign of the Baron he was after.

He shuddered at the memory of the voice the thing had possessed. Even for a herdbeast, it was unnatural. Orsin was determined to find out as much about the Baron as he could.

Though to do that he would need to actually find the fucking thing.

Orsin huffed in frustration, a long plume of breath coiling from his nostrils to quickly disperse in the sharp wind. Fortune was not smiling on his hunt for herdbeasts. Hopefully she would look more favourably on his hunt for provisions.

He turned over several rocks, but his luck in foraging there turned up no more than a few small grubs, barely enough for a mouthful. Not that he turned them down. Every calorie counted here on the icy tundra. Every mouthful was a bit longer he could stretch his reserves.

Orsin refused to turn back from his Trial simply because he ran out of supplies and began to starve. Hunger would not defeat him! No, if he returned it would be victorious or not at all.

His mind briefly flicked to his best friend. What was Torben up to right now? How many herdbeasts had he slain? Had he also encountered something strange? Was there a Baron stalking him?

There was no way to know. Orsin shook his head and returned to his foraging. He had to believe he would see Torben again soon, after they both returned victorious from the Trial.

He moved down from the small rise he had been following, checking stone after stone. Orsin was so focused on his hunt that he almost didn't notice when the ground began to warm slightly beneath his paws. Even then, he didn't think anything of it until he suddenly sank ankle deep in hot, putrid mud.

Orsin pulled his foot free with a quick jerk, the grasping power of the mud nothing before the sheer force of his muscles. A whiff of something foul, like rotting eggs, wafted up to his nose as he did so. He squinted ahead.

Small wisps of vapour curled up from the ground nearby. The wind quickly whipped them away. No wonder he hadn't noticed.

There must be some kind of geothermal spring beneath the tundra here, the hot water, laden with sulfur, seeping up slowly to turn the earth into a deceptive morass. Orsin carefully prodded the ground nearby with his feet, tracing the edge of the dangerous and deceptive marsh. There was no telling how far it extended, nor how deep he might sink if he tried to cut across it.

He certainly didn't relish the thought of wading through the hot mud. It would be an exhausting trek, and the wet stuff would quickly freeze to his fur once he was free of it. It would weigh him down until he was able to clean it off, and while there was water in these frozen wastes, there were hardly raging rivers full of the stuff.

So Orsin began carefully skirting the edges of the hidden marsh. So far as he could see, there was no way to tell which direction would be faster, but he was in no hurry, so it didn't matter. He chose to go right, if for no other reason than he wielded Muinnajhr in that paw more often than not.

The terrain was mostly flat, though a few small rises broke up the monotony, small spits of land and rock that clearly resisted the burbling waters beneath the marsh. Those bits of steady footing were welcome when they came.

It was cresting one of these small rises that Orsin was greeted by an unexpected bit of luck. A trick of the local terrain had resulted in the collection of some of the spring water into a small pool. It steamed in the cold, but the mineral content was clearly no bar to the local wildlife using this as a reliable source of water. Not only were there several sets of tracks to and from the pool, but there was a massive buck even now lapping up a drink!

Orsin grinned. Fresh venison was suddenly on the menu! He hefted his axe in his paw, adjusting his grip.

The reindeer suddenly raised its head. It hadn't smelled Orsin, not with the wind in his face and the stink of the marsh occluding his prey's nose, but some flicker of movement must have caught its eye. It stamped its foot and huffed nervously but didn't bolt. Not yet.

Orsin didn't' give it the chance to.

In one smooth movement, Orsin twisted himself up to his full height. As he did so he drew back his arm and rotated his shoulder, his muscles tensing and snapping his axe up and over in a powerful throw. The weapon in his hand released, turning into a whirling streak of slivered metal and flew true, covering the distance between the Fursja and his prey in the blink of an eye.

The blade of the axe bit deep into the reindeer's back, instantly severing its spine and causing the beast to collapse where it stood. Orsin ran toward his target, to reclaim his axe, as he was still in herd territory and the tundra around him was no doubt infested with various dangers and it would not do to be unarmed for long, and to finish off the reindeer quickly so the beast would not suffer any more than necessary.

His claws made quick work of the beast, slicing the hide free and tearing the meat into neat chunks. The body steamed in the cold air and Orsin dug into his first warm meal in days with gusto. The liver he ate with relish, and the kidneys, but the heart he carefully cut free and offered to Weihlaris in thanks. It may not have been a battle, but Orsin's weapon had flown true and felled his target in one blow.

That was something worth offering thanks for, lest such regard not follow him into battle, where he might need it more.

There was even the pool to wash the blood from himself afterward. Orsin considered drinking from it beforehand, but decided against it in the end. The smell of sulfur was too strong. Drinking the water might turn his stomach and there was plenty of fresh snow and ice to quench his thirst if he truly needed it.

It was a pity he couldn't linger here longer. It was a nice place, here between two gentle rises. There was shelter from the wind, there was water (although it was not the most refreshing), and plenty of prey that might just come to him seeking it.

The only real problem was the herdbeasts infesting the nearby tundra. There was no way he wouldn't soon be visited by some abomination or other, drawn by the scent of blood and the promise of death or a dying creature that was easy prey for the mutating sickness that the disgusting things spread.

He would likely be able to fight them off, if they came slowly enough. There was not enough here to tempt the larger beasts. Or at least Orsin didn't think there was. Though several rival herd abominations might all converge on the place, hoping to take whatever wounded animal was here for their own.

But whatever the case, the herd beasts would be drawn to this place. It was inevitable. The smell of blood on the wind would draw them.

Orsin paused. There was a thought. He'd been ranging across the tundra trying to hunt down the baron that had terrorised him, with little luck. Maybe he needed to change his approach.

Maybe he needed to find a way to lure the baron to him.

The more Orsin thought about the idea the better he liked it. If it worked, it would save him time and effort, allow him to choose the field upon which he met the baron in battle, and ensure he would be in the best condition possible for the fight.

And he knew he would need every advantage he could get, in this fight. The baron had been terrifyingly powerful. He shook his head. And the princes and queens even more so. Though he still believed a true warrior of Weihlaris could fell a prince single-handedly, it was a sobering thought.

Orsin turned his plan over and over in his mind as he stripped everything useful from the reindeer carcass before bundling the remainder up in the hide and hauling it up the nearby rise to bury it beneath a small cairn of stones. He didn't want the smell to linger long and put off other prey animals that might come to the pool to drink. He wanted to try and take one of the reindeer alive.

It had to be alive. That would make it a more tempting target for other herd beasts. The smell of blood would dissipate quickly, and the herd wanted living targets, right? The smell of death might draw them, but to make his trap truly tempting, the thing had to be alive.

Orsin carefully cleaned Muinnajhr, checking the blade for any small nicks or scratches. He nodded in satisfaction when he found none. He had done his work well. His weapon was truly worthy of the Trial. It would not fail him.

Nor would he fail it.

His paw tightened on the haft of the axe and, for a moment, he felt as if Torben were there with him. The blood of his best friend was forged into the weapon, irretrievably to the metal. His friend was with him, as much as the Trial would allow. Orsin could feel it.

He wouldn't let Torben down either.

Orsin hunkered down amidst the rocks to watch the pool and get an idea of how many prey animals came here for water, and how often. Which kinds of animals did he have available to set a trap for the baron? The taste of the reindeer was still on his tongue, coppery and rich, though the heat its meat had given his blood was already cooling in the tundra winds.

Hopefully Orsin could capture or wound another reindeer as big and healthy as the one he had just consumed, at the very least. If he had enjoyed it, he saw no reason why the herd would not as well. He had no doubt his plan would attract plenty of herd beasts.

Perhaps too many?

No. Orsin flexed his paws. He had slaughtered every lesser herd beast he had encountered so far, sometimes many at a time. If he did draw a large group of enemies, he was confident he could handle it.

After all, he was choosing the battlefield, and would know the best places to attack from and, should it come to it, the best avenues for retreat. Anything short of the baron arriving with a small army of herd beasts in tow, Orsin could manage.

He just needed the baron to show up for its free meal. A nice, strong reindeer, bleeding from a few superficial wounds, perhaps with a broken leg, should be more than enough to bring the nearby herd. As much as Orsin regretted the pain the beast would suffer, it was for the greater good.

Orsin needed to tempt the baron to him, and a nice tempting reindeer was the best option he could currently field.

And if that didn't do it?

He just had to find something the baron would find too tempting to resist.

Chapter 12

Orsin crouched in ambush, watching the approaching herd beast draw near to the bait he had carefully prepared. This was the strangest and ugliest of the several herd beasts he'd managed to tempt out with his new plan. Still no sign of the baron, but this monstrosity was a thing in and of itself.

It looked nothing so much like someone had cut two reindeer in half, then shoved the two front halves together and stitched them up with long, stringy cables of rot. There was a head to either end, and antlers to either end, though this specimen seemed to lack the thorny horns of others he'd seen.

The thing was damned hard to sneak up on, though, Orsin would give it that. It had come bounding over the nearby rise, drawn by the smell of blood and the cries of pain from the reindeer Orsin had captured and set out as bait. While one head snuffled at the wounded reindeer the other had kept watch, ears flicking as it turned its head to survey the nearby landscape.

The snuffling head, when it was satisfied with some unknown quality possessed by the wounded deer, suddenly made a deep, chesty sound and vomit-spat out long strings of sticky green-black rot over the injured animal. The thing screamed in agony as the stuff clung to its wounds. Even from where Orsin was crouched in concealment he could see the tendrils of rot moving of their own volition and *pushing* themselves into the open wound, writhing and pulsating as they did.

The herd beast vomit-spat again and more tendrils clamped on to the injured animal. The rot ran from predator to prey, unbroken, and even as Orsin watched the injured beast was split apart by tendrils of rot erupting from inside of it. The back half collapsed, steaming in the cold air, but the front writhed and wriggled and struggled on, even as it was pulled closer and closer to the herd beast that had attacked it.

Was the thing trying to add a third front half to itself? Orsin watched in fascinated revulsion. He'd seen several attacks so far, but never by this kind of herd beast. This was new.

As the prey was drawn near, the watchful back half of the herd beast finally allowed its vigil to slip. It stopped scanning the nearby tundra for threats and instead focused in on the struggling half-reindeer that would soon become another part of itself.

That was it. Orsin's chance to attack.

The Fursja warrior heaved himself up from concealment and began a powerful charge towards the distracted herd beast. The edge of Muinnajhr gleamed hungrily in spite of the lack of light and Orsin felt the thrill of battle thrum through his veins.

The herd beast detected his approach. How could it not? The thing wasn't headless. Quite the opposite. But it was still trying to incorporate its prey into itself, and connected to the struggling reindeer as it had very little ability to manoeuvre.

Orsin's axe flashed once, separating the head of the injured prey beast from its body and sending it spinning away. It was the least he could do for his sacrificial deer. At least it wouldn't suffer a life of abominations because of Orsin's actions.

The herd beast hooted a challenge at him, a curiously doubled sound, issuing as it did from two throats at once. The tendrils of rot, deprived of their prey, suddenly surged out of the now-useless body of the reindeer and reared up like serpents, dancing in the air almost of their own volition.

The smell hit Orsin like a ten-ton masonry block. It was thick and cloying and conjured images of bloated death in his head. He batted his axe in wide swings in front of him, keeping the tendrils at bay even if it did nothing to clear the foul scent from the air.

Orsin pressed forward, trying to get close enough to sink his axe into the flesh of the herd beast before him. The thing exuded so many sticky tendrils of rot, however, that there wasn't really a good angle for him to attack from.

The Fursja growled in frustration. Fine. He'd go through the fucking things then.

Orsin's axe whooshed through the air, moving in quick, powerful strokes. The edge of the blade aimed for the clump of tendrils closest to him, but rather than slicing through cleanly as Orsin expected it to, the rot instead clumped and clung to his blade, sticky and viscous enough to resist cutting.

He wasn't going to be cutting through anything like that. Orsin ripped Muinnajhr free from the clinging tendrils of rot, dancing back agilely on his paws to avoid the stuff which was crawling toward him. Long strands of green-black putrescence still clung to his weapon though, wrapping the head of the axe and rendering more than half of the blade useless unless he could clean the stuff off or find a way to cut through it.

Orsin retreated quickly, ranging blows down on the tundra as he did, his arms strong enough to drive the axe head into the frozen ground and the motion scraping off bits of the rot as he did so, until his axe was free of the stuff.

But the herd beast had not been sitting still as he did so. The thing advanced on him, in strange, twisting bounds, it's oppositional limbs working in tandem but not smoothly. Still, the thing was eerily fast. It vomit-spat another clump of rot at him, this one at range and fast moving.

Orsin hissed as a roiling ball of tendrils exploded near his feet. He narrowly missed being tripped up there! This thing was more dangerous than he'd thought.

Twice more he danced aside as the thing vomited at him. It's chest was starting to heave like a bellows. Hopefully it couldn't keep this up.

The next time the thing vomit-spat at him only a few weak tendrils dribbled from its mouth. Orsin felt a spike of excitement. An opening!

He lunged in, this time aiming to batter the thing's head in with the flat of Muinnajhr If it couldn't cut, it could still crush, and destroying the brain—or where the brain used to be—was often still an effective tactic in dealing with most herd beasts.

But his quarry dodged, whipping its head back and out of range with a deceptive swiftness.

Then Orsin heard the familiar heaving cough again. This time from the side. A mass of tendrils slammed into him and immediately began writing across his skin, seeking any open wound, no matter how small, to crawl into.

The thing had two heads! The other hadn't used any of its supply of rot, apparently. It had been held in reserve until Orsin got close enough to make good use of it.

Orsin roared and lashed out with his axe, driving the herd beast's other head back. He wasn't able to follow through on his attack, however, because the rot tendrils were fouling his legs.

He hopped backward, awkwardly, grabbing fistfuls of the stuff and tearing it from him in quick, painful bursts. Painful because each bit of rot tore some of his fur out with it. The stuff was almost as bad as tar.

His skin stung. Orsin could tell there were small tendrils of rot seeping into his body via the tiny wounds left by the patches of fur torn out by his own hand, but they were minuscule. He would deal with them after the battle. He had more than enough valendjahr for an amount of invasive herd disease this small.

Soon all the rot had either been plucked form his body or sank into his skin. Either way, it wasn't getting in the way of his next attack.

Orsin growled. There was still too much rot to allow his axe blade to be useful, and getting close risked fouling his footing in the rot tendrils that were waving around the beast. It was not a good matchup for his current situation.

But that didn't mean the warrior didn't have options. If a sharp edge couldn't prevail, there was still blunt force. And the tundra did not lack for rocks. Orsin secured Muinnajhr on his back and leaned down and picked up a large, jagged bit of stone.

The herd beast, while cunning, clearly had never faced a Fursja warrior before, nor any kind of opponent with ranged capabilities.

Orsin roared, charged forward a few steps, and launched the massive stone into the air. It flew fast and true, propelled by his massive muscles, until it slammed directly into the closest head of the herd beast.

The thing caved in like a rotten melon.

The remaining head trumpeted in distress, but half of its body had collapsed, becoming dead weight. The tendrils of rot writhed and began tearing at its own flesh, trying to rip itself apart so the remaining head could flee, but there was no way it was going to succeed before Orsin struck again.

And strike he did. With the tendrils distracted, Orsin charged. He left his axe at his back and chose instead to simply close the distance, grab the thing by its weeping black antlers, and use the full force of his muscles to slam the horny protrusions into the herd beasts skull, crushing it and pulping the brain matter beneath.

The herd beast collapsed, all the fight going out of it. The rot quickly began to sublimate into a noxious green-black vapour. Orsin immediately leapt back. There was no way he wanted to inhale any of that.

Orsin whiffed, his lungs working like bellows as he strained to catch his breath after the battle. That had been far closer than it had any right to be. It was a good reminder that even innocuous looking herd beasts could have hidden tricks that might trip up even an experienced warrior.

He moved back to his hidden campsite, reflecting on the past several days of baiting out herd beasts. While his plan had worked, to a degree, it wasn't catching his true prey: the baron. And he thought he knew why.

Orsin had been at this for several days. He'd baited herd beasts with three reindeer, a lone arctic wolf, a dire stoat (and that had been a challenging battle; the damn thing was damned fast), and a rangy snowbeast. He'd tempted out some of the changed artic foxes, a few variants of herd beasts clearly based on reindeer, and the dangerous odd variation he'd just fought.

Nothing he'd faced was a power on the level of the baron. They were all different, true, but there was still a pattern. They all had one thing in common.

Most of the herd beasts drawn to his bait animals were those inhabiting the carcass of a weaker creature than his bait. They had all had different powers and abilities, sure, and a few, like this most recent beast, were more dangerous than the rest, but in general it seemed that herd beasts sought out prey that challenged them, that was slightly more dangerous than the current base creature the abomination was formed of.

And if that held true on up the chain, then it was likely he wasn't going to be able to tempt the baron to him using injured reindeer. No. The baron, though it seemed to be some kind of ascended or advanced version of a simple arctic fox, was far too powerful to care about a simple reindeer. If it was also drawn to slightly more powerful prey as a way to improve itself or to spread the herd infection, then Orsin wasn't going to tempt it with anything he'd staked out as bait so far.

No. If his plan was going to succeed, one thing was very clear. Orsin was going to need some bigger bait.

Chapter 13

Orsin knelt down close to the frost ground and snuffed deeply. The animal he was after should be close. He could smell it. The musk was fresh, deep, and acrid at the back of his throat.

He was hunting a giant GauVark. It was not a beast Orsin had ever seen alive in person before, but he was familiar with the smaller, domesticated versions the Fursja kept for food and as working beasts in those few areas where the terrain would support farming. Familiar enough to be relatively certain the smells as correct, and to recognise the tracks the music accompanied. Deep, cloven hoof marks dented the frozen ground ever so slightly, a testament to the sheer size and bulk of the animal he was after.

Orsin was moving carefully through another patch of unnatural woodland, the trees a product of the herd blight more than any natural growth. There was an unnatural heat seeping from the trunks nearby that caused him to pant in a desperate effort to keep himself cool. He had become far too accustomed to the icy chill of the tundra. Here beneath the branches it was uncomfortable.

He did his best to move quietly. He didn't want to scare off his prey, not when he'd taken such care to set up this hunt. Not when it was his best chance at tempting the baron.

A branch snapped ahead of him. Orsin froze and looked carefully toward the sound. His lips pulled back in a feral grin.

Before him, in all its primordial glory, was the giant GauVark. The thing stood taller at the shoulder than Orsin, and it outmassed him by a substantial margin. Coarse brown bristles covered its hide, though even from this distance the Fursja could see just how powerfully muscled the thing was. It was crude, raw power all bundled up in one brutal package.

Two long horns swept back from the crown of the thing's head. As Orsin watched the GauVark used one of its horns to uproot an entire tree and cast it to the side as it began grubbing amongst the roots for something. It had a broad, porcine snout and a wicked pair of tusks as well, which, now that the tree was uprooted, tore the thing to bits.

The GauVark cast aside clumps of obviously herd-infected wood. There was a bestial cunning in its eyes, and a sense of powerful vitality that reminded Orsin slightly of the packet of valendjahrhe carried to ward off herd infection.

Did some creatures develop a natural resistance? The herd must hate that, if so. Orsin smiled. Better and better! This should tempt the baron all the more.

Orsin just needed to subdue the thing first.

He took a deep breath, checked his surroundings for any unexpected foes or herd beasts, stepped out from behind the tree, and roared out a challenge at the massive beast. The GauVark jerked its head up, piggish eyes zeroing in almost immediately on the Fursja. Narrow and red they stared at him for a moment before the GauVark's lips parted and a defiant scream rattled its tusks and answered Orsin's challenge.

Massive cloven hooves the size of cartwheels pawed at the ground, tearing great gouges in the soft ground. The heat from the trees had melted the frost and turned the tundra of a thick, green-black loam. With a reverberating squeal, the GauVark charged toward Orsin.

The Fursja wasted not a second, spinning on his heels and beginning to sprint away.

There was no way he was going to bring down something that big in single combat, not if he wanted it alive. He'd have to restrict himself too much. Kill it? Sure. Orsin was confident he could do that. As big as it was it was still pig-stupid and ox-stubborn. Not a terribly canny foe. But it was resilient, and big enough it might even manage to crush him if it caught him, so Orsin had to play it smart.

Orsin had to plan.

The Fursja warrior sprinted through the trees, dodging between them whenever he had the chance. The GauVark followed, using its horns to tear a wide swathe through the wood and barely slowing in it's advance as it did so.

But the trees did slow it, a bit. Enough that Orsin was able to extend his lead. Still, the GauVark was stubborn, and refused to give up the chase.

Good. That's exactly what Orsin wanted anyway.

A massive chunk of trunk suddenly slammed into the tree to his right. Orsin risked a glance back. The GauVark had hurled a tree at him! And it had nearly hit as well. Orsin dodged again, sacrificing a little of his lead to serpentine through the boles. He didn't want to get hit with something like that!

He managed to escape the edge of the wood unscathed, through not so far ahead of his quarry as he might have hoped. Now, on the open tundra with no trees to slow it down, the GauVark picked up speed. Orsin would eventually lose his lead.

The wind knifed across Orsin's face, drawing tears from his eyes. Still, the warrior sprinted forward, occasionally loosing a mocking roar. Every time he did so he was answered with a furious squeal from behind. The GauVark wasn't going to let up.

His lungs burned. Orsin was a warrior, and used to long periods of training, but a long-distance runner he was not. Not in the way many of his fellows were, and the last few weeks on the tundra hadn't helped. He had increased his endurance, to be sure, but he hadn't spent much time running at an increased pace. His legs and lungs were threatening open rebellion.

The terrain beneath him was an ever-present danger as well. More than once Orsin slipped or slid on a patch of frost, made deceptively slick by the hardness and smoothness of the ground beneath it. Each time he slipped the GauVark drew closer.

He was losing his lead. Bit by bit the beast at his back was gaining. Orsin had to focus all of his attention on staying ahead. If he slipped now, even for a moment, the GauVark would overtake him and he would be trampled and shredded by those razor-sharp tusks.

Orsin mounted a small rise and grinned. His destination—and the trap he had set for the massive beast behind him—was just ahead. He just needed to get there first.

The proximity to his destination lent new strength to his limbs and Orsin invested it all in a burst of speed. He ran ahead, eyes seeking out the specific chain of rocks that he had oh-so-carefully arranged earlier.

There!

Orsin ran, jumping smoothly onto the first, then skipping from one to the next in a quick, coordinated motion. Behind him the GauVark simply raged and charged forward.

It ran right into the thick, clinging mud of the hidden marsh. Momentum and its own fury drove it well beyond the edge before the beast even realised. Mud clung, heavy and grasping, to its limbs and the charge quickly slowed to a crawl.

The GauVark squealed in anger and began slashing at the terrain around it with tusk and horn. Orsin watched from his perch on the boulder. As long as he watched carefully and stuck to the stones he had placed around the trap area, he would be fine and free from the mud. The mud which would do most of the work in his trap.

He had gotten the idea from the rot-tendrils of that mutated reindeer from his first attempt to bait out the baron, actually. The stuff had impeded his movements a lot, and made what should have been a very easy fight for him much more difficult. He was counting on the mud of this marsh having the same or a similar effect on the GauVark, hobbling it to the point that he could knock it out.

What Orsin hadn't counted on was just how strong the GauVark was. The beast had powerful limbs, and while the mud was slowing it down, and its own bulk was causing it to sink, it was still able to move. Orsin, needing to stick to the boulders he had carefully placed around the marsh, was freer to move but only had so many angles from which he could attack.

The GauVark flung a massive blob of mud toward the Fursja. Orsin ducked, clinging close to the boulder as the sodden earth flew above his head. It looked like his enemy had not wholly forgotten him, though it was mostly concerned with extricating itself from the mire, a proposition that was easier said than done. The nature of the marsh made everything look like solid ground, in every direction, though if the GauVark was cunning enough it could follow the trail it gouged on the way in.

It didn't seem like it would be that clever, though.

Orsin leapt to another boulder, bringing him closer to the GauVark's head. His axe swept out once, twice, thrice, trying to connect with the side of the beast's head, but Orsin was just out of easy reach. He couldn't even manage to graze the thing.

And the GauVark, with Orsin in its sights, bellowed and flung more muck at the Fursja, trying to reach him that way when it couldn't trample him beneath its hooves. Orsin was forced to dodge, dodge again, and eventually leapt to another boulder, further away from the GauVark's head.

This wasn't working. He needed a different approach. Orsin panted, looking around him at the terrain.

He couldn't charge the thing because of the very muck he had used to trap it. And he couldn't reach it simply keeping to the boulders. The GauVark was too good at flinging mud. That wasn't something Orsin had accounted for. Even then, there was no guarantee it would keep its head near enough to one of the boulders to give Orsin a good shot at it.

Whatever he was going to do, however, he needed to do quick. The GauVark was within range of Orsin's safe footing now, but that could easily change if the dumb thing tried charging off in another direction, rolling away like a big, sentient boulder all its own.

Actually, that gave him an idea. It was reckless, and dangerous, but Orsin didn't have anything else to lose, so why not make the attempt. Nothing ventured, nothing gained, after all.

Orsin growled and leapt onto the GauVark's back. As soon as it felt his weight upon it, the beast went berserk, bellowing and trying to buck wildly to unseat the unwelcome Fursja pest.

The mud grasped tightly to the GauVark's legs, however. It was too mired to buck and pull itself free. The most it could do was shiver its back and try to shake Orsin off. And that was nowhere near enough to stymie a full-blood Fursja warrior.

Orsin growled and sank his claws deep into the GauVark's hide, pulling himself up along its spinal ridge until its head was within range. There was no doubt a massive, dense shield of bone supporting those horns and protecting the thing's brain, but Orsin was a Fursja warrior and his strength was not to be under-estimated! He hauled back and began to slam the flat of his axe-blade against the back of the GauVark's skull, ringing it like a bell until the beast's eyes rolled up in the back of its head and unconsciousness claimed it.

Fuck. The roar of victory that almost leapt from Orsin's throat strangled itself mid-celebration as the GauVark, no longer fighting the mud, quickly began to sink.

Orsin groaned. If he didn't act quickly all his efforts would be for nothing! The GauVark could easily drown in all this mud and leave Orsin without anything to show for all his effort.

He grunted and leapt off the GauVark's back, wading through the mud to seize the thing by the horns and haul its head up and out of the muck.

This was going to be a long afternoon.

Chapter 14

Orsin growled as the chill from the tundra beneath him seeped upward into his aching muscles. He had foraged for as much food as he could find since dragging that stupid GauVark free from the marsh, and gobbled down every bit of natural remedy and stimulant his skill had allowed him to find. It had been a meagre collection, but it had kept him going.

The GauVark was hobbled in a small depression between two rises. Orsin had to carefully hamstring the beast's back legs to keep it from charging off. Unable to move effectively anymore, the beast squealed in rage and pain, dragging itself around and leaving furrows in its wake. Orsin had treated the wounds to make sure it wouldn't bleed out. Now, all he could do was wait, to see if the baron would arrive and take this tempting piece of bait.

Orsin had taken great care in choosing the terrain. It was far enough from any herd-blighted greenery, the hollow was small, and the rises were well positioned to funnel any incoming herd beasts the baron might have with it into small groups. Too well did Orsin remember the baron healing by consuming lesser herd beasts. He was going to make sure that was a minimal advantage this time.

He also had two carefully planned escape routes, in case things did not go to plan. Orsin was confident he had the skill and the strength to take down this baron, but he wasn't an idiot. A smart warrior knew when to withdraw to return and fight another day.

And there would be many, many more days ahead of Orsin, and the herd would deeply regret that fact. He would fill all of them with blood and ichor, until either he died or the last of the herd taint was forever cleansed from the world. By Weihlaris, he swore it!

The GauVark squealed again and Orsin tensed, his paw tightening on the haft of his axe. Had a herd beast appeared? Was it the baron?

He relaxed after a moment of scanning the nearby terrain. Nothing that he could sense was present. The GauVark was just in pain and angry.

Not that Orsin could blame it.

Wait. Was that a flicker of movement along the rise across from him? Orsin squinted but the grey twilight of the tundra and time of year made vision one of his less reliable senses. The wind was perpendicular to him, neither betraying his location nor carrying any potential scent warning to him.

He watched, but he didn't see anything. Maybe it was a false alarm. Maybe it was a scout for the baron. If Orsin was lucky, time would tell.

Orsin waited. His mind occasionally wandered, but he patiently brought it back, time and again, to the task at hand. He had trained for this. War was long periods of boredom interspersed with brief flashes of action, blood, and glory. No Fursja made it this far without being equipped to deal with the waiting that was key to any successful combat encounter. This was no different.

So Orsin was well prepared when things finally did change. A flicker of movement appeared on the rise across from him once more. This time, however, he was able to see what it was.

First, one arctic fox appeared. Then another and another, in twos and threes. They circled the ridge, looking down at the wounded prey in the hollow, bait in the trap. Then there was a sharp yip from behind them and the pack flowed down and into the hollow, pinning and harassing the GauVark in place on one side.

Orsin's heart leapt within his chest, going from a steady tense drumbeat of anticipation to a Andrea line-filled flurry of activity. He knew that yip! That was the sound of the baron.

His prey had arrived.

The baron flowed over the rise across from him, white fur almost indistinguishable from the frosty tundra terrain. It moved carefully up behind the GauVark, creeping in unseen as the pack of arctic foxes in front of the wounded beast kept its attention pinned forward. Orsin could practically see the herd beast salivating at the thought of such an easy kill—or infection, whatever the baron intended to do with this prey.

Orsin shifted his weight, preparing to move. He had two choices: he could either charge the small pack of foxes and try to kill as many of them in a surprise attack as he could, limiting the baron's ability to heal, or direct a killing blow at the baron from the outset. If he managed to land it quickly enough and well enough, the baron would never get a chance to heal itself, because it would already be dead. And even if he failed, hopefully the baron would be so wounded that simply recovering from that first blow would destroy all of the support pack it had with it.

Of course if Orsin missed, or miscalculated, he would be facing not only the baron but also that pack of foxes. That was not a situation he relished facing again, even though this was terrain of his choosing.

Still, he was a warrior of Weihlaris! His was the path of glory, the path of the bold. He would gamble his life on the chance that it would net him the head of the baron and an excellent story to regale Torben with when they both returned home after the Trial.

Orsin's paw tightened on Muinnajhr's haft. The baron's attention was almost wholly on the GauVark. As soon as it commited itself to an attack, Orsin would move. It would be his best chance at catching the baron completely by surprise and his best chance at landing that hoped-for deadly blow.

The baron paused, sniffing loudly. Orsin held himself perfectly still as the herd noble below cast its gaze suspiciously at the rises to either side of it. He had been careful to cover his scent, but who knew what strange senses the herd abominations could bring to bear? If he was unlucky, his whole ambush could be ruined right here.

But the baron, after a quick examination of the surrounding terrain, turned its full attention back to the GauVark. The target was too tempting, perhaps, and greed overwhelmed good sense, even in abominations. Or the scent of the GauVark, as pungent as it was, overwhelmed the delicate senses of the herd baron. Orsin knew it had made his eyes water more than once.

The baron crept closer, And then closer still. It moved, lithe as a cat, intent on stalking its prey. There was no mockery here. None of that strange voice or any hint of it playing with its food. The GauVark commanded that much respect from it, at least.

Orsin would be insulted if it didn't so perfectly suit his purposes.

The baron moved in quick bursts, and Orsin rose, keeping low to the ground, and shifted position to behind another small clump of boulders. The arctic fox pack was far away, and too busy keeping the GauVark in place to notice him, and the baron likewise was too intent on its prey.

Orsin saw his moment and seized it. The baron was gathered to pounce, and the Fursja warrior rose from concealment and threw himself headlong down the side of the rise, using gravity to propel his momentum to even greater heights. He would need every edge he could muster.

He was quiet as he ran. No battle cry this time. No glorious shout to Weihlaris. Sometimes a warrior needed to strike in silence.

And strike he did!

Orsin aimed for the spine. Speeding almost too quickly for his feet to keep up, Orsin reached the end of the rise and used the last little bit of terrain advantage to launch his bulk upward, raising in his axe overhead as he did so. The Fursja warrior arced through the air, a furry missile of death, the combined momentum of his charge all poured into that leap, and that leap focused entirely on the torsion of muscles as he brought his axe down on his target.

Shin gin steel bite's deep into tainted white flesh. Orsin's axe buried itself almost to the hilt into the baron's spine. The abomination loosed a scream that made Orsin's ears bleed and he nearly lost hold of his axe, only keeping his grip through sheer bloody-mindedness.

Answering yips rose up in a furious chorus, as the pack darted towards Orsin and the baron. In their hurry, however, many of the pack forgot that the GauVark was still a threat. Tusks and horns flashed and several small white bodies went flying, trailing red blood and green-black ichor.

The baron screamed again, this time in rage. It was no rage on behalf of its pack, but every death was a bit of healing the monster lost the ability to realise. Still, as soon as the nearest fox was in range, it snapped it up and gulped it down, the flesh on its back immediately beginning to knit back together.

Orsin swore and tore his axe free, moments before it was sealed up irrevocably in the baron's back by the twisting, morphing flesh. He leapt down to the ground and set the blade to whirling around him. He sliced into every small fox form that he could, dancing away from the baron as he did so.

The herd abomination mostly ignored him, focused intently on healing what might have otherwise been a mortal wound. Orsin grinned. That would be a costly mistake!

He struck at the baron's hamstrings, slicing neatly through them, though the flesh twisted back into health almost immediately. The wounds were too superficial to last, though had they lasted they would have been devastating.

Orsin needed to strike deeper.

The baron twisted away from his next attack. And the next. But then another fox came within grasping distance of the thing's mouth and the baron couldn't resist turning to snap it up.

Orsin surged into the opening, burying his axe deep between the baron's ribs. White fur immediately turned black with ichor as the wound spat. A deep, bubbling yowl burst from the baron's mouth. Orsin must have sliced into a lung with that blow!

The baron was no simple beast, however. It's flesh continued to heal and the deep well of hatred and infection that beat in place of its heart turned to focus fully on Orsin. Fangs snapped and tails whipped, driving the warrior back and back.

Orsin danced out of the way, the terrain boxing him in as much as it had the baron, and he had to be careful not to come too close to the GauVark. That beast was likewise still alive and would happily gut him if he came too near.

Then it happened. Stone turned beneath his heel and Orsin's momentum turned from a graceful dance of evasion and death to a rough tumble to the ground. His wrist slammed against a protruding rock and his axe went spinning from his grip. Orsin rolled and scrambled, his leg flaring in pain from what was probably a torn muscle.

His prey advanced on him, thick, rattling breaths raking their way from his lungs.

"Little Fu-fu-fursja," the baron spat, blood frothing at the corners of its mouth. "I am coming for you. I am coming to add you to my collection. Oh yesss..."

Orsin scrambled backward, legs weak as water beneath him, unable to support his weight. His paws grasped desperately for his axe, but all he found was cold, frozen tundra. He was weaponless!

The baron lunged!

Chapter 15

Orsin twisted his body into a desperate roundhouse, bringing his clenched fist around with all the force he could muster and slamming the baron's snout away from him. The massive arctic fox-lord's eyes rolled and it shook its head as if trying to clear it. It was only a moment of distraction.

But a moment was all Orsin needed.

The Fursja warrior levered himself to his feet, eyes scanning the ground until they landed upon his weapon. Before the baron could recover enough to snap at him with its deadly jaws, Orsin flung himself bodily in the direction of his weapon, his paw closing around the haft moments before he tucked into a roll and narrowly evaded the snapping fangs behind him. He felt the hot breath of his foe on his fur and rolled up into a defensive position, Muinnajhr cocked behind him, ready to whip it around and bury it between the eyes of the baron at the first opportunity.

The baron stared at him, just out of reach, eyes glittering with hatred.

"The little Fu-fu-Fursja has fangs." It said. "Deep biting fangs. Truly, a worthy addition to the collection." It lolled its tongue at him, clearly laughing in the way of the arctic foxes.

It was a chilling and unnatural sight. Something about the usurpation of something so natural by something so unnatural just made Orsin's blood boil. But the herd beasts didn't seem to notice the reaction it provoked. It continued speaking.

"And you will be mine one day, little Fu-fu-Fursja. I will—"

Orsin had had enough of this thing's aberrant speech. With a roar he flung himself once more into battle. His axe spoke for him, lashing out and forcing the baron to fall back or lose its head.

Literally.

The baron growled and snapped at him, but the herd beast was moving more slowly. Not all of its injuries were healed, and there were no more little foxes nearby to help fuel the abomination's recovery. It was running low on resources and there were only so many tricks even a baron of the herd had access to.

Orsin pressed the attack. If he was going to kill the thing, now was his best chance, while it was already injured and far enough away from its home territory that it had neither the advantage of knowing the terrain nor of calling more of its kin to die and fuel the fires of its resurrection.

A tail slap nearly sent his axe spinning from his grip again but Orsin growled and managed to keep hold of his weapon. He spun the blade around him, turning the momentum of the herd beast's attack to his own advantage and slicing deep into the thing's tail, nearly severing it. Orsin blinked. That blow *should* have severed it. Those tails weren't so thick and strong that they should resist his axe. And the hide of the baron hadn't been that tough when he drove his axe into the thing's ribs earlier.

The baron yowled in rage and pain and immediately leapt back, away from Orsin. Even as he watched the thing's muscles waned and withered a bit as the beast channeled its remaining life energy to heal its tail. The wound vanished entirely in a flash.

Orsin's eyes glinted. What about the tails was so valuable? They had to be vital for the baron to dedicate itself in order to preserve one of them.

The Fursja warrior resolved to take another shot at one of the tails at the first opportunity. Any weakness he could exploit, he would.

But Orsin didn't get the chance. The baron stared at him, hate flowing from its eyes, but it did not throw itself back into the fray. When Orsin advanced, it retreated.

"Little Fu-fu-Fursja has fangs. Hateful fangs." The Baron growled. "I shall claim the fang for myself when the little Fu-fu-Fursja is collected. But not, I think, today. No. Not today. But soon."

The thing suddenly laughed, a wild, insane sound that set the fur at the back of Orsin's neck to rise. There was nothing of sanity as the Fursja knew it in that noise. It was a truly alien thing.

Then the baron turned and dashed away.

His prey was fleeing!

Orsin cursed and leapt into pursuit, his legs powering him up the rise over which the baron had already vanished. He crested the top and easily sighted the fleeing form off the baron dashing off across the tundra. It was headed back to its home territory, to that copse of herd-blighted trees!

He threw himself into the chase. If the baron made it back there, it would have no trouble at all healing. And there was no way it would fall for Orsin's bait tactic twice. He needed to finish this now!

So began a long and gruelling chase. The baron dashed ahead and Orsin followed. While the herd beast had the advantage in speed and knowledge of the terrain, it was wounded and in worse health than Orsin.

If nothing else, Orsin knew he was capable of fighting a baron toe-to-toe and prevailing. Not that it would count if he couldn't part the thing's head from its neck, but Orsin was confident that if he could just catch up to the thing he'd be able to do precisely that.

The blade of his axe felt thirsty.

Orsin powered through the exhaustion and aching muscles. His world narrowed down to a single point: the baron. He followed the flickering flash of white ahead of him, moving as quickly as he could. More than once he thought he had lost the trail, only to spy a small flicker of movement ahead, the tell-tale flick of those mocking tails, and the Fursja fell into pursuit with renewed determination.

He would not allow this victory to be snatched from his grasp so easily!

But fortune was not with him. As the day passed, and they drew nearer to that patch of herd-blighted land, mist began to rise up from the tundra, the warm air from the grove coiling across the land and giving rise to the noxious fog.

Orsin lost sight of the baron, and this time there was no way to get it again. The mist blocked his vision to too great a degree. Though Orsin was no cub, relying on only one sense to track his prey.

There was still scent to follow, though it was faint and fading, and the occasional track. The very heat that gave rise to the mist that helped the fox-lord also softened the landscape and made it possible for Orsin to spot regular tracks, disturbances in the soil that would not have been possible in the truly frozen tundra.

He nearly lost the trail across a patch of stone, however. The mist was thick and there was no soil to betray the tracks. Scent had long since been lost to the cloying smell of the trees and the sickening-sweet stench of herd-rot. But a smudged paw print showed him the way.

So Orsin followed, and the trail led him away from the grove, back to the tundra proper and out of the mist.

Clever baron. Trying to lose him like that. Orsin smiled. Not clever enough, however.

Orsin followed the trail, eyes locked to the ground. He had nothing but the tracks now, having long ago lost sight of his quarry and the scent trail gone stale. But Orsin pressed doggedly on. Giving up was not something a warrior of Weihlaris did lightly.

The landscape returned to that of the tundra he was used to: rock and frost and slow gentle rises and falls, long stretches of barren land with little to break it up aside from the rare boulders or the odd animal slinking along. Not that there was much motion that Orsin noticed. If it was not in front of him along the trail he was following, he wasn't interested.

But his perseverance was eventually rewarded.

There! Something huddled in a heap just ahead. Orsin forced speed into his fading legs and jogged forward.

He wasn't going to let the baron escape again! Not if he could help it.

But when Orsin drew near, it was not the baron huddling in fear of its life that he found, but the cold corpse of another herd beast. This one, while similar to the baron, was far more like a wolf than a fox. Well, its body was. There wasn't much left of its head to say for certain. The thing had been caved in with a hammer. All that was left were a misshaped lump and several spatters of bone and brain across the tundra.

Orsin felt an unexpected surge of warmth at the sight. One of his cohort had been here! That was the only explanation. Someone he knew had fought this herd beast, slain it, and lived to carry on the fight!

He walked the scene for a few moments, tracing out what he could of the battle from the disturbances in the frost and soil. It had been intense, from what he could see. There a spatter of blood where the herd beast had sunk its fangs into the unknown Fursja. Here a skid mark where the beast had clearly been knocked for a loop by a blow from the attacker's weapon. Something blunt, probably. There wasn't quite enough ichor staining the ground otherwise.

Orsin didn't even notice the time passing, gave not a thought to how he would have to backtrack and start again if he was to have any hope of picking up the baron's trail once more. None of that mattered. What mattered was that he felt a closeness to his people once more, a kinship in this moment of frozen violence. There was a unity of purpose here, a shared mission that echoed through the very stones!

The herd would suffer, would be destroyed; Orsin and his cohort would see to it.

There was proof, right here in front of him. Orsin sent a brief prayer winging skyward toward Weihlaris, a mixture of thanks for this moment and a request that the god look favourably on whoever had survived this battle. The sky looked back, slate-grey and impassive.

Orsin shudderd. Something about the sky above looked grim and unforgiving. There was a biting freshness in the air as well, one that made his tongue tingle.

It tasted like a storm was coming.

❈ ❈ ❈

Torben lunged backward, narrowly avoiding the cone of killing frost that sprang from the herd beast's gaping maw. At the beginning of the battle, that had been quite the threat but at this point Hjarsurunghad smashed the thing's jaw nearly to uselessness. The herd beast was in so much pain it's aim was suffering greatly.

Though he hadn't escaped the battle unscathed either. Torben was bleeding from several nasty bite marks, points of infections that would need to be cleansed, and soon. There was an irrepressible grin on the warrior's face, however, because he knew he was going to win.

He was Torben! He was mighty! Even if by his count Orsin had bagged slightly more kills than he had. That was partly down to the strange way his friend had been staking out animals and drawing herd beasts to him. Torben put the thought aside for later. He could puzzle out his friend's stange behavior after he slew the beast in front of him!

And honestly, a giant wolf-like thing breathing killing frost? That should count for way more than a pack of arctic foxes, even if they were herd-infected!

The wolf-thing lunged again and this time Torben brought his warhammer whirring around to meet its head from on high, like a carpenter hammering in a particularly stubborn nail. Chips of bone and globs of grey matter exploded all around the Fursja warrior as the herd beast collapsed, dead, at his feet.

Torben whirled Hjarsurung, sending bits of brain and small gobbet of fur flying in all directions.

Definitely worth more than a whole pack of foxes!

CHAPTER 16

Orsin crouched down close to the frozen surface of the tundra, sniffing carefully at the tracks in front of him. A subtle scent of rot and decay assailed his nostrils. He shook his head to clear the scent away. The baron had definitely come this way!

He had backtracked to the rocky area where he thought he had likely lost the trail and carefully went over the ground in a spiral search pattern until he picked it up again.

Orsin knew the baron now had a substantial lead. He was unlikely to catch up with it before the abomination had the chance to heal. Still he pressed on. He was a warrior of Weihlaris. He did not give up so easily.

Unfortunately, his prey was canny. The baron used its many tails to sweep away tracks when it could, ran over rocky ground as often as possible, and occasionally doubled back and shot off in a different direction.

Orsin stubbornly kept to the trail. He followed the scent when there were not visible tracks, made calculated guesses which direction the baron would flee along the rocky terrain when it cropped up, and relentlessly retraced his steps when the baron doubled back and tried to flee in another direction.

He had no idea if he was regaining any of the ground he had lost, but the trail did not seem to grow any colder.

Unfortunately he could not say the same of the air around him. A wind began to rise, ruffling his fur and trying to snatch the warmth of his body away from him via his breath. Orsin cursed. Too much wind and the shifting snow would make the trail much harder to follow, by obscuring tracks and dissipating the already faint scent trail even faster.

Orsin pushed himself to move more quickly. If he wanted the chance to find his quarry, he had to risk missing a track or a double-back. If he kept to his current pace, the weather would erase the traces he was after before he could find them anyway. It was not an ideal situation, but it was the only gamble he could make with the cards he held.

Was that a flicker of tail ahead of him? Orsin squinted. No. It was just a flurry of snow, driven by the rising wind. He pushed on, though the more cautious part of him whispered that he should give up on this fruitless chase. He was unlikely to catch up to the baron, and he was charging deep into unknown territory. There were all manner of dangers he might be missing in his single-minded focus on pursuing the baron.

He ignored the voice. He was so close! Orsin didn't want to lose this chance. He'd already bled for it. So he pressed on, moving more and more quickly, though he was increasingly uncertain if what he followed was truly the trail of the baron or his own wishful thinking.

Still, he pressed on until the howling of the wind broke through his focus, shattering the tunnel vision he had fallen into. Blinking, he glanced around himself. The light—always dim—had waned even further.

Orsin looked up into the sky. The steel-grey clouds were nearly obscured by the hard-driving snow. No soft, fat flakes, these. No, this was hard, harsh snow, small and sharp-edged, driven like caltrops into his eyes by the increasingly howling wind.

The Fursja had a name for storms like these: the Wrath of Weihlaris. They were sudden, unpredictable, and fell with the full, furious might of nature. As if all the world were the object of the god's fury.

He needed to find shelter. No Fursja warrior, hells, maybe not even a Queen of the Herd, could withstand the full fury of a storm like this without at least some kind of shelter. The snow would drive deep into the flesh, not that you would feel it, because the wind would steal the warmth from your flesh. If Orsin wasn't careful the wind would steal his life along with the warmth of his flesh and leave only a frozen statue standing on the tundra, dirty-grey snow drifting around him.

But seeking shelter now meant losing the Baron's tracks. The storm would obliterate them. Orsin would be back to square one.

With a growl of frustration, Orsin tore his eyes from the trail and looked instead for shelter. He couldn't kill the baron if he was already dead. Shelter now, find his prey again later. He'd managed to trick it once. With Weihlaris's aid, perhaps he could do so again. He'd hurt it. If he was fast and hit it before it could find more of those foes to eat and heal itself—no. Focus! Shelter now. All else later.

Orsin scanned the horizon. With a storm like this incoming he might even risk seeking shelter amongst the herd-blighted trees that seemed to be growing more and more all around. At least there would be some residual heat there from the infection.

But no copses stood out to his eyes. There were a few small rises, some strange collections of stone here and there, but no trees. Or if there were, he could not see them.

He growled again. He had pushed on too long! He should not have ignored the rising snow. He had been taught better than this. But his desire to slay the baron had consumed him. Orsin resolved to let this be a lesson, if he survived the coming storm. A true warrior was smart, as well as mighty and relentless.

The strange rocks called out to him for some reason, and, lacking any better option nearby, Orsin made for them. There would be shelter from the wind, and perhaps he could shift some of the smaller bits of stone to improvise a bit of shelter. Better if there were some grasses he could use for insulation. At the very least there should be some lichen. Enough of that and he'd have some insulation against the storm and a meal afterward.

If he was lucky. Though he had not been Fortune's favourite recently.

The wind was as cutting as any blade and Orsin's eyes swiftly began to water. He lifted one arm to try and protect his vision, but it did little to help. Even as he watched the moisture from his breath almost immediately turned to frost, coating the fur of his upraised arm. He could feel it on his muzzle as well.

Visibility dropped as quickly as the temperature. Orsin squinted against the elements, just able to make out large hulking shapes that he trusted were the rocks he was aiming for. Twice, he stumbled and nearly fell, his paws prey to rough stones and the uneven ground, but he managed to stay up and keep his focus on his destination. An ill-timed roll would be the death of him, now. If he lost sight of those stones he'd have no hope of shelter and a frozen tomb would be the best he could hope for. Weihlaris forfend that some herd beast find him before the last life left his body, or worse, somehow resurrected his frozen tissues with that fucking infection. No. He would make it. He had to make it.

And after what seemed an eternity in the deepest and coldest of the frozen hells, Orsin felt stone beneath his questing paw. He had made it to the stones and hadn't even realised! The visibility had gotten that bad.

With a prayer of thanks to Weihlaris, Orsin began to feel his way around the stones, looking for a nook out of the wind.

The stone was curiously smooth and flat. It didn't feel natural. It felt more like…like a wall! It must be.

Orsin had heard stories growing up as a cub of the Fursja settlements lost when the herd first came to these lands, and he'd found some of the other ruins himself in his first encounter with the baron. This must be more of the same.

He moved more quickly now, granted another burst of energy by this find. If these were ruins, there might be some proper shelter! There was unlikely to be any surviving supplies or food, but just a warm nook mostly out of the wind would be lifesaving.

If there was enough still standing, and he was very lucky, there might even be a fireplace somewhere he could use, and enough detritus nearby to burn. With the storm raging he need not fear the fire attracting the attention of the herd. The wind would whip away the smoke, and the driving snow would blind anything foolish enough to still be out in this weather.

Weihlaris must be smiling on him, in spite of the fury of his storm raging all around.

The stone suddenly vanished beneath his paws. Orsin felt a spike of panic but throttled it. He was no cub or green recruit. Fear was to be felt, and heeded if it was useful, and ignored if it wasn't. In this case he reached around in front of him and found the corner where the wall had called away. The wall had simply turned a corner!

Orsin followed it and relaxed immediately when the corner cut off the worst of the wind. It wasn't quite as large a relief as having a knife removed from your jugular, but it was close.

He could suddenly hear much better, out of the direct path of the howling winds. It was almost quiet. It gave the place around him an eerie feel, though knowing that his ancestors had once lived and laughed here before being driven out by the vile abominations of the herd did that as well.

It was dark, and the swirling snow in the air did Orsin no favors as he squinted, looking for a good spot to take refuge from the storm. He was out of the wind here, but someplace he could curl up and conserve body heat would be better. There were walls left, but they were so battered and worn that it was difficult to see that they had once been buildings. Orsin was unlikely to find good shelter there.

But he remembered how he had first taken refuge from the Baron, during that first encounter. There was a chance he could sniff out an old root cellar or something like that. While it was unclear what size this community had once been, from what Orsin remembered of the tales, there had to be some kind of storage beneath the ground.

A kitchen would be his best bet. Easier to recognise, and likely to have a small cellar for food and other goods. It's not like he needed much space, or to use it for very long.

It was painfully slow going. The low visibility and the shifting wind, combined with the extreme age of the structures around him, made finding what he was after a tricky prospect. The extreme cold was also sapping his energy.

Orsin was growing tired. And falling asleep could be a death sentence here. So he pushed through. It seemed like an eternity, but eventually he found what he needed.

It was barely more than a hole in the ground, and the door to the cellar was broken and useless, though that very flaw was what allowed him to spot it. Orsin grunted. It would do.

He set to hauling the detritus of untold years from the remains of the cellar. The fibrous bits from grasses driven here by the wind he twisted together in quick, rough knots and clamped under his foot. When there was enough space free, Orsin wriggled into it, out of the wind, and hauled the remains of the door over himself, stuffing the gaps with the knotted grasses, until he was as snug as he could make himself without also cutting off his oxygen supply.

Then, with the howling of the wind reduced to no more than a distant lullaby, Orsin curled up on himself and went to sleep.

Chapter 17

When Orsin emerged from his makeshift den the world had been scoured clean. Well, not clean, exactly. What snow was present was a dismal grey, rather than a pristine white, and tundra grasses—those bits that had survived the cutting wind anyway—poked up through the grey scum of snow in a mangy patchwork.

The tracks were gone. The scent was gone. Orsin would have to start his search up again almost from scratch. Though at least he knew that not even a baron could stand against a storm like that. It had to have holed up somewhere nearby. He was still close.

Orsin refused to give up. He had so nearly beaten the thing! And it deserved to die. Killing it would go far toward keeping his people safe. Any loss in herd nobility had to have that impact. And it would bring him glory. He could not deny that hunger. Wouldn't deny it. Killing a baron and bringing back a suitable trophy almost guaranteed he would be the most storied of his cohort.

Before he began his search for the baron, however, Orsin moved through the ruins. Part of him was looking for anything useful he might be able to salvage, but a larger part of him was satisfying his curiosity. What had it been like here, before the herd came? The thought was not one that he had entertained before. It had always seemed so far away, the time before the herd, and though the focus of his people was and had always been the extermination of the abominations, most anyone ever talked about was the war, not what life would look like when it was over.

Strange, now that he was seeing this place. He would have thought people would be happy to think about what things would be like, when it was over. Though that line of questioning did not go far. Orsin didn't have the energy for sustained contemplation.

Soon enough, thoughts of the past gave way to the necessities of the present. There was previous little to salvage that he could carry with him, though he did pick up a small fragment of stone with a few traceries of carvings still left to it, and added it to his supplies, as a reminder.

Once all was settled, Orsin set out to search the area. The day was clear, though it was still far from bright. Grey clouds still choked the sky. The air was crisp and clean and fresh, at least here near the ruins of the old settlement. Orsin could see a few spots on the horizon where wisps of vapor coiled into the air. Part of him now recognised these as likely herd-tainted groves.

He should get someplace high. A long view of the surrounding terrain would help him narrow down likely places to hunt for the baron, or at least might give him a glimpse of other herd beasts. The tundra was teeming with them, after all. Maybe another worthy target would present itself if the baron did not.

Any target would do at this point. Orsin had a lot of frustration and rage to work off. He had been so close to a victory! And to have it snatched away—he shoved the thought away. It was not gone yet. Merely hiding.

Orsin scratched thoughtfully at the walls. They had stood this long; they should be able to support his weight. And in the generally flat tundra, they might provide enough height to get a decent look at the surrounding landscape. It wasn't a huge advantage, but it was here. It should only be a matter of a few minutes to find one and scramble up to the top of it. If it turned out the vantage point wasn't good enough, he could make for whichever of the nearby rises looked the most promising as a vantage point. The view from the top of the wall would show him that much at least.

The stone of the walls had been quarried in large blocks, and though they had been fitted close and carefully when building the settlement, there were still small gaps for his claws to gain purchase where those blocks had been fitted together. His muscles bunched powerfully as they hauled his bulk up to the top of the wall. The roof that had once been attached to the tallest bit of wall still standing had long since fallen away, so he had nothing to stand on, but reaching the top Orsin was able to hook his arms over the edge of the wall and hold himself in place easily enough.

The nearby tundra was a white-grey expanse around the ruins of the small settlement. Here and there Orsin caught flickers of movement. Arctic hares had emerged from the safety and warmth of their burrows, to forage the grasses where the wind had scoured the snow away. A few caribou crested the rise to the west, and swiftly moved out of sight. Orsin had no way of knowing if they were regular beasts or herd tainted monstrosities.

There were no arctic foxes, so far as he could see, and no sign of the baron. There were two patches of unnatural green, one to the northeast, and one more west-northwest. The baron could have headed for either. If the baron naturally laired in such woods. It might have a small cave system somewhere, for all Orsin knew, magically dug out of the frozen tundra by herd-infested ants or something.

What horrors were out here, lurking beyond the range the Fursja usually raided? When was the last time a raid had driven deep into the heart of herd territory? And even then, how long did such attacks last? Long enough to discover secrets carefully hidden by the cunning intelligence that lurked in those twisted skulls?

Orsin didn't know, and the lack of knowledge was suddenly troubling.

There were other flickers of movement along the horizon, but Orsin was far enough away that he couldn't quite make out enough detail. It seemed like one large creature, perhaps the size of a Fursja warrior, but he couldn't be sure.

Perhaps it was one of his cohort. Orsin found the thought cheering, even if they could never meet. The rules of the Trial forbade it. The reminder that he was not out here waging a one-bear war against the entire herd species reignited the fire in his blood, however, and reinvigorated his competitive spirit.

Orsin resisted the urge to call out a greeting. He raised one paw in a salute, however. There was no communication there, merely recognition of a fellow warrior. There was nothing that could be construed as offering in terms of aid, or as a request for help. Just a simple greeting.

No response came, but Orsin had not expected one, really. Vision was difficult in the eternal grey light of the wastelands. Fine detail often escaped even the sharpest of eyes.

He descended from his perch on the wall and prepared to move on. He still had a baron to hunt, and dawdling would do no one any good. He had survived the storm, and had a reminder that others of his cohort were still out there, undergoing their own trials. All things considered, he had come out from the storm far better than he might have.

Another prayer went winging to Weihlaris. Orsin, thought he had lost his quarry and was beginning his hunt again nearly from scratch. He began to rumble an old ballad of ancient warriors quietly to himself as he angled toward the smudge of greenery to the north.

He would begin his hunt for the baron there, and slay whatever herd beasts he encountered along the way.

He had trekked along for nearly an hour when a chance glance behind him revealed that there was a familiar shape on the horizon. Orsin paused for a moment and frowned. That was definitely a Fursja silhouette behind him, wasn't it?

Even as he watched, however, the silhouette disappeared. The tundra was rising and falling enough here that it was plenty of cover. It made it easier to sneak up on prey, but also easier for hunters to stalk their prey, and Orsin knew he could be either, out here.

Why would anyone from his cohort be following him, though? No one in their right mind would risk violating the sacred boundaries of the Trial. It would be too great a dishonour. Even if one were to fail their own Trial, to endanger that of another?

Unthinkable!

Orsin watched for a long moment, but when the silhouette didn't reappear he shook his worries from his head and returned to his hike. The small patch of green on the horizons was growing and he couldn't be more than a couple hours from coming close enough to begin a careful search for signs of the baron or the servitor-foxes in the area.

After another hour he paused. There was a patch of boulders thick with lichen, most of them small and broad enough to be good hunting for grubs and fungus as well. Orsin took a break to forage and replenish his reserves.

He was just licking his jowls to catch the last of the scarce morsels when he saw something again. This time it wasn't along the horizon, no, the figure was far closer and it looked all the more like a Fursja for it.

He was definitely being followed. Orsin growled. What heresy was this?

Foraging forgotten, Orsin began to move once more. This time, however, he kept a careful eye on his pursuer. Whoever they were, they were definitely gaining. It wasn't that they were that much faster than Orsin, but he was moving at a careful, cautious pace, and whomever was after him was not.

It was like they were begging any nearby herd beasts to ambush them.

And maybe they were. It was a way to win glory, if you could survive. Making oneself a target was effective, if foolhardy. Usually it was the province of the very bold or the very desperate.

It usually resulted in warriors who were very dead.

Orsin was torn. Perhaps the other Fursja was in such a hurry they did not even see him. It could be coincidence that they were following so close to him. It wasn't like the tundra didn't make navigation difficult at times, and particularly in this region, with all the gentle rises and falls in terrain, it could be easy to miss another creature.

He should just slip away. It would be embarrassing for them both if they came face to face by nothing more than simple chance and endangered both their chances at the Trial. But before he could, the figure reappeared.

The approaching silhouette was definitely Fursja, and far too near! What had gone wrong that one of his compatriots would so violate the strictures of the Trial like this?

Torben? His mind asked, reaching first for his oldest, best, and best-loved friend in all the world.

But then he blinked and angled himself to get a better view. No. It wasn't Torben. The fur was the wrong colour, and where

Torben had a smooth expanse of glossy, chestnut fur across his chest and belly, this Fursja had a large, dirty-white patch, with some sort of splotchy shape in black fur in the centre.

"What's wrong?" Orsin called. "Why do you violate— "

The question caught in Orsin's throat, cold and bitter and sharp as thorns. Because he could now see, far too clearly, the face of this stranger, and it was no stranger at all. It was Sengetiid, one of the Fursja he had grown up with and who had so recently battled by his side as the cohort charged out of the gate.

But looking up into the face of his friend, Orsin's blood went cold. For Sengetiid, sleepy, grumbly, Sengetiid, was a Fursja warrior no more. The yawning black pits that had once been his eyes said that as clear as anything.

Sengetiid had been wholly taken over by the herd infection!

CHAPTER 18

Orsin stared into the ruined face of his friend, Sengetiid. The other Fursja seemed to stare back, but the gaping holes that were once his eyes made it hard to say for certain that was what he was doing. Traces of herd-rot, black and green, clung to the sockets like dried foam. Fresh spittle flecked Sengetiid's muzzle, and the strange pattern on his stomach fur that Orsin had noticed before bubbled and rippled with infection.

"Sengetiid?" Orsin asked, a bit stunned by the appearance of his friend.

He had already found the corpse of one of his friends and made sure to do right by his body. This, though, this was a whole new level of horror. Here was not a Fursja warrior, safe and scarred, nor the corpse of a noble fighter fallen in brutal battle, this was a walking corpse, a perversion of everything that Orsin's people stood for—and a thing out of Orsin's deepest fears and nightmares.

Sengetiid—what was left of Sengetiid—turned its head as if looking at him. Deep, rasping breaths rattled in his ribcage as his lungs heaved like a bellows. The walking dead stood before Orsin and did not move. It just stared with sightless eyes.

Orsin's paw tightened on Muinnajhr's haft. A deep, boiling anger began to rise in the pit of his stomach. This was an abomination, yes, but more than that it was a heresy! A violation of everything it meant to be a pure Fursja warrior. The herd had taken his friend from him, twisted him into this mockery of life, and turned a noble and powerful body to their own ends. It must not be allowed to stand!

He roared in fury and challenge, swinging his axe in a glittering arc in an attempt to part Sengetiid's head from his body in one smooth motion. He would rip this mockery of his friend to pieces, burn the infection from them, and give it a proper burial. On his honor as a warrior!

But the corpse-thing was fast. Incredibly fast. Though the motions were clumsy, it flung a paw up and deflected Orsin's blow. One of Sengetiid's claws went flying, sacrificed in the process, but Orsin's attack was otherwise ineffective.

In retaliation this thing roared, a wet, sucking sound that was a weak mockery to a true Fursja battle cry, but close enough to fan the flames of Orsin's fury even higher. How dare this thing!? It would pay!

The axe flashed and the corpse of Sengetiid lumbered and dodged in response. The corpse of his friend snapped and lunged, trying to sink its teeth or claws into Orsin, but the Fursja warrior dodged and whirled, his axe a deadly whirl of silver around him, keeping his flesh safe from violation.

"For Weihlaris!" Orsin roared, the defiant cry bolstering his spirit.

The attack he followed this cry with missed, but not because it was countered. Or not deliberately. The body of Sengetiid seemed to stumble back, slightly at the mention of the god.

"Lies—Leihlaris! God betray..." Sengetiid gurgled.

It was, like the rest of him, a mockery of the Fursja that Orsin had once known. But it was his voice. The thing was speaking, just as the baron had before it. Though with less ease and less sense.

Orsin repeated his fury and lunged once more, trying to turn the battle cry into a weapon all its own. But Sengetiid seemed enraged at the attempt and was not unsettled again. Though the corpse's movements were often jerky, they held a great deal of power and were occasionally deceptively fast and smooth.

The patch of herd infection on Sengetiid's stomach continued to bubble and leak, trailing long streamers of green-black pus from it every so often. Even amidst the sounds of battle Orsin could hear the gurgling and grinding of Sengetiid's guts as the herd-infection churned blasphemously within.

"Ba—baron!" Sengetiid gurgled.

Baron? Orsin's ears perked up at the word. Was there some connection between the fox-lord and this thing?

He leapt back as the thing attacked again, his axe lashing out and depriving it of a paw this time. The flow of battle made it hard to focus on questions like that. It was a dance of death, and distraction was a misstep that might prove fatal.

"No collect!" Sengetiid lashed out with his other paw.

Orsin dodged both the paw and the gouts of black blood that were jetting from the severed limb he'd just claimed. Infection everywhere. Even the blood was black. The infection had consumed every bit of his friend's body.

"I'm sorry, Sengetiid," Orsin growled. "I'm so, so sorry."

The thing froze, as if the utterance of the name it once bore was a conjuration that gave the speaker temporary power over the remains. Orsin didn't ask why, he simply took advantage of the opening. His axe flashed and great gouges appeared in the corpse's fur, blackened and gangrenous flesh showing through the wounds.

"Ha—hate you! Hate! Hate, hate, hate!" The ruin that had once been Sengetiid screamed at him.

It was the only warning Orsin had before the bubbling patch of herd taint smeared across Sengetiid's stomach exploded.

He had already thought it looked like an angry storm cloud, but the roiling of the rot only enhanced that illusion. Like a geyser propelled by the concentrated enmity within the remains of his friend, a vast gout of thready, string-like pus erupted toward Orsin, flying toward him like a hammer.

He only narrowly managed to dodge.

It was like the strangely doubled caribou thing all over again, but even worse. At least the pus here didn't seem to have a mind and a will of its own, but it smoked and roiled and turned the patch of tundra that it hit into a stinking, simmering morass as it ate into the earth.

Some kind of acid?

It did come from Sengetiid's stomach. It would fit with the strange noises his abdomen had been making. It was some kind of herd-enhanced projective stomach acid.

Even now, Orsin could see into the gaping hole where his friend's stomach and intestines used to be. A roiling mass of pus was even now welling up in it again, clinging to itself with enough surface tension to fill-in the strange cloud-like patch once more.

The thing would project another shot at him as soon as it was ready, Orsin was sure.

Orsin's eyes narrowed. It wouldn't get the fucking chance.

With a roar, Orsin used his position near the ground to brace his charge, and send himself hurtling towards his foe like a javelin. Muinnajhr whistled through the air, spinning in his hand and lancing out in quick, lethal arcs.

Sengetiid, perhaps disoriented from the acid-attack, or thrown off balance by the sloshing liquid inside of him, staggered back but did not manage to wholly evade Orsin this time. The axe bit deep and Sengetiid's left arm went flying off across the tundra.

The thing that had been his friend let out a gurgling laugh. Greenish-black foam sprayed from its muzzle and its head cocked unnaturally to the side to stare at him again.

"Collect you. Collect you. Stand by me in the collection, fuh-fuh-fuhrend!"

The sound of Sengetiid's voice, the mockery of that voice, would have made Orsin's blood run cold were it not for the fire raging in his gut. This thing had to go. He had to do it, not simply because it would bring him honor to end this mockery of a Fursja warrior, or because it was a part of his Trial, but because this had once been his friend, whatever it was now.

Orsin owed him much for the memories of warmth and camaraderie they once shared. He would not leave that debt to roam the tundra, uncollected, in this shambling body. No.

Another gout of acid sprayed out at him and Orsin, expecting it, nimbly danced aside. At least with this stuff he only had to worry about one point of origin, unlike those damned doubled-caribou. Even if it was difficult to look at the thing in the face.

"I will set you to rest, Sengetiid," Orsin called. "Though you have fallen, and you cannot hear me, I swear to Weihlaris that you will not continue to stagger about as this, this mockery of yourself. I will set you to rest, and I will burn this memory from my mind, so that I will always remember you as you once were. I shall tell your family that you died with honour, pursuing the Trial. That I found what was left of you and made sure to place you deep within the frozen ground, to ward you from the herd. This I swear to you, Sengetiid."

He wasn't expecting a reaction. The words just poured out, an offering to the memory of his friend, and to Weihlaris. It was perhaps a foolish indulgence, in the midst of battle, but this was no mindless beast turned herd-creature. This had been one of his peers.

Orsin felt it was right to offer that solace, useless or not, foolish or not.

It was *right*.

Suddenly Sengetiid stopped, froze in place awkwardly, like a puppet with its strings cut.

"No...collect..." came a croaking whisper from its throat.

A split second later, Orsin's axe obliterated the things entire neck, sending the head spinning off into the distance. Several more cuts neatly butchered the body and spilled a small tide of stomach acid out across the tundra to smoke and hiss itself into nothingness.

It took a long time for the last of the pus to sizzle itself into nothingness.

What had that been, there at the last? Some last fragment of Sengetiid, trapped and mad, in the prison of his own mind as the herd-infection ate away at him, body and soul? Orsin didn't know, but the question would gnaw at him in the dim twilight that passed for darkness in this place, in this time. How far gone was too gone, he would wonder. Where along the path was the point of no return?

Who could be saved?

He'd have to bury another friend, and bury him deep. Orsin sighed and threw his back into it. Sooner began, sooner finished.

When Orsin heaved the last stone into place and turned to gaze sadly at the battleground once more. Sengetiid—sleepy, grumpy Sengetiid—had been formidable, even in death. If he had been infected with a more cunning version of the herd infection, like the one that controlled the baron, he would have been a terror indeed.

He was just about to turn his back on the battlefield and resume his trek to the herd-blighted woodlands that had been his destination, when he spotted something strange. There was a thick, black liquid staining the snow. It looked like the same stuff as had erupted from the bubbling mass on Sengetiid's stomach.

Moreover, it existed off the battlefield as well!

Orsin retraced his steps. Yes. That mess on Sengetiid's stomach had been leaking, constantly! He could easily follow this trail. It would be a simple thing to track his friend's movements this way.

His brain turned over some of the fragments that had fallen from Sengetiid's raving mouth. He had said he was part of a "collection" and that he both loved and hated the one that had given him his gift. The one that had collected him.

The baron. It had sounded like the baron. After all, the thing had threatened to collect him, as well, during their last battle.

And if Sengetiid was a valued toy, perhaps the baron had kept it close. Maybe in one of its secret lairs? And even if not, a collection was something kept because of its value. It would be something that was valued and would be visited, possibly with some regularity.

Orsin could set up an ambush for the baron again!

And this time he wouldn't let the bastard thing escape.

Chapter 19

"Thank you Sengetiid," Orsin murmured to the memory of his friend as he stared down at the baron's lair.

The trail had led to one of the patches of greenery, as he had suspected, though annoyingly not the one that Orsin had been headed for when the corpse of Sengetiid had caught up with him.

Following a corpse to a copse. Orsin shook his head, the grim humor driving back the immensity of what he was about to attempt. The baron was holed up inside his lair, with his "collection" or at least part of it. Several small arctic foxes were milling around outside, one or two sniffling at the trail of black pus—long since sizzled away to nothing but ashy streaks—that Sengetiid's corpse had left behind in its flight from the lair.

Had part of his friend truly still been alive in there? The thing had paused, oddly, there at the end when he addressed it, and if it were wholly the baron's creature, why would it flee imprisonment?

But the baron was in that den. He knew that. He'd been watching, observing.

What he wouldn't give for a few barrels of oil and a lit torch. He'd love to roll them into that black, gaping hole and just thrust a torch in after. Let the whole thing blow deep inside.

Orsin knew better than to charge into that den blind. There would be no terrain advantage, and an unknown number of potential enemies inside. He had watched and he had waited. He didn't think there were many of the small foxes, but if there was a collection, there could be all kinds of herd beasts with unknown abilities inside. Whether or not the baron could command them, he had no idea, if they were even conscious, but he wasn't going to risk it.

The Fursja warrior was hidden atop a small rise, just to the side of the den entrance. He was at an angle that would allow him to see any activity around the entrance, but not directly across, to minimise chances he was spotted.

That and he had a plan to take care of reinforcements that required him to be right here.

In fact, if he timed things just right, his opening salvo for this fight might rob a large chunk of health and vitality from the baron before he even closed to melee range. He was less certain about destroying the smaller foxes around. If only he had time to hunt them and thin their numbers before he faced the baron—

And if wishes were soldiers, he would have an army at this back. Orsin shook his head. He had what he had, and it, and the strength of his arms, would be enough.

Orsin frowned. The only problem would be if there was another, secret entrance or exit to the den. He had carefully scouted the nearby area and had found nothing, but the herd was nothing if not surprising. Their very existence challenged expectation and the laws of nature. For all he knew one of these infected trees could pull itself up by the roots and reveal an exit.

Still, he had come this far, and he was this close. He would bring the battle to the baron and they would see who emerged victorious! As far as Orsin was concerned, their meeting had resulted in a stalemate or a tie. This would be the deciding encounter. One of them would not be walking away from this.

There was a flicker of movement at the entrance to the den and Orsin tensed, his muscles bunching and preparing themselves for the great push of what was to come. A long, elegant white snout poked out of the den.

The baron!

Slowly, the herd beast began to slink out of the den, its ears drawn back against its skull in clear displeasure. It barked a command to the pack of arctic foxes milling about outside the entrances and they dashed toward it immediately.

Orsin was already moving. His muscles strained and the bark of the herd-blighted tree in front of him crumbled beneath his grip, turning to dust rather than to splinters. It was spongy, the wood, and soft, but heavy. Orsin felt his feet sink deep into the soft ground, but it was still tundra, for all it was slightly thawed. It would bear his weight.

There were deep, cracking-tearing sounds from beneath the earth as roots snapped and soil shifted. Orsin's muscles strained as he lifted. Above him, the tree shook and trembled with the force he was exerting.

If this had been an ancient oak, rooted deep, or an ancient pine growing stubbornly out of the rock, this would never have worked. But these were herd-blighted trees. Their very existence was permeated with rot—the source of the unnatural heat all around. They were soft, for all they were heavy and tall, and they loosened the earth beneath themselves. They were shallowly rooted, as if the earth itself tried to reject their existence.

So Orsin yanked at the roots and the tree quivered and fell. Past a certain point its own weight turned against it and conspired to rip it form the ground.

And Orsin aimed it right at the entrance to the den.

The tree swooped down. The foxes all around had frozen at the unexpected sound, looking for the source, noses pulsing as they sniffed.

Their first instinct was their undoing. The tree came crashing down before they could move. Even the baron, with its enhanced reflexes, had been caught unawares enough to not move fast enough to fully escape the tree as it came crashing down. Though the fixers scrambled, the tree was inexorable, like Orsin's fury.

Fully half of the pack of smaller foxes were crushed by the branches of the tree as it hit, exciting in splotches of red blood and black ichor. They would be of no use to the baron. And the herd noble? Though it scrambled away from the den—arguing that there was no hidden exit after all—it did not move swiftly enough. The tree crashed down on its haunches, crushing its hind legs and snapping its spine.

A scream of utter pain and terror burst from the baron's mouth, echoing through the trees and across the tundra.

Orsin paid it no heed. He had allowed the roots to carry him and into the air, in a smooth arc that saw him propelled forward as inexorable as the tide, to land on the trunk and charge forward, paws pounding on the soft wood, a clear path between himself and his target.

The baron struggled, using its strength to slowly try and drag itself free from the fallen tree. The wood was soft, and it slowly cracked and splintered beneath the force exerted by the herd noble. Though it was heavy, and the baron wounded, there were enough foxes left that it could swiftly heal itself up again and become a deadly threat.

Orsin had no intention of allowing that to happen. He had fought the beast too many times. He moved as fast as his great strength would allow, turning his bulk into an implacable charge.

The baron's cry had drawn three or four of the smaller foxes into range. The baron greedily snapped them up, gulping them down whole, bones and fur and all, like some kind of serpent. A series of cracks echoed through the wood as broken bones twisted and surged back into place, healing unnaturally.

The tree shuddered. The baron, spine restored and legs once more functional, was able to exert even more force. But the weight of the wood still held the thing pinned, though clearly not for much longer.

The smaller foxes began to yip in alarm, sensing Orsin's attack. The baron turned to face the oncoming warrior, but there was little to be done. The branches limited its movements, and it had already shrieked out its cry for help. Whatever was coming was not here yet and would not arrive until after Orsin's charge was complete.

The fox-lord screamed at Orsin, pure sonic hell lancing out to assail his ears, but Orsin answered the attack with a war cry of his own, battering through the sound waves with the power of inertia, his own bulk, and pure determination.

The power of the herd noble was nothing in the face of Orsin's preparations, and hard-won experience. His axe lashed out, a gleaming arc that ended only when the Fursja warrior leapt from the tree, sailing up into the air and coming down with deadly intent from on high.

The baron struggled, but Muinnajhr was as inevitable as destiny.

The axe sliced through the spine like a hot knife through butter and Orsin spun away, avoiding the torrent of blood and ichor that spurted forth from the stump.

The foxes scattered. The body quivered and then relaxed into just so much meat, trapped still by the wood all around it. The head rolled to a stop amongst some fallen leaves and the air was silent. Not even a breeze moved through the trees.

Silence reigned for a long moment, as Orsin's chest heaved to restore breath to his lungs after the exertion.

"You will regret this," the baron's head said, unexpectedly, its eyes suddenly rolling around to focus on Orsin. "My Prince shall know, and your doom will come to you on sharp, skittering feet. Watch yourself little fuh-fuh-Fursja!"

The head suddenly erupted into a sick, cackling laughter. The eyes bulged, bloodshot and bulbous, until the entire head exploded in a tiny storm of viscera. Orsin dodged the steaming, streaming ichor. It would be exponentially more infectious than anything bled by a lesser herd-beast.

But the explosion of the baron's head had not been an attack, or not wholly an attack. As Orsin watched, each of the eyes coiled around on tendrils of nerve and coils of brain matter, small tentacles that each ended in a long, curving tooth or jagged fragment of jawbone. The things scuttled around, confused for a moment, then each one dashed off, fleeing in opposite directions.

Orsin didn't think. He just reacted, sending his axe spinning to slice neatly through one of the tiny monstrosities. It expired in a flash of grey goo. But the other escaped, scampering away into the the wood and vanishing.

He let it go. The thing was too small and too fast to track easily, and there was no telling what other creatures the baron's cry was calling down on this place. Orsin did not wish to risk being swarmed by maddened herd beasts.

No. He'd collect his trophy and retreat to the ruins he had taken shelter from the storm in. He'd rest there and decide what to do after.

Retrieving Muinnajhr, Orin stalked over to the baron's body. With one smooth blow he severed the largest of the tails, grabbed it, and turned to sprint away.

Laughter bubbled up inside him as he went. He had done it! He had slain a baron in single combat!

The glory was his!

Chapter 20

Orsin stared at the tail in front of him. The trophy looked much smaller than he expected, in the diffuse light of what he assumed was morning. It was impossible to truly know the hour, nor how long he had slept, safe and secure in his hidey-hole in the ruins where he had weathered the storm, but it felt like morning.

A baron. He had felled a *baron* of the herd single-handedly! By any measure, he had passed his Trial, provided he survived the journey home. Glory to Weihlaris!

Eve the sky seemed to smile upon him. The grey clouds that so often shrouded the heavens above the tundra had cleared. The sky was still more grey than blue, but there were no clouds. No hint of snow. The light, such as it was, was a bit brighter.

Home.

Orsin massaged his left shoulder with his right paw. He had torn something in that battle, either in tearing the tree up by its roots or in driving his axe through the spine of the baron. He'd not noticed it in the heat of battle, but after sleeping once more on the cold tundra, even insulated as he was by the ruins, it ached.

Small injuries like this could add up, if not tended carefully. And too many of them could spell doom in facing a herd-beast. Every day out here was a danger.

Home.

Orsin couldn't help but think of it, after the seemingly-endless days he had already spent out on the tundra. The battles he had won were glorious, to be sure, but every warrior dreamed of the comforts of a roaring fire and hot mead once in awhile.

He could head back. He had certainly struck a glorious blow in the war against the herd. Weihlaris himself must be pleased. He had survived the storm. He was granted the clear sky above right now. And none would fault him if he did return.

He could see his parents again. He could sit in front of a roaring fire and eat roast boar and drink honey mead. He could face the Warlord with pride and honor, and he was sure to receive a great blessing from Weihlaris during the ceremony for those who pass the Trial.

Or. That single syllable echoed in the vaults of Orsin's mind. Or.

Or he could continue his Trial. He had managed to slay a baron! The taste of glory was better than any honey-mead. It was richer, and darker, and oh how bright.

And there was something else going on out here, far from the regular raids of the Fursja warriors, something that escaped notice when they mounted their regular sorties into herd territory in an attempt to cull vast swathes of the beasts and eliminate as much of the nobility as they could.

That idle boast—it seemed so long ago now! To slay a herd prince. Maybe he was riding too fast and too furiously on the warrior's high, but it actually seemed as if such a goal might be within his grasp.

Had he not defeated a baron already and survived? Sure, he had nearly died the first time, and the second it escaped, but he had *done it*.

Could he do even more?

If he went home now he would never know. His next trip here, and every one after that, would be part of a cohesive force of warriors. This was the time to take his true measure. This was the time to show his god precisely what he was capable of. This was the time to strike a blow against the herd and drive deep into their territory and uncover their secrets.

How often would the warlord allow him to do something like that?

And there was also a small part of him that wondered if his word that something foul was afoot out here would be taken seriously, would be heeded, if he went back now. Yes, he had slain a baron, and the trophies he had claimed, the scars on his body, and the chants of the shamans would all prove that, but would it give enough weight to his words that the Warlord himself would listen? Or the council?

Orsin almost didn't believe it himself.

Then there were the practical concerns. He had supplies and body fat reserves enough right now to make it home. That would not be the case if he ventured deeper into herd territory. He would have to scavenge even more than he had been doing so far, and there would be less and less food that was safe to eat. Less and less food would be completely free of herd taint.

He would have to be very wary indeed. The herd beasts would be stronger, more deadly, and he would be alone, with no one to watch his back.

He might die out there, alone. Or worse, be turned into some foul abomination. The fates of his friends weighed heavily on him. He could still see their faces, cold and covered in dirt as he buried them beneath tundra soil and stone.

Did he have an obligation to carry their tales home? Was it greater than the call to glory? What about the service to Weihlaris?

All these thoughts and more whirled around in Orsin's head as he stared at the severed tail of a noble of the herd beneath a clear, cold sky.

Torben would press deeper. Torben would continue the quest for glory. Torben wouldn't stop now.

Not until he had the head of a herd prince at his feet.

Orsin rose. The thought of his best friend drove him on. How could he return now, even if he *had* slain a baron, knowing that Torben would be urging him on, a maniac smile on his face?

No. He'd go deeper. That was the right thing to do.

Orsin scoured the ruins once more in search of anything useful, but aside from a few bits of fungus to line his stomach, he came up empty. Ah well. There would be other ruins.

He set out across the tundra, heading for the patch of greenery that he had guessed—wrongly—had held the baron's den. It was in the path to the depths of herd territory, and more than worth a look. Barons of the herd were not common, but of all the nobility they were the most common.

And Orsin would need to find another if he was going to have a chance to track down a prince. A plan was already beginning to form in the back of his mind. He would let it grow as he travelled, then turn it this way and that, until he was certain it stood the best chance of success.

The tundra was clear of herd beasts, though not of the signs of their passage. Orsin frowned as he passed several different kinds of herd sign. Most of them seemed to have been headed in the direction of the baron's den.

Perhaps they had headed to answer the call the baron had screamed to the uncaring sky right before Orsin had deprived the fucker of its head.

The Fursja warrior felt his lips curl up in a feral smile. Well, if they had, they arrived too late to either help the baron or avenge its fall. Though from the looks of things some of the beasts had fallen themselves.

Orsin spotted a few large corpses in the distance, between his current spot and the copse where he had slain the baron. He hesitated, but then decided to trek over and investigate. It was only an hour or two out of his way, and he might learn something. Had they perhaps collapsed dead when the baron died? That would be useful. If killing a herd noble caused those herd beasts that owed it fealty to also die, well, imagine what would happen if they managed to finally slay the Queen!

But when Orsin arrived he found the beasts most certainly did not die from natural causes. He inspected no less than three and every single one had their heads caved in with some kind of blunt weapon. Bits of skull and brain matter were slung liberally around the nearby tundra.

Orsin felt a familiar warmth kindle in the pit of his stomach. One of his cohort had been here. Perhaps they even managed to help cover his escape, all unknowing. Perhaps not. In any case, it would have had no bearing on his battle with the baron and was no violation of the strictures of the Trial.

It was a pleasant reminder, and Orsin took it a sign he had made the right decision in trying to delve deeper into herd territory. Even if he fell there were other Fursja to carry on the fight.

Torben would carry on the fight.

Orsin allowed himself to walk over the battles, tracing the signs of the struggle and seeing a familiar warhammer as the weapon that deprived these beasts of their lives. There was no way of knowing which of his cohort had been here, Orsin revelled in the idea that his best friend might be so near.

Idly, he brought his paw up to the blade of Muinnajhr and ran the pads of his fingers over the cold surface. Somewhere, deep inside the metal, a single drop of his best friend's lifeblood beat like a heart. Somewhere, in this vast expanse of tundra, a drop of his blood likewise beat within the metal of Torben's warhammer.

Not so far apart, though Orsin could not see nor battle beside him. They were connected with a bond inviolate. Nothing and no one could break that. Not distance. Not some herd beasts. Not the Fates themselves.

I look forward to seeing you again, my friend. Orsin thought. *I cannot wait to sit with you before a roaring fire, the two of us, with full flagons and full bellies, exchanging stories of our time out here. What are you doing right now, I wonder?*

❇ ❇ ❇

Torben watched as his best friend in the world made the bravest—and possible stupidest—decision possible.

Orsin was heading deeper into herd territory.

Torben slung Hjarsurung over his shoulder and smiled. Brave! Well, looks like the adventure was just beginning.

A herd baron! Torben had crept into the wood once everything was over. Several large herd beasts had charged in. Torben was still cleaning bits of many of them off his hammer. He'd not been so close that he would interfere, but he heard the cry from the wood he'd seen the tiny form of Orsin enter. He'd been exposed on the tundra when herd beasts suddenly surged up and began converging on the wood.

It had been quite the scramble, crushing as many of the nearby ones as he could. Good exercise, all glory to Weihlaris!

To kill a baron in single combat! If Torben wasn't so delighted for his friend he'd be jealous! Not that his own assistance—entirely appropriate and from a distance—hadn't been been a factor in ensuring Orsin made it away from the battlefield alive. The glory of it all!

Torben grinned. Orsin would be able to pull so many beauties with that story when they got back home!

His friend was really blossoming out here on the tundra, truly growing into a fierce and formidable warrior. Torben had always known they would both pass the Trial, would both do honor to their family and to Weihlaris, but seeing something like this!

He couldn't wait to see what would happen next.

Torben grinned and swung his warhammer around by the thing at the end of its handle. The whirring noise accompanied him as he cheerfully fell into a slow job, following his best friend deeper and deeper into herd territory.

For glory!

Chapter 21

It got warmer the deeper Orsin pushed into herd territory. It was a gross violation of nature. Previously, the further North he had pressed, the darker and colder it got. Now, with the herd-blighted woodlands growing thicker and more frequent, he found himself alternating between freezing in the natural tundra wind, and beginning to sweat as he hauled his warrior's bulk through the increasingly hot and humid patches of greenery that he carefully made his way through.

He hadn't seen more of the arctic foxes yet, but he'd run across at least three different kinds of mutated caribou. Thankfully only one of them had been the kind that projected those strange living tendrils of rot, and that one was also a solo encounter. The other herd varieties of caribou he'd met had been in small herds, but not nearly so dangerous. They had been bulky, in one case, and emaciated in the other. The emaciated ones were mangy, and Orsin could clearly see their bones beneath their withered hides, but they were *fast* and their bones not nearly so brittle as you would expect.

The worst thing, though, was seeing so many more of his people infected with the herd taint. It wasn't that many, compared to the infected beasts he encountered, but every one was unique in a way the lesser herd-beasts weren't, and every one was a dagger straight into his heart. To be torn from the embrace of Weihlaris like that, to be stripped of honor and purpose, reduced to merely a shambling, rotting puppet-thing.

Orsin had faced three of his former kin, since leaving behind the grave of Sengetiid. None of them were so well preserved as his friend had been. It was as if some part of the spirit of the Fursja rejected the infection, and fought on, even once past the point of all hope.

The first had been a cruel fusion of Fursja warrior and GauVark. The torso, head and arms of a Fursja warrior and been merged onto the GauVark where the head and neck should have been. The battle had been long, and dangerous, and Orsin more than once was forced to use the trees around him to press his mobility advantage versus the corpulent beast that charged after him, roaring and squealing.

Fortunately, it was not so powerful as the one he had captured to tempt the baron, and the two halves did not work in perfect harmony. Orsin had lured it into charging full on between two massive trees where it had wedged itself, and, once stuck, chopped it to bits with Muinnajhr. It had been sweaty, bloody work and the rot had run thick across the tundra before he was finished.

The second was nothing more than bones, though strange herd-infected vines were wound through the ivory jumble and curled up inside the skull like some kind of grey brain-matter. The bones moved as the vines moved in response to Orsin's approach, but no skeletal warrior arose.

He had split the bones down to splinters and scattered them, before slashing through the vines and retrieving the skull for burial and blessing. The list of the dead was growing in his mind, and his father's skaldic tricks, while useful, were a bittersweet blessing. Sometimes Orsin wasn't sure he wanted to be the bearer of all these memories.

The third and last was by far the worst. It was so old as to be nearly skeletal, with only a bare few patches of fur remaining over a hide long since dried and tanned by exposure to the elements and the tundra winds.

It had also been only a cub when it had fallen to the herd infection.

Orsin had no compunctions about fighting the little demon. Whatever it had been, now it was nothing but a vessel for putrefaction and horror. It needed to be ended, and the cub that it had once been deserved to rest.

The thing was canny though, and fast. It had a whole network of tunnels spread beneath the ground and even up through the trunks of several of the trees. It attacked quickly and retreated, leaving small, stinging lacerations from its unnaturally bone-white claws. It was a battle of attrition and Orsin struggled mightily to end it. Though end it he did, eventually. He caught a flicker of movement out of the corner of his eye and swung Muinnajr around, allowing the little beast to neatly bisect itself on the razor-sharp edge.

Orsin buried it as he had the others, with a prayer to Weihlaris and a sprinkling of sacred herbs to help place the soul to rest.

The image of that wizened little body, however, continued to haunt him as he moved deeper into herd territory. He moved more quickly than he needed to to escape that patch of greenery and find the fresh, cold air of the tundra once again. How long had that tiny body been host to a herd parasite? The Fursja did not field child-soldiers, and it had been centuries since this area had been home to any of his kin.

How old was the baron he had slain? How many years had it prowled the tundra? How many Fursja, humans, or Lurgirs had fallen to it? To the herd in general?

Suddenly the scope of the war he was fighting hit him in a brand new way. He had always known this was an old war, but now that he was out here, fighting it amidst the haunted expanse of its most ancient battlegrounds, he was truly in awe of the sheer scope of the struggle.

"Weihlaris help us," he muttered to himself and the cold tundra winds.

He moved quickly across the tundra, not because it was cold and he wished to warm himself, but because the deeper he moved into herd territory the more herd creatures there were all around. Orsin was a lone warrior in enemy territory. He needed to choose his battles carefully.

There were still scattered rock formations, old ruins, and the gentle rise and fall of the terrain. Orsin made use of each and every opportunity to pause, scan the surroundings, and choose the next piece of his path.

He was halfway between the ruins of a small village, almost entirely erased by time and strange herd vegetation, when a dark form came hurtling over a small rise and dove for him.

It had once been some kind of wolf, that much Orsin could see, but now the thing trailed a dark mist of some kind, possibly a cloud of spores, and they poured from its mouth with every breath. Viscous fluid dripped from the thing's front two fangs, like venom from a snake, and it snapped and growled at him.

At this point his reflexes had been honed by not only years of training but also weeks of existing on a razor's edge here in the tundra, fighting herd animals of all kinds. Orsin narrowly missed being caught in those fangs, but still he dodged and his axe came spinning around in a brutal counter-attack.

The wolf danced away from the blow, growling in frustration. Orsin swept his axe through the dark mist that coiled in the wolf's wake. He held his breath and took several steps back. Whatever it was, he wanted to keep it as far from his lungs as possible.

The wolf circled, eyes narrowed as it looked for an opening. Orsin set Muinnajhr to spinning around him, a silvery dance of death. Let the wolf come. Orsin would split it in two.

The herd beast darted to the side, clearly trying to circle him and go for the hamstrings. Some instincts held true, even after the infection had sunk deep. Orsin was learning that there was almost always at least a small echo of what the beast had once been in its herd-mutated form. Even if things changed, there would be something recognisable.

The wolf before him seemed to have an obsession with attacking from behind. As soon as Orsin whipped around to face it full on, it would dart to one side or the other, attempting to catch the Fursja from a lateral angle.

It was a pattern, and one Orsin was happy to use. He let the wolf circle, watching carefully out of the corner of his eye. As soon as the thing started sprinting toward him Orsin prepared his blow. He would have to time it just right. If he turned too soon his enemy would break off before he was in range, but if he timed it just right he could catch the wolf as it leapt for his exposed hamstrings and fell it in one blow.

And the plan worked almost perfectly. The wolf attacked. Orsin waited and swung his axe just in time to make the herd beast's death a certainty.

But right before Orsin's axe split the wolf's head it losed a terrible, echoing howl. The sound of it turned his blood to jelly and, had he been any less a true warrior of Weihlaris, might have caused him to lose his nerve, turn, and flee.

But Orsin's rage burned hotter than whatever fear-mongering sorcery the herd beast unleashed upon him. His courage drove the axe blade true and split the skull of the damned thing wide open. Brains and chips of bone flew through the air and Orsin whirled his axe to send the herd ichor and gobbets of flesh flying off in clean arcs.

Answering howls came, however, echoing all around.

Orsin's ears flicked in irritation. Wolves were pack animals, and it seemed that this one was no exception, even though it carried the herd-rot. It sounded like it had quite a few siblings, actually, and Orsin knew better than to face unknown numbers in an exposed position like this.

He turned and considered his options. He could easily fall back to the last ruin he had used for cover. It wasn't much more than a few tumbled stones in lines that said walls once stood here, but it would be cover. His scent would be strong there though, and the wolves would easily find him.

There were two other options. He could try from a small collection of boulders, or make a beeline for a swampy bit of herd-tainted greenery. He could smell the rot from here and if his nose could pick it up, it was sure to sear the nostrils of the herd wolves. There were a few trees there amongst what smelled like it had to be brackish water, vast things with roots like spider's legs. They would bear his weight with little issue. So long as they themselves were not alive and blood-thirsty abominations, he should be able to get a vantage safe from the wolves.

Decision made, Orsin headed toward the swamp. After stowing his axe, he clambered easily up into the branches of the first tree that looked solid enough to support his weight, concealed himself behind the drooping, moss-like foliage, and watched.

After seeing the sheer size of the pack that came boiling out of the hills Orsin decided he had made the correct call. There were dozens of the wolves, several even larger than the one he had killed. While he could have taken several of them with him to the arms of Weihlaris, he was not so certain he would not have been completely overwhelmed if he had to face all of them at once. They were fast and their teeth were sharp and who knows what other herd tricks they were hiding.

The pack roamed about, finding his trail, clearly, and splitting off into two groups to chase down the scent. The one that ran off toward the ruins he paid little mind, but the one heading toward his swampy bit of land held his full attention. If they braved the swamp...but no. His guess had been correct. The wolves showed little desire to wade into the swamp, and even whined a bit, sneezing at the scent.

After a bit of snuffling around the edge of the swamp, the pack wheeled and headed off after the other half of itself, toward the ruins the Fursja warrior had so recently left behind.

Orsin waited until the pack had cleared out then carefully made his way deeper into herd territory.

Knowledge and glory awaited him.

Chapter 22

It began at first as innocent tendrils of mist, creeping along the ground, weaving through the glittering, frosty blades of tundra scrubgrass. Before Orsin quite knew it, however, the fog was ankle-deep and thick enough that he could not see his feet. It began to rise in plumes, thin tendrils coiling upwards like a sea of dancing snakes.

Orsin blinked in the grey half-light that continually suffused the tundra at this time of year. Several compass points all around him were marred with herd-tainted greenery. The interplay of hot and cold air all around, of unnatural moisture and plant life, caused all manner of strange weather effects. Most were localised. He had noticed them becoming more and more common as he pressed deeper into herd territory, however, and he assumed they would continue until he went too deep that the tundra fell away and there was nothing around him but the hot, dripping jungle that had no right to exist anywhere, let alone here, near the frozen roof of the world.

A curious mix of heat and chill washed over his feet as he hiked forward. Curious, Orsin lifted one to look at it. A faintly green-white frost glittered on his fur, turning every hair into a crystalline spike. It brushed away easily enough, turning back into fog as soon as Orsin flicked his paws across it and sinking down to join the growing cloud beneath him.

It was up to his knees now. Orsin glanced around him. The stuff was rising and thickening in every direction. There was no way out of it that he could see, so he oriented himself toward one of the taller herd-groves and began to power through the mist. If he could get to one of the warmer patches, the fog should fall away. He really didn't relish the idea of trudging along this deep in herd territory with next to no visibility. There was no telling what might lurk out there, or take advantage of the fog's veil.

The fog continued to rise. It came to his waist, and then to his chest, growing thicker and thicker. It almost seemed to cling to his limbs as it swirled around him, disturbed by the wind of his passage. The occasional wafting coil of mist even made it to head-height on him now, and when Orsin breathed in the vapor it tickled and stung his nostrils. There was a curious, minty scent to it, fresh and sharp and too-sweet.

It was almost pleasant, actually. Orsin snorted. It would be the first thing he'd encountered out here that was, aside form the occasional fungal delicacy he'd scrounged from beneath the rocks.

Orsin licked his jowls. He hadn't found any tempting tidbits from his scavenging in days. The deeper into herd territory he went, the scarcer food was. At least, the scarcer food which he trusted enough to eat was rare. There was plenty of other food if he wanted to risk infection. There had been a strange purple fruit, long and rounded and thick, hanging from the trees he'd passed the day before yesterday. They had smelled sharp and fresh and slightly acidic but he refused to pull any down from the trees or risk the thick, white sap that oozed from the cracked ends of the ripest of the bunch.

The frost tingled on his tongue and was immediately replenished by the clinging fog. It was actually kind of invigorating. Orsin felt himself grinning and he picked up speed, his eyes still locked on the massive tree rising above the fog banks.

Though the fog rose quickly enough that in short order even the tree he had been using as a guide vanished from sight. Everywhere he looked there was nothing but the fog, filled with a diffuse, grey light. Sound was deadened, and smell, and Orsin felt almost like he was pushing his way through a cloud of incredibly soft and delicate wool. The kind of thing his mother might wrap a particularly valued family heirloom in.

All sense of time vanished. Orsin kept walking. Something in him wanted to pause, to stop here in the mist and drink in the peace, but he knew if he did he'd risk losing his bearings entirely, and would eventually run afoul of some herd beast or other. What had the terrain looked like before the fog cut off his vision? Was the grove he was aiming for at the top of the rise he was on or the next?

Orsin would have thought that the fog would roll down the rises and gather in the valleys, but it seemed to cling like a desperate thing evenly across the earth. Even to his limbs. Tendrils of it wrapped around him, moving with the air from his passage and leaving a sparkling trail of stinging frost all over him.

Then, at the very edge of his vision, a shadow darted through the fog. If it didn't disturb the rising mist with its passing, he might have thought it a trick of the light, but the whirling vapors told him clear as day that something was in this fog bank with him.

Orsin drew his axe, the weight a comforting tug on his muscles. Oddly, the mist almost seemed repelled by the metal. Where his fur and most of his armor developed a thin, glistening layer of frost, the stuff eschewed his weapon.

The shadows flashed again. More than one, this time. Or was it? Whatever it was—or whatever they were—it was fast.

No. There were definitely at least two of them. Probably more. Weihlaris help him. Orsin was getting very tired of hate herd beasts that hunted in packs. Was it the foxes again?

A bolt of adrenaline shot through him at the thought of facing another baron, here, in these conditions. His head suddenly cleared, the edge of battle cutting through the fog that the mist all around appeared to have wrapped his brain in. Something strange was going on here. He needed to get out of this mist, find someplace with clear lines of sight and make whatever beast that was behind this pay with its life.

Three shadows flickered at the edges of his vision this time. With their lives, he mentally corrected himself.

It wasn't the foxes, Orsin decided. He hadn't heard any of the tell-tale yip, nor had any of them made a play for his hamstrings. The foxes would have attacked by now. No, this was something else.

Something that was having fun with the hunt.

He tried tracking the flickers. There seeemed to be no pattern to them. They appeared and disappeared, almost always at the edges of his vision. When he did manage to catch a bit of a glimpse, however, it didn't tell him much.

There was a flicker of white fur, noticeable because it was paler than the grimy snow or the coiling green-white mist. Whatever it was, it was definitely bigger than the arctic foxes he'd faced. Well, not counting the baron. The baron had been a thing on a scale all its own.

And it had fangs. Orsin caught a very brief glimpse of sharp teeth against a pale green background. The thing's insides were green it was so full of herd-taint! And it seemed to be breathing out the fog, somehow.

But before Orsin could snatch more than these few, fragmentary impressions, the thing was gone. He tried to follow, but it was too fast, and they appeared at random all around him.

They were definitely hunting him. The flickers at the edge of his vision came more and more frequently. Four, then six, then possibly as many as a dozen all at once. They moved so fast it was difficult to count all the motion.

Why were they holding off? Orsin growled. If they came just a bit closer he could slice them apart with ease. They were fast, but so was he. They just needed to come within reach.

But the things stayed stubbornly away. It was unlike any other herd beast he had yet encountered. Usually the damnable abominations charged right at him, or at least tried to harry him from the sides or go for the hamstrings.

These little fuckers, they just kept circling him. Taunting him. Playing with him.

He tried charging at one as soon as the flicker appeared, but the thing just danced away and was lost in the fog. He picked up speed, moving faster in an attempt to get out of the mist, any direction would do so long as it would clear, even just a bit. But the fog remained thick all around him.

There was no sense of time. How long had he been wandering in this mist? How many hours? Or was it just minutes? He should have found his way to a rise or some trees or something by now, surely.

The flickers of movement kept coming. Though it was getting harder to pin them down. There were either too many of them and he was losing track, or whatever it was that was hunting him was changing how it stalked him.

Orsin blinked. His paw looked fuzzy. The edges of Muinnajhr were filmy and the axe seemed almost to ripple before his eyes.

His eyes. Something was wrong with his eyes. He'd thought it was just the fog obscuring his vision, but it was something else.

The mist. He'd been breathing it in for who knew how long. It tasted funny. It felt funny. Was it laced with herd infection? It didn't feel like it. If it was, it didn't feel like any of the other times

Orsin had brushed up against that foulness. But there were many terrible things out there that had nothing to do with the herd.

This wasn't one of those. Not this deep into herd territory. But it was something. Poison? Orsin cast about, looking for any hint of a landmark, but all he could see in every direction was the fog. He had no idea how far or close he was to the edge of it. Safety could be two steps away to his left and he would never know.

Orsin blinked. His head had begun to swim. The frost on his fur was thicker than ever, though he furiously brushed it away. It turned back to fog, but the fog just turned back to frost.

His nose began to burn and his stomach flopped. Acid bit the back of his throat, minty and cloying, an echo of the taste of the fog. Orsin growled.

Poison. A coward's weapon. Of course the herd would have beasts within its ranks that employed such a vile tactic.

He stumbled. The ground suddenly seemed much less steady beneath his feet. Had he stumbled into a marshy area? No. It was the fog.

Orsin shook his head in a vain attempt to clear it but that only made things worse. The world whirled around him and he staggered unsteadily to the right. His paw spasmed and he very nearly dropped his axe. Only iron determination enabled him to maintain his grip.

But it was too much. The world had been sent spinning and it didn't stop. The fog swirled around and around and Orsin had to clench his teeth closed against the acid bile of vomit threatening to burst from his throat.

He had to get out of this fog. He needed—

Orsin got no further than that. His eyes rolled up into the back of his head and he collapsed to the ground, unconscious, the fog swirling around him with malicious glee.

Chapter 23

A death scream, high and shrill and piercing, ripped Orsin out of unconsciousness. Instinct saw him roll to his feet, axe at the ready, and through his head was still muddled, he still managed to focus on the sound. It was the only thing that was new and different. The fog still swirled around him, but that scream? That he could follow.

Orsin charged towards the sound. He felt the ground rise up beneath him. A small rise! Thought he could not see it, he was climbing it.

But the exertion wasn't without cost. The fog had coiled deep within him. As Orsin charged forward, the breath he needed to move came at the cost of a deep, wracking cough. Something thick and wet flew from his mouth. Blood. He was coughing up thick, black clots of blood from his lungs. The poison was eating him from the inside out!

He stumbled as he crested the rise, expecting to continue on his upward trajectory, but his feet found no purchase there, and he nearly fell over himself onto the broader, flatter top of the rise. But the mist swirled and he found himself in a small clear space. The fog was dissipating here, a small eye in the storm of poison slowly swirling all around.

Orsin coughed again, splattering crimson across the dirty grey snow clinging to the top of the rise here. But it was not the only color flecking the grey. Small splashes of grey matter and mint-green colored the snow as well. At the edge of the clearing in the fog he spotted a likely source. A white-furred foot, tipped with wicked green claws, lay unmoving.

Off to his right he saw the top of a tree peeking over the fog. He'd gotten turned around, gone off course when he couldn't see past the fog. Orsin hesitated. Did he investigate the corpse at the edge of the fog or did he charge back into and hopefully through the cloud of poison, toward the tree that he'd been using as a guide before he lost sight of it before?

A hiss of rage was all the warning he had. Something came hurtling out of the fog toward him. It was at least a meter long, thin and sinuous and covered in dirty white fur that would blend in naturally with both the native tundra landscape and the grey-green vapors of the mist all around.

Orsin whirled, a motion that set off another fit of coughing and hacked at the thing clumsily with his axe. It was a clumsy counter, lacking in the force a true warrior of Weihlaris should be able to exert, but the poison was sapping his strength and still clouded his vision.

The *eisvesle*, at least that's what it looked like, though Orsin had never seen one grow to such a size, nipped at him with sharp teeth, dancing out of the way of the Fursja warrior's clumsy blows. It missed, rage blinding it and making it almost as clumsy as the poison made Orsin.

"Stand still you little weasel," Orsin growled, though his foe was no *little* weasel.

It chittered at him, dancing back before launching itself at him once again. Orsin swiped at it but missed, his filmy vision throwing off his aim. The eisvesle landed between the Fursja and the corpse at the edge of the mist and exhaled, thick tendrils spilling from its mouth, reaching out to knit itself to the larger body of fog nearby.

The clearing shrunk, a tiny bit.

No! This was the only clear air he had nearby! Orsin could not let this thing close the hole in the bank.

He roared a battle cry and thrust himself forward, wringing every bit of speed from his poison-weak muscles. The eisvesle, mouth open and focused on some arcane process by which it knit the mist to the fog, was too slow in moving this time. Muinnajhr struck, an arc of lethal silver, and split the thing's head in two.

More grey matter splattered across the dirty snow, followed by a few jets of viridian blood. These things were steeped in herd-taint! But they didn't show the overt rot that many beasts he'd encountered did. Were they perhaps *born* already infected?

He was deep within herd territory now. Such abominations might be possible. They certainly had stranger powers than the other herd-beasts he'd encountered so far. Something like this didn't seem like a simple infectious mutation. But he was no shaman, no specialist in studying the enemy. He as a warrior. His solutions were a bit more simple.

What he did notice, however, was that with the death of another eisvesle the fog began to dissipate more around that side of the clearing. The beasts seemed to somehow shape and control the fog as well as breathe it out. With this one dead, the stuff seemed to be thinning.

He could actually see all of both corpses, now. His vision was steadying the more lungfuls he took of cold, clear air, though he still fell to hacking up globs of blood and pus.

The poison was insidious stuff.

The other eisvesle, the one whose death screams he followed, had been crushed. Orsin could see the place where its spine had been broken by blunt force trauma, and then the soggy messy that had once been its head. Something had come down on it with incredible force. There was even a clump of brain matter sticking out of the thing's left nostril.

He had no time to ponder this discovery, however, as more furious chittering came from all around him. The beasts seemed to have a greater than usual care for one another, some kind of advanced herd connection. It drove them wild to see one of their own destroyed, apparently. The scent of their own blood, spilling across the tundra, brought them charging forward, most signs of their previous slinking, stalking behavior gone.

Fine with Orsin. They were easier to hit when they weren't just dancing away at the edges of his vision. And the more he could kill, maybe the more this damned fog would dissipate.

Muinnajhr was a comforting weight in his paw. The axe's edge glinted green with the blood of the eisvesle he had killed, which had turned to a glittering frost. Yet another bit of evidence of the connection between the beasts and the damnable fog.

Shadows flashed at the edges of the mist. Orsin tensed, throwing a glance behind him. These things were fast. If they managed to flank him…

Before the thought could manifest to anything more than a faint worry, two eisvesles burst from the fog, streamers of mist trailing from their open jaws. Fine with Orsin. If they were breathing out fog, they weren't going to be able to bite him. The most they could use were their claws, and he'd not give them a chance.

Muinnajhr split the spine of the first, but a wracking cough threw off Orsin's aim for the second, and the thing danced away, diving back into the fog. The eisvesle he had hit was still struggling to breath out mist, though, so Orsin reversed his strike and severed the thing's head. Then, because it seemed the beasts were easier to fight when they were enraged, he seized the head by a convenient ear and flung it into the fog.

"Come on you fucks," he roared. "Come and try to avenge your fallen!"

Orsin didn't expect that they could understand his words, but the message of that severed head should be clear enough, even for the dumbest of herd beasts, which these most certainly were not.

Two more charged out of the mist. This time their jaws were primed to tear into his flesh, not to dispense more of the poisonous mist. Orsin, his head clearing by the moment as he breathed in the fresh air, slashed out with Muinnajhr. Stomach and intestines spilled out as one of the eisvesle came too close to his weapon. It screamed in agony, drawing yet more of its kin from the fog bank to throw themselves at the Fursja warrior in rabid fury.

Muinnajhr whirled, a silvery arc of death. Orsin's muscles screamed at him but he forced himself to fight on. The fog almost boiled with eisvesle, as the long, lithe forms shot forth, each trying to tear him to bits. There was no order to their attacks. It was wave after wave of furry, poisonous rage.

The tundra around him became slick and muddy with venom-green blood and more than once Orsin had to carefully leap back to avoid being baited onto slick ground. Once he nearly slipped on a pile of entrails, the swiftly cooling organs treacherous as the eisvesles he had torn them from. But still he fought on. He would not fall. He would not allow this damnable fog to rise once more and sink its poison into his every pore.

His chest was a pit of fire. His throat rasping and rough, like meat studded with broken glass. His vision blurred again, though this time with exhaustion. The poison had sapped his strength and left him weak.

But his will was the will of a warrior! He was a servant of Weihlaris! The herd would not claim him! Muinnajhr sang through the air, parting fur and flesh, driving back the eisvesle and with them the mists that the brought, until Orsin was alone in a sea of gore, the fog fading fast all around him.

He flinched at a flicker of movement at the edges of his vision, but when he turned there was nothing there. There was nothing around him at all. Nothing living, anyway.

Orsin stood, chest heaving with exertion. Was that the last of them? Had he somehow managed to kill them all? The mist was nothing more than the few faint tendrils it had been at the beginning, and even as he watched those too began to fade. Either the last of the eisvesles were dead, or they had fled in a cowardly rout.

It was impossible to know for certain. Orsin had been all but blinded by the fog and never got a good count of just how many of the beasts there had been in the vile pack. At least a dozen, sure, but there were fourteen or fifteen corpses all around him, if he included every one he could spot from the top of the rise.

There were also a few more that had been crushed, perhaps as many as five or six. That was definitely not the work of Muinnajhr. In any case, more than a dozen corpses lay strewn across the tundra.

His lungs hurt. Each breath sent small needles of pain shooting through him. And the fog—it had been filled with some kind of herd taint. He needed to get out of here, find a safe place to camp, and treat himself immediately. There was no telling what might be metastasising in his lungs even now. He needed to burn the sacred herbs, inhale the smoke, and offer prayers to Weihlaris that he made it through the night without succumbing to some new kind of herd infection.

The thought of a pack of these things inside Fursja held lands, running along the rooftops, filling whole villages with this fog, infecting countless innocents while evading and dancing away from the blades of the Fursja warriors...it would haunt his dreams.

He should go now. Find shelter. These things were vindictive. He'd seen that much. If any escaped there was no telling what they might bring to the area in their quest for revenge.

Herd beasts were more intelligent than he had thought, and the way they communicated...if there was one of these things at the baron rank...Orsin shuddered. The fox lord had been bad enough!

A cough wracked his body. Shelter. Fire. Herbs. He needed to go, and now.

With one last wondering glance at the bodies of those eisvesles that had been crushed to death, Orsin turned and loped away from the battlefield. There was a collection of stones near the horizon with suspiciously regular edges. It might be another Fursja ruin where he could take shelter.

He prayed to Weihlaris that it was.

Chapter 24

Orsin was lost.

Once he had burned the sacred herbs and dosed himself liberally both with the smoke and a paste made from their crushed leaves and melted snow, Orsin had fallen into a deep sleep. He'd found another cellar and secured it as best he could against any wandering herd animals that might happen past. His preparations must have worked because he had not been disturbed.

But he had no idea how long he had slept. It could have been hours or days. Likely at least one or two days. A storm had swept through while he had been asleep and covered everything with a fresh coat of dirty driven snow. There would be no following his own tracks back the way he had come.

When he awoke he felt incredibly weak, but he was no longer coughing up blood. The herd poison had been driven from his system. He was hungry, but that was no measure of time either. He was almost always hungry. The lack of safe foraging in this area saw to that.

Worse than his loss of a sense of time, however, was the fact that the fog had robbed him of all familiar landmarks. He was utterly lost and had no idea where he was or which way he might travel to move deeper into herd territory.

Climbing the few standing walls here, in the ruins of the Fursja settlement, was of no use. They did not go high enough for him to see anything useful. And while he had been following a large tree, there were a few he could see from his position, and none were distinct enough for him to be able to tell them apart, or to recognise the one he had been using as a landmark.

The sky was an eternal grey. Even if the clouds parted at this time of year there were not nearly enough stars to use for navigation. The best he could manage was a very rough guess as to his direction using the sun as a reference point, but the territories he moved through were vast, and twisting. There was no guarantee he'd be able to find his old trail, or backtrack along it. There had been enough storms to see to that.

What Orsin needed was a higher vantage point.

There were the trees, of course, though he did not trust the soft, herd-blighted things to support his weight in the heights he would need to climb, if he could even find one truly tall enough to serve his purposes. He might wander out of herd territory before he could find one that suited his needs.

There was another possibility, however. In the distance, thanks to his vantage from the top of the wall, Orsin could make out what seemed to be a larger outcropping of rock. More than a rise, it might be a proper tor. If he could scale to the top, he should be able to see far enough in all directions to find his way once again.

Yes. That was what he would do.

Decision made, Orsin scoured the ruins once more for anything edible or useful and then set out. The weather was clear and crisp and the air still smelled like new-fallen snow, for all the stuff was dingy and grey all around instead of white.

At one point he startled an arctic hare, and the way it fled from him told Orsin that it was untainted by any herd infection.

Some quick axe work and he was soon snapping down morsels of raw flesh and cracking the larger bones to suck out the marrow.

The small meal somewhat assuaged his stomach but Orsin still felt a deep hunger. He had expended a lot of stored energy fighting off the poison. His skin felt looser around him. Not much, but a little. Enough that he wasn't going to turn up his nose at any source of food.

The tor rose off in the distance. It was several hours journey away, at least. Orsin settled in to a ground-eating stride and kept his senses peeled for any roaming herd beasts that might offer him trouble. The last thing he wanted was to be ambushed again by something as strange as those fog-breathing eisvesles.

Orsin was lucky, he knew. If someone—and he was sure it was a someone, not a something—hadn't crushed that handful of the beasts, and their death cries hadn't awoken him, he'd likely be a shambling, rotting host for herd-taint at this very moment. Lucky, or blessed by Weihlaris.

He wondered which of his cohort it might have been. He couldn't imagine it would be anyone else. There were stories of course, of mad Fursja rangers, living out in the wild, waging a solitary war on the herd while living off the land. But so far as he knew, they were just that, stories. The only Fursja he had encountered out here had been his cohort, dead, or both.

The wounds had been crushing ones. Not that that narrowed it down much. Warhammers and mauls were as popular as axes and swords amongst his generation. Though he could easily think of several of his cohort who were too lazy or too cautious to venture this deep into herd territory. Even that, however, wasn't a guaranteed way to account for possibilities. He himself had seen how easy it was for herd beasts to lead Fursja warriors astray.

It could be anyone.

There were surprisingly few signs of herd activity, and what few there were only grew less as he walked on and the tor grew in prominence at the horizon. Was he heading further away from herd territory? It was possible. Orsin grimaced. Soon enough he'd scale that tor and find his bearings. Until then he might as well content himself with scavenging for more food.

Keeping an eye out for attack, Orsin turned more of his attention to the terrain. As he drew slowly nearer and nearer the tor, he noticed something odd. The plant life was slightly different here.

In fact, he recognised many of the herbs peeking up from the soil or between the thing, rank tundra grasses. They were the sacred herbs that were used to create the remedy for herd infection!

At first he stopped at every specimen and carefully harvested it, to increase his own stores. But Orsin began to realise that the herbs were not rare here, if anything it was the opposite! They seemed to grow everywhere, thicker and thicker the closer he got to the tor.

Orsin squinted at it, now that it took up more of the horizon. Was there something special about that place? Or would the herbs vanish before he got there.

He would find out soon enough, he supposed.

Perhaps this was the reason there was so little herd activity though, the herbs being so prevalent. Even in their untreated state they might be unpleasant for the herd beasts to encounter. This might be an oasis in the middle of their territory.

If nothing else, however, it was reassuring to increase his stock of herbs. He couldn't bring himself to fully let his guard down. He had suffered too many mishaps recently for that, but Orsin was not going to turn down the favour of Weihlaris when it presented itself.

Each time he harvested, he was careful to offer prayer of thanks, and, occasionally a small offering of his own blood. It was only right. The herbs preserved his life, he should offer them some of his in exchange. May it be well received and ensure that the plants thrived and continued to be a thorn in the side of the abominations.

Orsin knew the herbs were hard to cultivate. They resisted domestication as fiercely as the Fursja resisted the herd. While small amounts could be grown, and the magic of the shamans stretch that supply almost infinitely so long as the warriors using the herbs kept the faith, seeing this many of the plants in one place was almost unthinkable.

How many more surprises were lurking out here in the depths of herd territory?

Orsin shook his head. It was too bad. If these plants did have a minor ability to keep the herd at bay, it would be well worth cultivating them. Though he suspected herd nobility could drive the lesser beasts into a frenzy of destruction that would destroy those fields when it came to war.

No, his people would not win this war as farmers. They were warriors!

As nice as it might be to have another, simpler weapon to deploy against their ancient enemies.

It took several more hours to reach the base of the tor. It rose from the surrounding tundra, a blunt, rounded cylinder of stone. There was no mistaking it now, no losing sight of it beyond a rise. It soared above the rest of the landscape, massive in comparison to the relatively flatter lands around it.

Was the air cleaner? Or was it just the effect of hiking for hours through the dense beds of holy herbs? What was this place? Orsin was convinced, now, that it had been important to his people once, before the herd drove them from these lands. There was a peace here that wasn't present across the rest of the tundra as he had experienced it. A wounded peace, to be sure, but a peace of sorts.

Stone eventually replaced the tundra scrub grasses and holy herbs and the thin, frigid soil they rooted in. There was little purchase for anywhere here except lichen. Orsin greedily gathered all he passed, and turned over a few stones though without the plant life to feed on grubs were far scarcer. He managed some bits of fungus, even more of the astringent delicacy he hadn't tasted in weeks now. Though it was not enough to completely quell his hunger, it helped. It helped a great deal.

Orsin squinted at the tor. The walls of the thing were too sheer, too steep to have a path as such, but there certainly seemed to be a way from the bottom to the top. He spotted what had to be artificial hand-holds, carved long ago into the rock. While they were long since worn by the elements, they did not look wholly natural. Maybe once there had been ropes, or wooden support pegs, or other climbing aids, but not nothing remained by the holes, too regular to be anything other than deliberate.

He could see the path he would ascend. It would be dangerous, the rock icy and slick with frost, but he was strong, and there were ledges upon which to rest and handholds to grip with his claws. It would be difficult, hauling his supplies with him, as meagre as they were. He was half-tempted to leave them here, at the base of the tor, and pick them up upon his return, but there was no guarantee he would be descending on the same side.

No, he might descend the opposite side, if that looked to be the best direction to move in. Returning here would then just be a waste of time and effort. And while circumnavigating the base of the tor would be easier than climbing it, it would take a great deal of time as well. No, to be on the safe side he'd just have to haul his supplies up with him.

At least there weren't that many.

Orsin hefted his bulk and began to climb.

Chapter 25

Orsin's paw slipped, the frosty stone slick and treacherous. His warrior's bulk shifted dangerously and a small cascade of pebbles, dislodged by his unsteady weight went clattering down the cliff face. Muscles screaming, Orsin clung with both legs and one arm to the face of the tor, teeth gritted. Carefully, he sought out the paw-hold once more and carefully worked his way in until he had a firm grip.

He had lost count of the number of times he had slipped. The cliff face, even with the paw-holds left by his ancestors, was no easy path. Orsin growled deep within his chest, however, and hauled himself another arm-length upward. His claws quested for each crevice, testing them one by one until he found. a grip that would hold, strong enough to haul himself up, feet mirroring paws in the quest for purchase and stability.

Time and again he repeated the process. His world narrowed down to a single point of focus, the cliff face he was climbing. It was a good thing this place was surrounded by those fields of herbs and that he was now several lengths off the ground. If he had to worry about pursuit from herd beasts this ascent would go from dangerous to almost certainly lethal.

Eventually, however, Orsin's questing paws found no more stone. Instead he hauled himself up and over the lip and onto the broad expanse of the tor. He rolled onto his back and panted, his arms and legs on fire. The air here was much colder than the tundra below, though at this moment Orsin relished it. The climb had left him dangerously overheated.

When he had recovered enough, he carefully levered himself up with a groan and looked around him. The top of the tor was mostly stone, mostly flat, and was host to several kinds of moss and lichen Orsin had not seen before. None, however, appeared to bear any herd taint, so he happily scraped up several samples and, finding them good, proceeded to refill his energy stores with them.

It would likely take years for the ecosystem to fully restore itself, but that was not Orsin's concern.

The tor was massive in breadth, but Orsin didn't cross it immediately, nor explore far across its surface. He had climbed up here to get his bearings, to find out which way he should journey next. His attention was all on the horizon.

Looking back the way he had come, he saw several patches of herd-blighted greenery in the distance. Glancing in the opposite direction, across the wide expanse of the tor and to the horizon beyond, he saw the same. As far as his eye could see, all was herd territory.

He shook off the thought. There were other directions. A glance to his right and there was less greenery. From here he could see beyond it to the scrubby tundra and small scatterings of ruined Fursja settlements. He thought he could see the one where he had taken shelter from the terrible storm, the Wrath of Weihlaris, but he couldn't be certain at this distance. Though it did tell him which way he would need to journey to return home.

That must be South, he decided. Which meant that the deeper reaches of herd territory would be in the opposite direction, to the North. Orsin turned and squinted through the twilight toward the northern expanse in the distance.

At first it was hard to make out much beyond the general grey expanse and the increasingly thick patches of green. His eyes slid over the expanse of enemy territory, almost absently, knowing that this was indeed the direction he would need to travel. And then he blinked. What was that?

The green was so thick there was practically no tundra left at all. So why was there that large grey patch? And why was it rising out of the trees like a stubby mountain? It looked like stone, yes, but it was far too smooth to be natural. A cast dome like that—Orsin blinked.

That dome…he'd heard of that dome in tales and ballads! They were not always sung, for they were always as tragic as they were glorious, and warriors did not like to dwell overmuch on defeat, but that dome?

That was the home of the herd queen and her attendant princes.

Orsin's blood went cold at the same time his gut burst into flame. A deep, primal growl rose up from his throat. The heart of the enemy. How he longed to rip it out with his bare claws.

But even as he looked upon the seat of his foe, the cold wind whipping past him cooled his ire and stopped him from immediately charging forward towards it. It was a nigh-unassailable fortress. Fursja armies had crashed and broken against the stone of that dome, never so much as cracking it.

That was the tragedy of all those tales. Yes, the warriors fought valiantly, and were welcomed into the bosom of Weihlaris for their fearless battle fervour, but it always ended the same way. A scant few survivors escaped to tell the tale, limping back through enemy territory carrying what knowledge had been gleaned in the hopes that the next attack, or the next, might win through where they had failed.

As the dome was still standing and his people were still embroiled in this endless war, it was clear that their hopes, as of yet, remained unfulfilled.

Orsin stared at the dome. How could he hope to succeed where whole armies of warriors had failed? Weihlaris was with him, he knew, but he was still a green warrior, in the midst of his Trial. He did not yet have the might of a true berserker. He did not bear the sacred mark of Weihlaris which would grant him even more power.

What could he, alone, do?

Doubt gnawed briefly at him before he backhanded it from his mind and his heart. He was a warrior of Weihlaris! The question was indeed, what could he, alone, do!? That was the entire point of this Trial.

And Orsin knew what he wanted to do. Something no Fursja had done before. Something to eclipse the feats of all who had come before him.

He would slay a herd prince.

If he could do that, if he could strike them, alone, so deep within their territory, so deep within their home, where they felt safe…what might that do? How worthy might that act be in the eyes of his god?

He had already slain a baron. A prince would be an even greater, challenge, yes, but it was a worthy one. It was a worthy foe.

Orsin felt a wild grin slide across his jowls. This was what it meant to be alive, to be a warrior in service to his people! He would face the enemy and it would fall before him, or he would fall before it. Either way, in so doing he would truly know himself and know his worth.

He moved immediately toward the edge of the tor, glad he had brought his equipment up along with him. There would be no tiresome delay in heading toward his goal! He knew the best direction to head.

He paused before he began his downward climb, however, clearing away more moss and lichen, bolstering his reserves as he carefully studied the terrain between the tor and the dome. It would not be an easy journey. There were few landmarks to follow.

In fact, most of the terrain he would be passing through would be herd-blighted greenery of some kind, woodlands or possibly even jungle, close to the dome where the growth was thick and a haze of vapor—poison mist or simple moisture trapped between the heat of the plants and the cold tundra air blowing above them. Orsin could spot precious few landmarks. There was a finger of stone that rose above the trees not too far from the tor. Probably a particularly well-built remnant of Fursja ingenuity. He would head for it, first. Maybe he could find something useful there, some knowledge that might help him.

If nothing else, it was likely he could find shelter there from the herd beasts all around, and it was pleasant to have a reminder of his people, for all it was a sad one and a testament to their long ago defeat.

Fixing the other landmarks in his head as best he could, knowing that things would likely look very different from a perspective on the ground, Orsin checked that his supplies were secure and began his descent.

Here, too, were the remains of an ancient pathway his people had once used. Again, the wood and ropes—if there had been any—were long since rotted away, but handholds and crevices and ledges there were aplenty.

Unfortunately there was more moss growing on this side of the tor as well, making things even more slippery. As if the frost hadn't been bad enough. Orsin felt his worldview spin down to a single point again, as he focused tightly in on making his way down without falling to his death.

Initially, the enthusiasm for realising his next destination buoyed him. He felt energised as he had not felt in days, and his muscles happily complied with everything he asked of them. Plus it was easier to lower himself down than to haul himself up, though he did not want gravity to be too helpful a friend.

It was a long way down and the rocks below were sharp.

But then he discovered he was not the only living being on this side of the tor. Perhaps it was because this side of the tor faced herd territory. Perhaps the sacred herbs did not grow so thickly around the base of the place on this side, but there were all manner of nests playing host to herd-tainted birds.

Orsin discovered this the hard way, startling a sleeping specimen that looked somewhat like a seagull with a wicked, serrated green beak. It exploded away from its nest in alarm, the sudden sound and movement nearly causing him to lose his grip and fall, but he managed to hold on, claws digging desperately into the stone.

That lone gull, however, began to cry in fury and more and more avian voices took up the cry. Soon Orsin was forced to deal with a whole flock of birds dive bombing at him and attempting to peck his eyes out.

Orsin made his way down to a ledge. It was broad enough to stand on, and he was able to draw his axe and swing it before him in a silvery whirr of death. Gull after gull perished on that blade, falling in streamers of blood and feathers.

Eventually, he managed to kill enough of them that the rest flew off, sqwuaking in distress, but not before their leader, a large gull with a wingspan nearly as long as one of Orsin's arms, took one last swoop at the warrior.

Orsin slashed at the gull, and missed. Worse, the ledge beneath him cracked and he was forced to scramble to grab on lest he fall. He managed to save himself, but the gull flashed by again, razor beak slashing, tearing open the back of Orsin's paw and causing his grip to spasm.

Muinnajhr fell, spinning end over end until it vanished from sight below.

❈ ❈ ❈

Torben held one paw up over his eyes, squinting to see what was happening up above. He had been too far behind his friend to catch up with him before he had nearly submitted the tor. And there was no way he would risk climbing up after him. Not only was Torben unwilling to risk the fall, there was no way to avoid coming face to face with Orsin and violating the strictures of the Trial. The tor was large but not *that* large.

And he was unwilling to risk his own glory as well. He was here to make sure they both came home, if he could, but he would do so by helping from the fringes. He would not and could not risk the wrath of Weihlaris.

Torben would not risk not being granted the mark of a true berserker.

And there was nothing he could do to help his friend from down here. Not with whatever he had done to anger all those birds. Though if he had not, Torben might well have lost him. It would have been very easy for Orsin to descend the tor while Torben was too far away to track him, and going around the perimeter of the entire rocky outcrop would have takes ages. There would have been no guarantee he'd be able to pick up his friend's trail after that as well.

His eyes tracked the flash of silver as Orsin's axe fell and Torben shook his head.

It was a sad, sad thing for a warrior to be parted from his weapon under the best of circumstances, but to be disarmed by birds?

His greatest service here on the tundra very well may be never telling this story to another living soul.

Chapter 26

Muinnajhr! Orsin stared down the cliff face toward where his axe had gone spinning away. A deep, furious growl built in the depths of his chest and rattled up his throat until it burst between his fangs as a howl of pure rage.

The herd-infected avians fluttered back for a moment, taken aback by the sheer volume and the fury. The reprieve didn't last long, however, and soon the bird, emboldened by the lack of the silvery arc that had been defending Orsin, began dive-bombing him in even greater numbers.

Orsin pressed himself back against the stone of the cliff. He couldn't climb down like this. He needed time and care to find and test the hand- and foot-holds. He wasn't getting down until either he, or all the birds around him, were dead.

His claws lashed out, as deadly in their own way as Muinnajhr, though not as sharp nor with as much reach. Feathers flew and black-green ichor splattered against the rocks around him. Back and forth Orsin and the birds warred, neither able to gain the upper hand. Orsin was larger, with deadlier natural weapons, but the birds were faster and had the advantage of numbers.

The birds were clearly as frustrated as Orsin was, as the leader of the flock, a large, black-crested thing that had once been some kind of gull, let out a piercing cry. The rest of the flock began to fly to the leader, slamming into a massive, roiling ball of feathers. Black ichor began to seep along the wings, turning them black as bodies rent themselves asunder and long, stick strands of herd-venom lashed out and pulled flesh and bone back together, re-knitting many bodies into one, massive bird.

The thing roared at Orsin, vast wings beating unsteadily to keep it aloft. It's beak was wickedly serrated, composed of the beaks of the whole flock fused into one, flesh-rending nightmare. Massive, beady clusters of eyes, two in the head and one on the chest, blinked in a cascade of lids. Four legs, rough and spiky with leftover talons exploding out of the scaly, yellowed flesh, curved beneath the body. Each leg ended in three or four wickedly bladed talons, as serrated in their composite nature as the beak was.

The thing opened its maw and shrieked hate at Orsin.

It was at least twice his size. The Fursja warrior had no idea how it was staying aloft, but it was. And it was clearly eyeing him up in preparation for an attack.

Unlike the flock it had been moments ago, the mega fowl would have no trouble tearing him from the cliffside and shredding him for dinner. Orsin glanced around, looking for something, anything that might be a weapon or a crevice in which he could press himself out of reach of that deadly beak and those terrible talons, but there was nothing in sight.

He glanced down. There was no sign of Muinnajhr from this height, and jumping would almost certainly kill him. He was still trapped between two terrible choices.

Orsin paused. Or was he? Yes, if he simply jumped, he'd likely die from the fall, if the bird didn't tear him to shreds first, but what if he had something to cushion the blow? Something he could ride all the way down?

A feral grin split his face. The mega fowl was barely holding itself aloft. With Orsin on its back it'd start to fall, but far slower than Orsin would, with no wings of his own. He just needed it to get close enough, jump on its back, ride it down to the base of the cliffs, find his axe, and finish it off before it could finish him off.

It was a stupid plan, dangerous in the extreme, but it was better than his alternatives.

"Come on, then," he roared, trying to provoke it. "Come at me!"

Dozens of eyes blinked and zeroed in on him, fury glittering across them. That jagged maw of a beak slit open again and shrieked back at him before the massive beast lurched clumsily toward him. Power had come at the cost of mobility, in this case.

That was to Orsin's advantage. He dodged the thing's first attempt, lunging to the side and clinging desperately to the rock face. The talons that narrowly missed him gouged deep into the stone, impossibly sharp and strong.

His eyes widened. Fucking herd mutations. You could never tell what would change, what would be more dangerous. He needed to steer well clear of those talons if he wanted to live long enough to finish the Trial as he wished.

Twice more the thing swooped at him, and twice more Orsin narrowly escaped being eviscerated by those wicked talons. How many more deadly attacks could he dodge? And though it was ungainly, it had a lot more staying power than he had thought. It was only slowly losing altitude.

This time, though, this time Orsin was sure. He had to be. He'd only get one shot at it. As the bird shrieked and flew at him again, this time coming in along a line just below Orsin's eye-level, the Fursja warrior bunched his leg muscles, pushed off agains the cliff face, and sprang through the air, claws extended, arms pinwheeling, to land on the back of the beast.

He scrambled for a grip, claws tearing furrows of feathers free and casting them to the wind all around. They swirled around his face, a white and black flurry, making it hard to see. The bird shrieked in outrage at his presence and immediately turned into a barrel roll to attempt to fling him off its back.

But Orsin was Fursja. He was born with claws and he knew how to use them. Hours, weeks, years of training had honed his muscles and his grip until it was as relentless as a steel trap. He dug his claws deep into the dripping flesh of the bird-thing and held tightly to it.

The thing failed to dislodge him. There were cracking sounds coming from deep within it, and Orsin could see flashes of the cliff face as the bird tried to slow its descent and simultaneously fling him off.

They were falling fast. Not as fast as he would have if he had jumped, but fast.

Suddenly something pierced the center of his left paw. Orsin roared in pain and yanked his paw free. A beak and several feathers and gobbets of flesh trailed after it.

The bird had somehow moved one of the beaks around inside its body to stab him!

Orsin growled and slammed his paw back down, shoving the pain aside to bury his fist deep into the bird. It thought it could dislodge him like that? It'd have to try harder.

Much harder.

The bird suddenly launched itself into a spiralling barrel roll once more, trying to fling him off. This time the effort was accompanied by beaks stabbing up out of the thing's flesh, trying to dislodge Orsin that way. The Fursja warrior roared defiance and pressed his claws deeper, until he found a spot where a composite rib adjoined the knobby mess of bone that was the thing's spine.

He wrapped his claws firmly around it as the bird shrieked in pain and hate and held on.

He was going to ride this thing all the way to the ground, and when it hit, if there was anything left, he'd tear it apart with his bare fucking claws.

The ground was coming up fast. It had to be. Orsin couldn't see it from his position on the back of the bird, but the thing was increasing the intensity of its struggles. It was afraid.

Good.

Though Orsin's pleasure was short lived as a clump of flesh next to him suddenly bulged. Another beak erupted, but this one was still attached to the head of a bird. The herd-thing struggled, like a chick emerging from its egg, to tear itself free of the surrounding flesh and take wing in the air.

The thing was turning back into a flock! If it fell apart too soon, Orsin would hit without any cushion. He could not allow that to happen.

Orsin roared and began tearing furiously at the thing's flesh with his free paw and raked its back viciously with his legs. Green-black ichor squirted into the air, acompanied with the smell of rot and fistfuls of stained feathers. Orsin tore at the flesh, clawing his way deeper, seeking the vital organs that powered this monstrosity.

And there were many of them. Tearing away a vast ribbon of flesh, Orsin suddenly saw through the ribs he clung to with a vise-like grip. Pulsating sacs, composite monstrosities formed of dozens of hearts and livers and kidneys, chained together into large organ-globs, all wrapped around one another and sheltered in the stained ivory vaults of the thing's ribs.

Even as he watched they were pulling apart slightly, moving around like oversized grubs, seeking to form systems and pull themselves free of the monstrous bird they had become. Orsin roared and drove his claw deep into a pulsating mass. Maybe it was a secondary heart, maybe it was some kind of spleen or other organ. The things ruptured beneath his attack and the herd-beast beneath him shuddered.

More and more birds began to wriggle up from the flesh around him. The wings to either side started showing great holes. As many of the beasts as could escape, were trying to now.

On the plus side, they were so desperate to pull themselves free that they no longer bothered to attack him. On the other paw, the fewer birds made up the massive herd-fowl he was on, the rougher his landing would be.

He couldn't stop it. All he could do was slow it. Orsin redoubled his attack, hauling and clawing and forcing the larger bird-beast to react and try to throw him off, distracting all those little component bird-brains from trying to flee. If the organs were in use, trying to preserve themselves, they wouldn't be able to fly off.

At least Orsin hoped that would be the case.

Then he felt it. Momentum ceased and gravity slammed him into a bursting sac of flesh and bones and organs. Bile and blood and ichor exploded out of the beast beneath him, and Orsin felt the shattered bones of the beast drive themselves bodily through him in at least four places. He would have roared in agony but all of the breath had been forcibly driven from his lungs by the impact.

It took him several long moment to regain his breath, but he was alive. Most of the bird could not say the same. A few smaller specimens still weakly tried to pull themselves from the mass of ruined flesh, but most of the organs and eyes had been shattered beyond use, even if there was plenty of bones and muscle tissue and feathers.

Orsin pulled himself free from the wreckage of the monster and staggered away. His paw, shaking, grabbed great handfuls of the sacred herbs from the pouch he still carried with him and poked them into his wounds. He muttered a prayer when he had enough breath to do so and stumbled across the tundra.

Muinnajhr. He needed to find his weapon. With his wounds he needed every edge he could get to fight off any of the birds that might return.

At least there was enough of the herb growing nearby to drive off most of the land count herd beasts. It rose around Orsin's feet as he staggered forward, struggling to focus his bleary vision on anything bright or shining that might lay on the ground nearby. His axe had to be nearby. The bird was too weighted down by him to have been able to fly far.

Muinnajhr was here, somewhere. He could feel it. His weapon was a part of him. He would always recognise it, would always be able to feel it.

Was that a flash of silver off to the left? Orsin turned to stagger in that direction. Yes. That felt right. It had to be!

Orsin fell to his knees as he neared the axe, his wounds throbbing. He reached out his paw, still slick with ichor and cramping from having held so tightly to that beast's rib as he rode it down to earth.

Muinnajhr.

Orsin sighed as he felt whole once more.

CHAPTER 27

Orsin's breath wheezed in and out of his throat. He must have cracked some ribs when he hit the ground, in spite of the cushion of flesh he had ridden all the way down. His body ached and pale green and grey pus—cleansed herd infection being forced from his body by the sacred herbs—oozed out of the wounds across his body from where the bones of the mega fowl had pierced his body.

But he had Muinnajhr, and he knew the direction he was headed in next. He just needed to lay low here, where there were fewer herd beasts, until he recovered. He just needed some strength back.

Orsin slept, then, a deep, healing sleep that was almost hibernation. If he lost hours or days, again, he did not know. He only knew that when he awoke his fur was matted with dried pus, his eyes were clear, and his wounds had turned to the tell-tale pale green scars that spoke of herd-related tribulations.

His muscles groaned and ached as he stretched but they did not flare with white-hot pain. What damage or tears there were had had some time to heal, but was not completely gone. More than hours, possibly a day or two.

His fur hung lanky from his form and his stomach growled. Healing took a lot of energy, possibly more than fighting. He needed more food. His bodily reserves were dangerously low.

Orsin began by rooting under the nearby rocks. Grubs and fungus he found aplenty, perhaps thriving because of the lack of herd beasts or other predators. It would not fill him as easily as a couple sides of venison, but it was better than nothing. When the worst edge of his hunger hadn't been blunted he began making his way toward the dome he had seen in the distance form the top of the tor, foraging for more food as he went.

His paw strayed frequently to Muinnajhr as he went, reassuring himself that his weapon was one more secure on his person. Being parted from his axe was not something he had ever seriously considered would happen. The bond between a warrior and his weapon was a sacred thing. But now that it had happened, Orsin carefully considered how difficult his life would become without Muinnajhr.

Orsin was unlikely to make it out of herd territory if he lost the weapon, truly lost it. There were too many threats that his claws could not deal with alone. Not to mention the spiritual pain he would feel without it. It would be like losing a piece of himself, as well as losing a piece of Torben, given the drop of his best friend's blood that burned within the axe.

He certainly wouldn't be able to fell a herd prince without it.

Orsin's thoughts turned to his goal. It was a war, a campaign in miniature. There were tactical and strategic objectives to consider. He had found the location of the dome, yes, and traced out a path to reach it. That did not take into account the other challenges, however.

He would need to locate a prince within the dome, somehow. Orsin did not know how many princes there were, but the dome was massive, easily larger than any three Fursja cities, if not bigger. He needed to locate a single target within that dome.

The baron had a link to the lesser herd beasts of its type. It made sense that it might run the other way. He might be able to call a Prince by tracking and ambushing another baron. Or perhaps the barons were called before the Princes? Could he track one back that way? Did the herd hold a kind of twisted court?

Orsin didn't know, but it seemed possible. He would have to keep his senses peeled, see what he could uncover as he moved deeper into herd territory. With the grace of Weihlaris, he would find a way.

But that was not the only challenge.

The Prince would have attendants. He would need a way to deal with them. Orsin was mighty, and he believed in the strength of his arm and the might of Weihlaris, but he wasn't delusional. No matter how mighty a lone warrior might be, a single Fursja against an army was not a winning strategy.

He needed a way to move mostly undetected through enemy lands. It was an impossible task, but any edge he could think of to increase his odds would be welcome. And several minutes later Orsin stopped dead in this tracks.

What was he thinking? He was walking through one! The herbs all around. They were somehow keeping the herd at bay. Could he lay in a store of them and use that to set up a perimeter for his camp when he needed to rest? Or could they somehow mess with his scent trail enough to break any herd beasts that might try to follow him? There had to be a use for the stuff.

Orsin began to gather herbs as he went, stowing them in small bundles, quickly braiding the stems together. Memories of being a cub and helping his mother in the kitchen with the food stores came to him. They had braided together strings of onions, and sheaves of wheat for various festivals. His paws were not so nimble as hers, but he knew what to do. He could secure several parcels and packets of herbs.

By the time he reached the edge of the herb fields and the open tundra between them and the rising forests and jungles of herd-tainted greenery, Orsin had a substantial supply of herbs and had filled his growling belly to a small degree. He kept an eye out for more food, however. He was still hungry and needed more food.

A set of tracks, possibly a small herd of caribou, presented themselves after he had been trudging through the tundra for an hour or so. There was greenery on the horizon, close enough that he could see individual trees, but he was not in a patch of it. He was in herd territory, but Orsin held out some hope that there were still normal animals in the vicinity.

It was easy enough to track the caribou. They were not trying to hide their presence. That alone argued they weren't herd beasts, to Orsin's mind, though that may have just been his stomach talking. Still, he tracked them down, taking care to always keep one eye on the landmarks he needed to follow to get to the dome. He wouldn't risk losing sight of his way again.

Orsin caught up to the herd two hours later. They had abused to drink greedily from a small spring. Though it was not much of a herd. There were only three of them. Maybe there were more, further ahead and these were the stragglers. In any case, Orsin did not waste his fortune. They were here, and well within range.

He lunged into a fast sprint, moving as quickly and quietly as he could, the haft of his axe firm in his paw. He slammed into the beasts like a force of nature, his initial attack nearly taking the head off of one and hamstringing one of the legs on another. His axe flashed in quick, brutal arcs. It was a fast and efficient killing. In less than a minute three dead caribou were splayed out on the tundra around him.

Orsin's breath plumed in the frigid air but he did not pause to rest. He immediately began to field dress the caribou. There was no telling how long he had before the scent of blood brought something down on this place. He needed to extract the richest organs, as much of the meat as he could carry, and move on.

He paused when he carved into the first caribou. All of the organs had a slick coating of green-black slime on them. Herd infection. The meat was tainted. It was not yet become an abomination, but the process had begun and there was no way he could safely eat the meat without also consuming a massive amount of sacred herbs. It wasn't worth it. Not yet. He wasn't in straits that dire.

The second caribou was also infected, but not to as great a degree. Orsin managed to salvage the liver and part of a haunch of venison from the back right leg. It wasn't much and he would carefully rub the meat with sacred herbs to be safe, but he needed the meat.

The third caribou was the least infected of the three. Orsin quickly went through and grabbed the fatty organs, slicing a piece of the liver off with his claws to chew on as he worked. The rich, coppery flavour filled his mouth.

What he wouldn't give for a flagon of ale to go with this meal! And a roaring fire and the camaraderie of his friends.

A distant howl, guttural and rasping, broke the image. Orsin began to work faster. Some herd beast or other had clearly scented blood on the wind and was on its way in the hopes of finding easy prey to infect. He needed to grab as much meat as he could, but he dared not linger. If he was not safely away, he risked being hunted by an unknown herd beast.

Orsin preferred to conserve his strength for the journey in front of him and the Prince he intended to slaughter without mercy.

He swallowed the chunk of liver he had been chewing and packed away the last of the meat, slinging the haunches he's harvested over his shoulder. With a glance and a sniff in the direction he had heard the howl coming from. The wind was against him though, so there was nothing to smell and he saw no movement amongst the rising and falling tundra.

Orsin curved away, diverting from his ideal path just enough to put a small rise between himself and the carnage he was leaving behind. Out of sight, he could then angle back toward his path and the landmarks that would lead him to the dome. As he went he slipped more food into his mouth, chewing carefully as he moved so as not to inhale when he meant to swallow.

It was an uneasy thing, eating meat that had been attached to a herd-tainted creature, even though he was fairly sure he was only consuming the safe portions. The infection had been mild, and slow. That was not something he was used to seeing. The herd usually infected creatures directly, injecting the mutagenic venom directly into their victims.

That didn't seem to be the case here. Orsin hadn't seen any obvious herd-wounds. No, these caribou seemed to have fallen prey another way.

As he thought about it, even in the third caribou, the one least infected, the stomach had been thick with green-black infection. Was it something they had eaten? There was herd tainted vegetation all around. Perhaps the caribou had fed on the greenery and been slowly infected that way.

Just what the Fursja needed. Another way that herd infection could spread. If innocently animals were infecting themselves without any agency from outside herd beasts at all, there was no telling how their enemies ranks might swell! And this infection was subtler, harder to spot. Caribou ranged far. What if a tainted beast made it near the wall and was taken by a wolf or a Fursja hunter who was not paying close attention? The infection could quickly get out of hand, possibly even cross Vaeggdor itself!

Orsin added the terrifying thought to the list of things he needed to report back when he returned from his Trial. Were these new developments? Or were they secrets the warlord kept from the wider populace for some reason? Orsin didn't have any answers, and no use for the questions, really, save to pass the time.

He pushed them aside. He had other things to think about.

Like how to find and slay a Prince.

CHAPTER 28

Orsin panted in the unnatural heat as he pressed his way through the herd-tainted grove. The trees had continued to grow larger and larger, and closer and closer together as he made his way deeper into herd territory. Yesterday, vines had begun to appear, strange flowering things whose scent reminded him of the tang of the poisoned fog he had fought his way through.

He avoided their fruits.

Food had grown increasingly scarce. There were fewer and fewer normal-looking animals. The plants he had been suspicious enough of already, but after seeing the infection radiating out from the stomachs of those Caribou he had mercilessly slaughtered for food, he was even warier now.

The thought prompted his stomach to growl. While he had bulked up his reserves, he hadn't eaten anything truly fresh or satisfying in three days now. He was hoping the next patch of tundra might prove more fruitful, for while the patches of herd-infected greenery were growing larger and more frequent, there were still, curiously, open spaces of tundra throughout. Orsin didn't know why, he just knew they were a welcome reprieve.

It was hard going. The heat, needing to press himself through the increasingly thick and vicious greenery, avoiding any foolish battles that would risk spiralling into small wars he had little chance of winning, the pressure was mounting. He still managed to slay the odd herd beast. How could he not, when opportunity presented itself or he was caught by surprise?

The last surprise had been a serpent. He'd taken it for yet another hanging vine, but the mottled thing reared up to strike at him as he passed. He'd narrowly avoided the fangs and what was surely an intense dose of herd-venom. Anything that was built to poison or infect other things before being infected had to be exponentially worse once the herd had mutated it.

Orsin didn't feel like finding out, and his reflexes were fast enough that he managed to part the thing's head from it's body with one swift blow. The fangs had melted the greenery beneath them as the severed head stared at him with glassy eyes. Since then he'd encountered more than a dozen snakes. The increasing heat seemed to breed them, somehow.

Everything combined to make each step deeper into herd territory more difficult. Orsin was a determined warrior, but he was still Fursja. He was mortal. He did not have the stamina or stubbornness of the gods. Every inch forward was increasing in the effort it took to move.

He reminded himself what he was fighting for. This was the Trial, the true measure of his worth in the eyes of Weihlaris. If he stopped now, if he fell to the side, his life would mean nothing. And Orsin craved that meaning. He would prove to his people and to the gods that he was worthy! He would be recognised for his might and for his valour!

But it was not simply about him. It was about his people as well. He thought about the horrors he had seen visiting themselves upon his parents, his friends and neighbors, upon the city he had grown up in. The thought of that city looking like the ruins he sought shelter in chilled him to the marrow and ignited a fierce determination to defend them. And to do that he needed to slay more herd beasts, pass his Trial, and return with what he had learned to better arm himself and his people against the ongoing threat that endangered not only them but also the world.

If the herd thrived so well here, in the frigid tundra growing their rotting groves, he didn't want to consider how fast they might spread in the warm, soft Southlands.

It was strange, that the herd seemed so attracted to heat but first appeared here in the frigid tundra. There were tales and songs of the first time they came to these lands, of course, but they were amongst the most ancient of commonly-told tales. Orsin knew from his father that there were other, older tales, but the skalds did not often tell them, as they spoke of a time where the Fursja prospered and did not face the implacable enemy. Orsin's father thought the tales were being preserved for the days when the herd was finally vanquished, but Orsin thought perhaps that they simply weren't repeated because who would want to listen to them? It was such an impossible thing to imagine.

Peace. Prosperity. No such thing as the herd.

What had they even done to prove themselves before their ancient enemy appeared? Fight off the humans who had sought to conquer Fursja lands? That seemed such a paltry threat in comparison to what his people now faced.

He remembered the tale the shamans told of when the herd queen first arrived. There had been strange motions in the stars above, and lances of fire across the skies. Thunder without a storm had rolled across the land and an entire city had vanished, leaving only a smoking crater behind.

Shortly thereafter the first herd beasts had appeared. The details escaped him now, if there were any included in the tales, but the herd grew swiftly, and many Fursja became infected, turning against their own. Whole villages turned on one another out of fear.

It was a dark and terrible time.

All the shamans agreed that at this time the herd queen first appeared. It was she who had infected the animals, the Fursja. Though now that he thought about it, none of the shamans ever seemed to agree on *what* exactly, she looked like. Though perhaps that was because she moved from host to host, abandoning one for a stronger whenever it was available. Or perhaps it was because she was simply so terrible that no mortal mind could comprehend what they saw, and so there were as many tales of what she looked like as there were survivors that had seen her from afar.

Orsin knew of only one survivor who had seen her up close, Brunnerjohrn. But the tales did not speak of her appearance. The Princes, however, it was generally agreed that they all took the forms of great beasts. Having experienced a flock of birds becoming one massive bird, Orsin would well understand how that might come to be.

Torben had always been fascinated by those tales, actually. Orsin remembered his friend capering around the fireplace when they were both just cubs. He would always beg for stories of the greatest and more fearsome herd monstrosities. And Orsin's father would always laugh and oblige. Orsin himself as a cub far preferred to hear of those mighty heroes who rose to join Weihlaris after they fell in battle. He remembered driving his father up the wall asking for details that no one could provide. What had Hjarald done with his hammer? And how big had it been? What metal was used in its forging and how had the warrior gotten the dragon hide to wrap the hilt in? Where was that story? Why was the maiden Hildebjara bound in enchanted slumber with chains of fire? How come they didn't burn her fur?

On and on and on the questions would come, until his father drove him away with playful swats and a command to go out and do something to earn these pieces of story. Usually some chore or other that Orsin's mother had needed someone to do for longer than she liked to wait.

As often as not Orsin would drag Torben along, promising that if he helped his father would be more inclined to share more stories of terrible and terrifying beasts. It wasn't completely a lie. Orsin's father was always in a better mood when he had fewer chores to do. And it gave the two young Fursja time to play and laugh and grow together.

Torben. Where was he now? What had he faced so far in his Trial?

Orsin grinned as he slowly pushed his way through a thick patch of vines, eyes peeled for any hidden snakes. Torben was likely ankle deep in blood and viscera, trailing a chain of severed heads behind him—one for each kind of beast he had slain. The more fearsome the better.

He stumbled, foot turning on a patch of uneven loam. It took him a moment to right himself. The heat was pressing down on him like a boulder. Orsin blinked his eyes to clear them, panting in a desperate effort to cool himself.

What would Torben say to him now?

Get up, lazy bear! Guts and glory await! You'll never keep up with me at this rate. Honestly, if you don't push at least a little harder I'm going to have to choose someone else to carry my shield. Can't have my good name associated with any slackers!

Orsin grunted and pushed himself upwards and onwards.

Unfortunately, on the other side of the tangle of vines were more vines. And this time Orsin was certain he saw movement amongst them. Snakes. He was swiftly coming to hate the herd-tainted snakes more than any other creature he had faced, including the baron. The way they moved...he shuddered.

He stood and watched for a moment. Yes. There were more snakes than vines ahead. Trying to get through that nest unbitten would be a tall order.

Should he turn around and go back? Look for another way? He had been marching and fighting all day. He was tired and did not wish to risk making a mistake. One bite from those herd-vipers he could survive, even a half-dozen. But it would consume a great deal of his supply of herbs, and there was no reason to take stupid risks if he didn't have to.

Was there some other way through?

Orsin looked around for inspiration. Eventually his gaze settled on the large tree to his right. He longed to lean on it to rest but didn't dare. There was no trusting herd-tainted vegetation. But perhaps it *could* help him.

He grinned and whirled his axe around in a silver circle. Glancing over at the tangled nest of snakes, Orsin quickly began chopping at the base of the tree, carving out a careful wedge on the side facing the nest. Once he had made a large cut, he switched and began chopping on the opposite side of the tree. In no time there was a wet *crack* and the tree began to fall, toppling directly toward the nest of snakes, falling as he intended.

It toppled quickly, the weak and soggy wood falling under its own weight, to crash down like a pile driver on the tangled mass of snakes and vines, smashing them to the ground and proving a clear path for Orsin to spring through, if he was quick. There would still be a few snakes to avoid, but it would be far easier this way than fighting his way through the tangle.

The snakes were so disoriented, Orsin only had to fend off one set of snapping jaws before he was through and beyond, pushing through increasingly smaller and thinner trees as another patch of tundra opened up in front of him. He pressed through as quickly as he safely could, relishing the lessening of the heat and the freshening of the air.

It was a welcome lessening of pressure. Though the threat of the herd remained, the heat was gone, and the roving packs of beasts on the tundra were easier to spot, generally, than the ones hiding within the foliage. The tundra here was not the same as the tundra he had crossed earlier, however. As Orsin squinted he could see the fallen shapes of decayed trees and occasional stumps beneath the icy coating of grey snow.

Interesting. So herd-tainted forest had once grown here but something killed it off and it had yet to recover.

But what?

Had a massive beast like a herd prince rampaged through, and knocked down all the foliage? He didn't see any signs of battle or tools which might have felled the trees artificially. No. They had been torn down, some ripped entirely from the ground. Many were just shattered masses of splinters.

Wind? A storm? Lightning from the gods? There was no way to tell. Instead, Orsin took a deep breath, relishing the clear air.

It smelled of snow. Orsin took another breath. Yes. The scent of snow was on the air.

He glanced to the sky.

It promised trouble.

CHAPTER 29

The wind was rising. Hard, gritty snow was once more lashing across Orsin's face, drying out his nose and stiffening his fur. While not a storm truly worthy of being called the "Wrath of Weihlaris," it was not far off. To be safe, Orsin was hunting for shelter from the driving wind and snow, but before he managed to find anything, a howl rose up behind him.

With a keen warrior instinct, Orsin immediately knew that he was not only the hunter, but the hunted. Some herd beast must have picked up his trail and was following through the rising storm. Orsin gritted his teeth and stopped looking for shelter and instead began looking for a defensible position. The howl was too close.

Grey shapes, almost impossible to see against the grey backdrop of the tundra and the grey snow driven across it by the wind, flickered at the edges of his vision as he cast a look behind him. It was a pack of something wolf-like. He couldn't make out any greater detail than that, other than something about the movement wasn't quite right. They lumbered a bit more than loped. Their movements were slower.

Up ahead he caught sight of a vast shadow which split the whirling snow around it. Orsin put on a bit more speed. It was a large rocky outcrop. It looked natural, not like the Fursja ruins that also dotted the tundra.

It would do. At least he'd have something at his back to keep him from being surrounded. Orsin gripped his axe tightly and adjusted his path slightly.

The wind howled in his ears, and the beasts howled in the wind, but there was something else there. Something that sounded strangely familiar, for some reason.

He couldn't place it. It was too faint. Orsin shook his head to clear it. He needed to get into position.

The rock rose up, higher and higher as he drew near. Soon he was right in front of the dark stone, pitted with frost and centuries of driving winds. Orsin whirled, Muinnajhr gripped firmly in his paws, eyes squinting against the driving wind.

No sooner had he managed to brace himself than the howls split the wind, drowning out the sounds of nature with unnatural, monstrous cries. Shapes flickered through the driving snow, half seen and menacing. They were drawing closer slowly, stalking him now rather than chasing. And their numbers were growing. More and more shapes appeared, though Orsin's choice of place to stand his ground limited their approach to a half-circle.

His back was covered by the stone promontory.

"Come on then," Orsin roared in challenge. "Come and die!"

The wind snatched his words away, mutating them as surely as any herd-taint mutated flesh, and then threw them back at him, strangely hollow and twisted.

"Come...come..."

Orsin ignored it. He had enemies in front of him that commanded far more attention. And they were finally coming into view, though some hidden instinct of his whispered to his warrior soul that there were more of them holding back. Something larger, and far worse, lurked just out of sight, biding its time.

The herd beasts, when they drew near enough for him to pick out some details, were the size and general shape of wolves. Their grey fur blending in with the snow all around. Though their claws were longer, their limbs thicker. They moved with a lumbering, ungainly gait, as if still not used to their own limbs somehow.

The shape was slightly wrong. Their muscles were too thick, their coats fluffing out in the wrong places. Orsin squinted. Actually, up close they looked...they looked like bears.

More than that, there was something vaguely Fursja-like about them. It was almost as if someone had come across a wolf, and with eldritch powers unknown, reached out to reshape the wolves like a potter reshapes clay, pulling and bending, bulking and twisting, until the wolves had taken on this new semblance, neither one thing nor the other.

This uncanny resemblance was made even worse as one of the beasts rose up on its hind legs, its spine twisting unnaturally as it attempted to stand on its two hind legs. It took two staggering steps forward until it fell forward and resumed moving on all fours.

Orsin felt a chill seep into his bones that had nothing to do with the howling gale around him.

Then they were on him, lumbering toward him, two to either side while the rest of the pack held back. Sacrifices, attempting to suss out his weak spots. Orsin had no intention of giving them anything. With a roar he charged forward, splitting the skull of one of the two to his left and slashing through the spine of the other before darting back to the stone before he could be flanked or hamstrung.

The other two paused, seeing the brutal efficiency with which he had destroyed their pack mates, but after a moment they resumed their approach. Orsin let them come to him this time. They split as they neared, trying to flank him, but he was a Fursja warrior and Muinnajhr spun and whirred in his hand like a living comet of death, and Orsin had no trouble laying open the two herd beasts and painting the tundra around his feet with their stinking ichor.

He whirled his axe around, slinging the sticky fluids from it off into the roaring gale. The pack shifted but did not move, keeping a perimeter. It was an unnatural act and Orsin felt unease spark to life in his gut.

There was something strange going on here.

Then he heard it, the words echoing once again on the wind.

"Come...come..."

He looked into the storm, trying to find the source of the words. He had thought it was just his own voice, twisted and thrown back to him, but he had not spoken this time.

This was something else.

Orsin squinted. There was a figure, shadowy and indistinct in the driving snow, standing behind the wolf-bears. It loomed at least as tall as he did, though it was thinner. And now that he was able to pick it out from the surrounding storm, he managed to also pick the eerie, keening croon that was coming from the figure form the surrounding wind.

"Come...come...come home. Home. Come home. Come!"

There was an infinite sadness in that voice, matched only by the madness that also crooned through the words. Orsin felt his stomach curdle. It was a feeling that was becoming more and more frequent, the sense that he stood in the presence of one of his people who had been taken and twisted by herd infection.

"Come and get me then!" He roared back at it.

There was a pause, then the figure shivered into motion. The limbs moved jerkily and it advanced, coming closer and closer until Orsin could see it clearly through the rising blizzard. It was one of his people all right, but perhaps the most horrible twisted specimen he had seen so far.

It had once been a Fursja, that much was obvious, but it resembled Orsin as much as the bones of a distant ancestor might mirror the fat, fleshy form of a living descendant. The figure was thin, though its fur seemed in very good condition. At least that's what Orsin thought until he saw the way it moved.

That wasn't fur. It was…it was like very fine coiled thread, made of some kind of thick, glimmering herd-infection. Larger strings of the stuff were attached to each of the fingers, larger still were the ones attached to hands and arms, to feet and legs, a fine webwork of strands that twisted impossibly around the body and moved it mechanically, like some sort of macabre mockery of a puppet at a children's show.

All of the threads coalesced and attached to the head, pulling in and out as if by unseen mechanisms. Every thread thrummed when the thing took a breath, every limb quivered with each word spoken. And that it could speak at all was a mystery, for it looked nothing so much like the Fursja's face had been stitched up, long, jagged threads zig-zagging around the thing's muzzle, as if to hold it closed. Yet as Orsin watched, those selfsame threads quivered and moved the jaw up and down as it spoke again, urging Orsin to *come*.

The eyes were worse, each one cris-crossed with jagged X-like threads. How it could see, Orsin did not know, but those sightless eyes followed him as he shifted to one side, making sure he was in the best defensive position possible.

This, he suddenly knew, was the thing that had reshaped the wolves. The reason they resembled Fursja as much as they did (though that scant similarity was a horrific mockery at best) was because it had somehow used the threads that controlled its movements to reshape them. The jerkiness of those wolf-bears was because those were not their natural forms, not their native muscles.

Orsin cocked his head. Or were they jerking around because it was somehow also controlling them, like puppets? The thing practically puppeted itself. Were there unseen threads connecting the Fursja-thing to the brains of its creations?

It certainly had some kind of control over them. They were holding themselves too still, too ready. Orsin kept part of his attention on the pack, as they could swarm him at any time.

Another two pair of wolf-bears peeled off and approached him. Orsin growled. He feinted charging ahead, just as he had last time, and the pair he aimed himself at split immediately, having learned from their predecessors.

But it was only a feint. Even as he moved, Orsin switched his trajectory, darting over toward the opposite pair of wolves, dispatching them with brutal efficiency before retreating to the stone that guarded his back and facing the other two wolves.

They stared at him, blinking, before slinking back to rejoin the pack.

His foes had learned they could not face him two at a time.

"Come...home."

The thing spoke again, the sound of its voice reedy and thin. Though it was more demanding this time. Orsin got the sense that it had a limited measure of patience and he would eventually run through it all.

Well, he wasn't going to wait until the thing chose to go all out on the attack. If he was going to win with the odds stacked against him like this he was going to need every advantage he could get, including the element of surprise.

The wolf-bears stood in a half-circle. There was no easy way to flee. The blizzard was still gaining strength and without the stone at his back the danger of being surrounded on all sides was too great. Especially when he didn't precisely know what other abilities the Fursja abomination might have.

No. His best shot was direct action. A quick and lethal attack designed to inflict maximum damage in a short amount of time.

Orsin's eyes played over the situation quickly once more, assessing strengths and weaknesses. There weren't too many options. It didn't take long to come to a decision.

Cut the thread and all the puppets would fall. If he had any luck at all, that is. Orsin gripped the haft of Muinnajhr tightly and squinted into the oncoming wind. He'd have one shot to get this charge right.

With a roar of defiance, he sprang into action, pushing off against the stone at his back and charging forward toward the twisted mockery of a Fursja before him, axe held high.

CHAPTER 30

Orsin charged forward, howling defiance in the face of the wind, the wolf-bears, and the abomination that had once been one of his people. Muinnajhr slashed as he went, crippling wolves to either side of him and his bulk muscled them out of the way, sending them tumbling into the snow with pained yelps and snarls.

He paid them no mind. All of his attention was on the abomination that commanded them all, the twisted, once-Fursja puppet-master.

And it's attention was on him.

It cocked its head to one side, a strange, childlike motion. It was as if it could not believe Orsin would dare approach it, or that he could possibly mean it harm. But when Orsin's axe swept down, it moved slightly to the side, causing the blow to miss its head, though the warrior still managed to slice through one arm at the shoulder.

The axe passed through the thing like a hot knife through butter, as if there were no muscle nor bone there, but only threads before a pair of sharpened shears. The arm fell off, landing in the snow with a thump, but even as Orsin adjusted his stance and prepared to swing once more, the claws of the severed arm exploded from the end of the limb, trailing long back threads, and launched themselves back to the main body of the thing he was fighting. They connected, and the threads began drawing the limb back to the body.

There was no ichor. No blood. Everything the herd-taint had mutated was bound up in those sinewy threads.

Orsin growled. No. It would not knit itself back together so easily. He swung again, severing the threads before the arm could pull itself back to the body. This time it quivered and remained still. It had no more claws to use as projectile needles.

He spun, slashing with controlled strength and precision at the exposed joints of the monstrosity. The threads were thinnest there, easiest to sever. It danced away, jerkily, it's unpredictable motions making the battle lopsided and strange. Wolf-bears threw themselves at him, but Orsin managed to dodge or disable them, no longer taking the time for a solid kill. He couldn't afford to. He had to cut this thing apart before it knit itself back together.

He could put the wolf-bears down permanently after he removed their leader.

He took wounds. The fight was too intense and there were too many enemies for him not too. The burning pain of herd-venom began to seep into his flesh. He roared and fought on, pushing through the agony.

Orsin had plenty of valendjahr. So long as he was standing at the end of the battle he would purify himself and be fine. He simply needed to win.

And to do that he needed to cut this abomination apart.

The Fursja warrior threw himself fully into the battle. His first minor victory came when he successfully severed the thing's left leg and the knee and kicked the limb far enough away that it could not reattach itself. The abomination's movements got increasingly erratic then.

Orsin was able to open great rents in the thing's body, but the threads always knit themselves back together as fast as he slashed them apart. Unless he could remove a mass of them from the central snarl, it was a never-ending battle and a losing proposition.

Fortunately, the thing was still controlled from the head. That was obvious. And Orsin had grown adept in parting herd monstrosities from their heads.

He cut off the second leg at the hip. The abomination before him only had one functioning arm and half a leg. It bounced ungainly across the tundra. That it was still moving was nausea-inducing, but Orsin had it precisely where he wanted it. Finally, with one smooth blow, he sliced through the threads that attached the head to the neck and the rest of the body parts, sending it spinning off into the snow.

The body collapsed without any motive force as soon as that happened.

Orsin felt a flare of victory. However it was fleeting. As his eyes turned to seek out the head, to make sure the thing was truly dead and done, he caught sight of a wolf-bear, injured but still mobile, limp over and take the thing in its jaws. Threads exploded out from the head, threaded on several claws which still, somehow, remained attached to the thing. The wolf-bear darted over to the severed arm and the claws reached out and snatched it up as well. Then it turned and ran back into the snow, a howl bursting form its mouth.

It was getting away.

Then answering howls echoed through the wind.

Orsin froze. That had not been the whole pack! There were more wolf-bears out there! And that thing, though mostly destroyed, was still alive.

As much as any herd beast was alive.

He growled, considering whether or not to pursue or wait here near his defensible position for them to return. He quickly applied some of his sacred herbs as he was waiting, for his body had begun to quiver with the heat of the herd-venom coursing through him.

There were shadows on the horizon, barely visible through the driving snow. Orsin squinted. More of the wolf-bears, he could tell from the size and the way they moved, but there was another shadow there as well, larger and hulking. Fursja-sized.

Was there another of those commanding abominations nearby? Just what he needed. Orsin growled. Well, he had defeated the first one, he could handle another.

But then a battle cry came to him upon the wind, wild and defiant and very, very alive. The sound of a Fursja warrior in the throes of battle rage. One of his cohort!

Orsin froze. He knew that battle cry. He knew that voice.

Torben.

The snow was driving, blinding. The wind whipping the grey granules to a fury. Orsin could barely see through the blizzard, but he thought he could pick out the massive form of his friend, surrounded on all sides by rampaging wolf-bears and there, at the back, the head of the thing that was controlling the entire pack.

His feet began to move, his heart lurching into motion long before his head could raise any questions about the Trial, about the cost of his actions of the price of honor. Because his best friend was in front of him, and he was going to die if Orsin didn't do anything.

Orsin charged forward, all thought driven from his mind. He moved on pure, adrenaline-fuelled instinct. Every breath thundering through his body beat with the need to save and protect. But even as he charged forward, growing despair reached up to clench around his fist with icy fingers.

He wasn't going to make it!

❈ ❈ ❈

Torben roared in defiance. This pack of things had been stalking Orsin long before his friend had noticed them. Torben had pressed on through the rising storm, determined to take out as many of the fucking things as possible while he could, giving Orsin the best chance possible to deal with the other half of the pack.

They surrounded him now, these wolf-bear-abominations. Lances of fire shot through him with every move. He'd already been bitten several times, and he could feel the herd-venom coursing deep through his veins. His mouth frothed green with the sacred herbs he had tossed back to try and stave off the infection until he could end the battle and treat the wounds directly.

Three of them came at him this time, their movements jerky and uncoordinated but deceptively fast for all of that. His warhammer slammed into one, snapping its spine. Torben immediately used the impact to reverse the momentum and whirl the hammer around to smash through the skull of another wolf-bear, crushing it and sending gobbets of brain matter skidding across the frozen tundra to lose themselves in the driving grey snow.

The third managed to tear at his legs, though it missed the hamstrings. Torben drove it off with a glancing blow from his hammer, before whirling his weapon around and breaking majors joints in a succession of blows: right front shoulder, back right knee, front paw.

He killed the beast, but at the cost of yet another wound. There were so many now, each burning with a sick fire, and too many wolf-bears still standing. Torben growled his defiance and shook the thought form himself. He was a warrior of Weihlaris! These foes would not best him! He would put them all in the ground in service to his god and his best friend.

"Die, herd scum!" Torben bellowed and threw himself into the fray.

His hammer smashed a bloody path through his foes and a red haze clouded his vision as Torben lost himself in slaughter. Onwards he rampaged until something new gave him pause, shaking him slightly from his rage.

The severed head of a Fursja seemed to have been stitched to the back of the wolf-bear in front of him, with a few claws clattering along side of it, connected to the head by strange, black thread.

"Come...come...come..." the thing crooned at him. "Come...home."

Torben roared his refusal, of the suggestion and of the abomination before him. He raised his warhammer, muscles screaming in agony, herd infection burning through his veins, and prepared to launch an attack.

Then a sudden pain thrust itself deep into his core and Torben felt the shock of it freeze him in his tracks. He gasped at the sudden penetration, feeling something moving deep within him. There was a curious warmth all around the area, startling in this frigid environment.

One of the thing's claws had shot out and pierced him through the heart.

When it retracted it pulled his heart with it, the organ bursting out of Torben's chest. The wolf-bears howled in triumph. But Torben couldn't hear them. He could not hear the wind. All he heard was a strange roaring in his ears, and even that was growing fainter and fainter.

He was going to die.

But he had a breath left. He had one more moment, though the light was fading. With the last of his strength he lifted Hjarsurung, his soul cried out to Weihlaris for this one last moment of grace, and his heart, though it had been ripped off his chest, sang with determination to do one last thing for the best friend he loved so much.

He would crush this beast and Orsin would carry on.

Make me proud, buddy.

Then Torben, with the last of his strength, brought his hammer down on the unsuspecting abomination before him. Weihlaris must have guided his hand, because the blow hit squarely and the thing exploded like a smashed pumpkin.

The wolf-bears around began to yelp and jerk, but Torben did not notice. He had collapsed to his knees, the last of his strength spent. He didn't even feel it when he fell to the side and splayed out.

The light began to die in the warrior's eyes. He took one last shuddering breath and released it, sending his soul to the arms of Weihlaris, and one last prayer into the world, his last thought of his best friend.

"Orsin…"

But when his friend arrived, all that remained of Torben was his unmoving body and his warhammer, swiftly disappearing beneath a grey veil of snow.

CHAPTER 31

Orsin's world froze. The snow seemed to cease its falling, to hang suspended in midair. The wind could not touch him. It *dared* not touch him. All sensation vanished. Time ceased its flow. Orsin's vision narrowed down to a single point, a blot of darkness in a colourless void, the centre of which was his best friend, Torben, falling to the ground.

Lifeless.

Impotent, helpless, Orsin watched from afar as the twin stars that were Torben's eyes guttered and went out.

Dead.

Torben was dead.

His oldest friend, his best friend, wasn't there any more.

The body lay splayed across the snow, crimson blood leaking from countless wounds staining the grey snow several shades of pink and red and green and black. The snowflakes hanging motionless in the air all around seemed to shine like a whole galaxy of stars. It was strangely beautiful. There was peace on Torben's face, mixed with the defiant triumph of his last, heroic act.

Red and green and black, so stark against the grey of the snow and the severe clarity of the tundra.

Herd infection.

The green and black leaking from his friend's veins was herd ichor. The taint of the abomination. The mark of the enemy.

Time stuttered, moved forward once more, though somehow Orsin felt as if he were wading through honey. Everything around him moved so slowly to his mind. As if he were beating faster than the heart of the world.

He watched as one of the wolf-bears, the one that still had several threads tangled through its flesh from the thing that had been commanding the herd, snarled and sank its teeth into Torben's throat, blood spouting from the jugular, from the noble heart of his friend that had not yet ceased to beat, though the soul that once dwelled in the body had already departed.

The wolf-bear drank and as it drank Orsin watched it change. It began to swell, muscles twisting and bulging, spine lengthening and straightening. Green-black ichor boiled in streams from its eyes as the herd infection soaked in the might that had been Torben's, claimed it as meat for its unholy feast, and grafted it onto its host the wolf-bear.

The thing hulked into monstrousness, rising up to stand on two legs, arms bulging with muscles and muzzle pulled back in a mockery of the true Fursja form. This was a beast uplifted to a terrible parody of nobility and power.

Orsin felt a deep growl building within him, vibrating against the curious effect that had slowed time all around him. The herd had harried his people down through the centuries, stole countless lives, ruined innocence, warped nature and profaned all that was holy, and now, now that they had stolen his best friend from him, the person he loved more than any other in all the world, they were going to steal Torben's very essence to fuel the creation of yet another abomination?

No. Orsin vibrated with fury. He tasted copper on his tongue and the galaxies of grey snowflake stars that hung in the sky in this frozen moment suddenly turned red. All he could taste was blood. All he could hear or feel was the pulsing, pounding thrum of blood through his veins. All he could see was red, red as blood.

He was the power in the veins. He was the pulse of life. He was the implacable right hand of Weihlaris himself and he would not be denied.

These fucking *things* had taken from him. No. No, no, no. Fuck no. They would fucking pay. He would fucking tear them into tatters of flesh and smear their ichor across the tundra. He would grind them down to nothingness and extract every iota of suffering he could from them in payment for their gross violation.

He would have his revenge. Torben would be avenged. Torben—Torben.

The world flared red. Pure, primal fury, the likes of which Orsin had never before felt, suddenly burst forth from a deep and sacred well somewhere in the center of his soul. He heard a voice as if from on high, echoing across the heavens and though he knew not the words Weihlaris spoke—for who else could it be?—he knew what they meant.

Death. Death to the abominations.

Time snapped and resumed its flow. Orsin howled, a pure juggernaut of fury, and began sprinting toward the newly formed herd baron, wobbling weak on its newborn legs. It would die aborning, Muinnajhr delivering it death a single breath after its apotheosis.

Howls rose all around him. Wolf-bears, thick with herd taint, began to fling themselves at him in wild defense of their new-created lord. They seeemed to boil out of the hills, darting forethought from the shadows where they had lurked in numbers far greater than he had realized before.

There was nothing in Orsin's mind now but blood and battle, however. Numbers were meaningless. There was only the flow of the battle, the pulsating, pounding drumbeat of war. He felt it thrum through his feet as he charged forward.

Muinnajhr whirled, a silvery arc of death that quickly began to trail streamers of green-black ichor from it. Orsin ripped his axe brutally through the neck of one wolf-bear and into another, where he suddenly twisted his arm and used the flat of the blade to split the skull open like a watermelon. Blood and brain matter cascaded around him as he charged forward, hatred and fury and righteous fucking anger driving him forward.

A pair of wolves lunged at him from the left. Orsin swatted them away with a casual backhand. His fist alone, fueled by his fury, pulped flesh and snapped bone and the two wolf-bears flew off in a chorus of pained yelps and whines. On his right, three of the things menaced him, but with the strange, red-tinted clarity of battle, Orsin was able to face them simultaneously, raking Muinnajhr across eyes and throats and forepaws, mutilating the things so severely that they fell to the ground writhing and useless from their pain and wounds.

He crushed their skulls beneath his feet and he charged over them, forcing his way closer and closer to the thing that had stolen Torben's blood, stolen his friend's essence. More wolf-bears threw themselves at him, wild and furious, but Orsin carved a bloody path through them all. There was no counting now, no thought for honor or glory, there was only fury and the iron will to see justice done on the body of the thing that had wronged him, the thing that was an affront to the gods themselves.

There was a blessed purity to his purpose, a fierce and bloody joy to the flawless accord between his desire for blood and the dictates of the pantheon that ruled his people. His wants and the wants of his god were the same in this moment, and that unity lent a religious ecstasy to the bloodthirst that pulsed in his veins and drove him to exact implacable revenge.

And the focus of all his hate was not three lengths in front of him. The newborn baron was already massive, and scraps of several wolf-bears littered the tundra around its feet. They had been consumed to fuel its growth. Even as Orsin watched another wolf-bear was split by burrowing threads, snipped apart and then drawn up and sewn into place on the back of the new-formed baron.

This baron stood three times Orsin in height. There was a cruel intelligence flickering in its eyes, but the face was still and new, it moved clumsily, not used to its limbs, though the power in them was evident. Mountains of muscle cascaded in ranges along its limbs, and when those limbs split into fingers and toes, they were ended with wicked claws, furred with small curls of thread where they fused to flesh. A tongue, long and black and forked like that of a viper flicked forth from its mouth, to coil and trail along the three rows of fangs that sprouted from the thing's mouth like razor-sharp knives.

It took a breath as if to speak, but Orsin knew no fear and would brook no syllables to fall from that profane mouth. He roared with the voice of Weihlaris as he charged forward, causing the thing to flinch before the holy fury before him. It even took a step back, and the green light in its eyes snickered and dimmed for a moment, the fear beating within it reducing its intelligence to that of any mere beast, if only for a moment.

It didn't last. The thing braced for Orsin's charge a split second later, bringing its limbs up to meet the lethal edge of Muinnajhr as it sliced through the air toward it, the power of Orsin's limbs driving it forward with such force that the air itself seemed to split and whirl around the blade, coiling off into two errant breezes that wailed in fury, disappearing into the grey and uncaring tundra.

It was not enough—could *never* be enough—to stop Orsin's charge. Onward the warrior drove, fuelled by the flame burning within him. Muinnajhr flashed, glittering and lethal arcs carving through the air to seek flesh and open wound after wound which wept green-black ichor.

The baron danced back, lashing out with its claws. If it drew blood or opened rents in Orsin's flesh, the warrior did not know. He certainly couldn't feel them. There was only the red haze all around him and the purpose that drove him. He felt nothing but the fury pulsing in his veins. He saw nothing but the crimson-mantled figure of his enemy.

The enemy that would soon be lying defeated at his feet.

Orsin ducked and wove, his body moving with the speed and strength of his will. It almost seemed to pass beyond mortality in that moment. The forces of the world, gravity, inertia, anything that might hold him back were cast into abeyance. Movement was an expression only of will and his skill in battle.

His axe whirled, his limbs lashed out, and the baron fell back before the onslaught. Orsin pressed the advantage, never wavering, never pausing, until the baron stumbled. Then he struck.

Orsin's axe lashed out, setting the baron on its back foot. He kicked out, a mighty blow shattering his enemy's knee and yanking its legs out from beneath it. The herd baron tottered, and Muinnajhr drove deeply into the thing's shoulder, momentum forcing the thing to fall backward, crashing brutally onto the tundra, helpless and open before Orsin's might.

The baron flailed on the ground, scrabbling for purpose but to no avail. It was as if the earth itself reached up to hold Orsin's foe in place for him, but maybe it was simply that his fury had driven Muinnajhr so deeply into the baron that it had passed through its flesh and into the frozen earth beneath.

It had to be done with his bare claws. His fury and bloodlust would be satisfied with nothing less. Orsin ground the axe head deeper, pinning the thing in place, nailing it to the frozen tundra beneath its back. Then he backhanded it, eliciting squeals of terror and pain before hauling back his arm and slamming it down into the thing's chest.

Flesh parted before his claws, ribs snapped. Orsin twisted his shoulders, braced himself, dug in with his other claw, and then ripped the thing's chest wide open in one vicious movement, exposing the black and beating heart at the centre of the thing. Threads coiled and pulsed around it like veins.

Like a striking snake, Orsin's hand lashed out and seized the pulsating organ. With one brutal jerk of his arm, he ripped it forth from the body of his fallen foe. The heart came easily, trailing black threads like coils of smoke and a final, despairing cry burst forth from the newly elevated baron's lips and the thing died.

The heart in Orsin's hand pulsed once more. Then twice, before stilling after the third and final beat.

It turned to green-black paste in his paw as Orsin crushed it without further thought.

The other wolf-bears had long since died or fled. But with the death of his foe, Orsin's fury died with it. The red haze that had clouded his vision flickered and faded away, leaving him with nothing but the grey, grey expanse of the tundra all around, though not even the wind dared stir and disturb the triumphant warrior.

Chapter 32

Orsin stood shivering, his limbs weak and his mind reeling in the aftermath of his berserker rage. To feel so weak, after feeling so powerful...it was humbling. No doubt this was the wisdom of Weihlaris, to keep warriors humble and thus alive, but it was a bitter thing to experience.

At least he stood alone on the tundra. So what if he stood in the teeth of a howling blizzard? He stood triumphant, his foes dead at his feet.

It was a worthy tribute to his fallen friend, a worthy recompense for the life of his friend, so hideously ripped away.

Or it should be.

Orsin struggled to think. His mind was clouded, his feelings blunted. The wind was rising. The snow still whirled.

He needed shelter.

There wasn't any. Orsin moved slowly. A flickering coal of determination managed to stay alight in the Ashfield left in the wake of his berserker rage. The corpse of the nascent baron steamed in the air, dripping with green-black ichor where he had ripped it open.

It was large enough to shelter by, and the heat pouring off of it from its decay would ward off the worst of the chill. His flesh crawled at the very thought, but survival in that moment was greater than any squeamishness. There were no other choices.

Orsin hunkered down next to Torben's body, drawing his friend's corpse into his arms. Then he hauled the corpse of the massive herd baron up behind him, twisting and snapping the body so the fur curved around his body and blocked the wind.

The stench was unbelievable, but a thick heat emanated from the corpse as the herd infection burned itself out on the corpse, desperately trying to repair or resurrect it.

It would not succeed, but its vain attempts would see Orsin through the blizzard. When it passed, the herd taint would be gone and Orsin would remain. But just to be on the safe side Orsin extracted a pawful of the sacred herbs and began to chew them as exhaustion carried him down into the depths of sleep.

When Orsin awoke, the blizzard had passed. A small drift of snow had accumulated, but he broke out of it easily enough, shouldering away the cold remains of the herd baron and lifting Torben's body free from the clinging snow.

Looking across the tundra, Orsin could see nothing stirring. There was no sign of herd beast, nor of prey. Orsin sighed.

He could really use a nice, fat arctic hare right about now.

Orsin would have to do without, however. He gently set Torben's remains down on the frozen ground and stared at what was left of his friend. Torben's sightless eyes looked skyward, as if seeking Weihlaris in the grey expanse above.

A flicker of rage kindled itself amongst the ashy expanse that extended throughout Orsin's soul in the wake of his berserker rage.

Why? Why had Torben perished? He was as skilled a fighter as Orsin, if not more so. He was certainly more confident and had been looking forward to the Trial more than anyone. He had trained so hard.

Was this the will of Weihlaris? How could that be? How could Torben fail the Trial and Orsin be sitting next to his corpse, still surviving, still fighting?

Orsin paused.

He didn't need to carry on. He had passed the Trial. He'd gathered plenty of glory, won victory after victory. He could gather up Torben's remains and return home. No one would gainsay him.

Not even Weihlaris.

But what a bitter price to pay.

Orsin felt his eyes sting, though there was no water in them for tears to fall. He was wounded, he realised then. The superficial wounds of his rage had all healed overnight, either by the grace of Weihlaris, the effects of the rage that suffused him, or the influence of the sacred herbs he had consumed, but there was still a pain lancing deep within him.

Never again would he hear his friend laugh. Never again would they chase after the bright and beautiful Fursja maidens around the fire while sipping stolen honey-mead. Never again would they share stories or spar in the early morning.

Torben was gone, and his departure from this world had ripped a piece out of Orsin's soul.

He had heard of things like this. Deep soul wounds that warriors received on the battlefield. Some healed from such things, or claimed they did. Others did not. Some carried on, always wounded but still fighting. Others wasted away.

He was just so tired. The rage had burned him up inside, hollowed him out. Orsin felt empty, distant. It would be so easy to just…let go. To pack up Torben's remains and trudge home with them.

Not even Weihlaris could fault him.

The thought was a bitter one. Orsin had never before doubted his god, but to see his friend cut down in battle, somehow, it gave rise to a host of questions that it were better Orsin never voiced, though he could not quiet the asking of them in his own mind.

What was the point of war? Of glory? What was the point if his loved ones still died? Why should he fight so hard to protect a world that did not care?

Did the soft southerners send warriors to the fight? No. Did they send food or supplies or weapons? Some, perhaps, but far more often than not they charged an arm and a leg for their goods.

What good were such things in a world where Orsin had to stumble through life bereft of his closest friend?

He howled, then, in grief and rage and loss. He poured his pain into his voice and sent it screaming across the empty expanse of tundra all around. It didn't matter who or what heard him. Orsin would not be denied this expression of pain. It was a festering wound that needed to be cleansed and here, in the middle of nothing, he knew of no other way than to assail the heavens themselves with his emotion.

Then he laughed. He laughed and chuckled and snorted.

Torben would be making so much fucking fun of him right now if he could see him.

Maybe he could. Orsin, still laughing, flipped a rude gesture upward at the sky, for Torben and Weihlaris both. Voyeuristic fucks, spying on his grief like that.

No, Torben wouldn't want him to return home with his bones. Torben would want him to carry on the fight and avenge him even further. Torben wouldn't stop.

Torben would have hunted until he found a herd prince and figured out a way to bring the thing down.

Now *that* would be a worthy sacrifice to the memory of his friend. Though to do that Orsin would have to delve deeper and faster into herd territory. It was not something he could do carrying Torben's remains. He would have to leave his friend here, to sleep beneath the tundra's frozen soil.

Possibly forever, if he could not return to retrieve the remains and bear them home.

Orsin hefted his axe and began to use it to cut deeply into the tundra soil, carving out a worthy grave to receive Torben's remains.

"I'm sorry, my friend," he said as he worked. "You did not deserve this. You were bright and you were mighty and you were worthy. I have to believe I will see you again, someday, in the Halls of Weihlaris. We will drink then, and trade the stories we should have traded before the fire when we returned home. Mother and Father—"

Orsin paused. He was not the only one who had lost Torben. When he returned home—if he returned home—he would have to deliver the news.

That thought frightened him more than anything he had seen since the beginning of the Trial or before.

"You should be there, with me, you idiot." Orsin shook his head and continued to dig. "I can't believe you were so close, I—"

It was in that moment that something clicked in Orsin's mind. The Fursja silhouettes he had occasionally spotted nearby, the ones that had given him strength and renewed his purpose, those had been Torben. The dead herd beasts he occasionally found, crushed by an unknown weapon, those beasts had died at Torben's hammer.

His friend had been shadowing him this entire time. Never so close as to risk violating the Trial, but always close at hand. Torben had been with him not just in the drop of blood that beat within Muinnajhr, but actually nearby, working in concert with Orsin without actually directly aiding him or violating the strictures of the Trial.

"You, you—" Orsin looked to his friend. "You should be here with me, still. We should finish this together."

And he would. Orsin looked over at Hjarsurung, Torben's warhammer. It was just a shadow in the snow, drifted over by the driving wind of the blizzard last night.

"You were a true warrior," Orsin said, once the grave was completed and he had carefully tucked Torben's remains into it. "You showed me that, even at the end. You gave me the gift of knowing what it was to die with honour, to die in glory, to die for the right reasons. One last lesson. Thank you for that." Orsin shook his head. "Though I'm not forgiving your fucking ass for dying. That was a fucking stupid thing for you to do. Leaving me all alone like this. And I'll have to figure out what to say to Mother and Father—"

Orsin paused. Then he leaned down at the edge of the grave and carefully cut three locks of fur from Torben's corpse, tying them up with small knots of tundra grass. Muinnajhr's edge made easy work of it.

"Right. I'm dragging at least this much of your ass with me into herd territory to find a prince and kill it. You always bragged you would, well I'm not letting you off the hook! You're going to help me whether you like it or not."

Orsin smiled sadly.

"I remember when we were cubs and Father would tell us stories. You said even back then that someday you'd grow up to be a mighty warrior and be the first to slay a herd prince in single combat. Well, you were right about becoming a mighty warrior, and I'll be damned if I'll leave you here and not take you along with me so you can see me beat your ass to your dream."

Orsin chuckled softly.

"Goodbye for now, my friend. I can't linger here much longer. Not if I'm going to go out and beat you to killing a herd prince."

Orsin began to murmur prayers for Torben's soul and for his own course, calling out to Weihlaris with everything he had. There were enough to fill all the time it took for him to replace the soil and the sod. Then, as he field-stripped the head of the herd baron he had killed, to raise up as a grave marker for his friend, he told himself stories of their time as cubs, remembering the adventures they had got up to, and the trouble that usually landed them in.

He rooted some sacred herbs in leftover soil, stuffing the skull of the herd baron and planting the herbs in the sockets where they eyes one gleamed so hatefully.

"I'll be back," he promised when all had been done. "I'll slay a prince and return here to tell you about it. Then I'll take you home."

Orsin glanced back at the horizon, in the direction he thought would lead him there. Home.

"We'll go home."

Then, with nothing else left to say or do, Orsin shouldered Muinnajhr and Hjarsurung, resting one over each shoulder and feeling the pulse of Torben's presence within the weapons and the bundles of fur tucked safely away.

He had a prince to slay.

CHAPTER 33

Orsin whirled Torben's warhammer and smashed one of the squirrel-like herd beasts against a nearby tree. The things were tiny, but fast, and they had razor-sharp fangs. Another new beast, though not much of a challenge all on their own. Orsin had seen them strip a fully grown caribou to bone in a matter of seconds when there was a swarm of them, however, so he moved ahead cautiously.

All the caution in the world however couldn't dim the flares of pleasure he got at the death of each and every herd-tainted abomination. Every one was sent heavenward with a prayer for Torben and for Weihlaris. Then he ground their remains beneath his heel and moved onwards, deeper into herd territory.

Torben's warhammer fit his paw like it was made for it, as smooth and natural as Muinnajhr. The two weapons were weighted slightly differently, but Orsin was taking full advantage of each and every skirmish to hone his skill in dual-wielding the weapons. He almost had the knack of using the difference in weight and momentum to help fuel his blows. He could spin the heavier warhammer much like a counterweight and spiral his arms in a roundhouse blow that gave extra weight and force to the slicing arc of Muinnajhr.

The two weapons worked well together, just as he and Torben had.

It had been a week since he'd left Torben behind to rest beneath the frozen tundra. He thought of his fallen brother every day, and every day when a new herd beast presented itself for battle, Orsin brutally destroyed it.

He felt his lips twist into a snarl. He would wipe every last herd beast from the world. He would wash it clean in a sea of blood and then, and only then, would he consider it just recompense for the loss of Torben.

Orsin game himself a moment to consider what it would feel like to hold the beating heart of the herd queen in his palm and crush it into paste, just as he had with the herd baron he faced the night Torben died. It was a sweet dream though he knew it was just that: a dream. Whole armies had fought the herd queen and all had fallen to her. She was a force of nature like unto a Demigod. He knew better than to think he could fell her on his own.

At least not until he discovered a secret weakness. Perhaps he would be able to rip one from the mind of one of the herd princes right before he slew it. That would make his achievement all the sweeter, truly.

But to do that he first needed to find the dome. He needed to discover a way in and carefully choose a battleground that would play to his strengths. And he wouldn't do that daydreaming of easy victory.

Orsin had work to do.

So he shouldered his weapons once more and pushed deeper through the thickened greenery. The closer he came to the dome, the thicker the greenery and the fewer patches of untainted tundra he found. Though they still appeared, odd patches of pristine, cold beauty, like oases in the desert.

Somehow, nature was fighting back.

The thought sent a fierce excitement through him. The herd were far from invincible. The land itself wished to rid itself of the vile taint of the abominations. Even here, so far from home, alone in the midst of his trial, Orsin had the land and the gods on his side.

There were far worse allies to have.

A patch of greenery shifted slightly and Orsin lashed out with Muinnajhr. There was a startled yip and a whimper before the herd beast died. He paused to look at it. From the looks of it, it had once been some kind of arctic fox, but in place of fur it had somehow begun to grow moss. It made the thing incredibly difficult to spot in the herd-tainted jungle all around.

The fucking taint even blurred the line between beast and plant. Orsin shook his head. Was there nothing sacred? Must this taint violate every natural law?

Orsin turned his eyes to his surroundings. The foxes had been pack animals before. It was likely that remained true. Where there was one there were likely to be more. And he wanted to kill as many of them as possible.

He quickly worked out the trick to spotting them. While their camouflage was good, they were still limited to the moss they grew in place of fur, and patches of moss that looked like foxes were unnatural enough to stand out to his eyes when he was specifically looking for them.

Orsin waded forward, alternately crushing and slicing, littering the floor of the jungle behind him with corpses. He considered picking up a tail as a trophy, but he quickly dismissed the idea. It would just be extra weight. He did not need to carry anything unnecessary with him. He still had a long way to go and he had to conserve his strength.

Food was scarce.

Orsin's stomach growled as a heavenly scent came to his nostrils. What was that? It smelled like honeyed mead but a hundred times more intoxicating! There was also the scent of roast boar and some kind of fish, fresh and succulent.

His mouth watered. Before he knew it, Orsin found himself pushing more and more quickly through the greenery. He almost lost himself to the needs of his body when he reached out to push a branch out of his way and suddenly found his paw stuck to it with some kind of incredibly sticky sap.

It cost him a good deal of fur and possibly a layer of skin to tear himself free. What was this? Some new and horrible mutation? He sniffed it. It smelled heavenly, whatever it was. It took an effort of will to to stick the stuff in his mouth.

Orsin shook his head and took a step back, slapping himself on the face with his untainted paw. The pain cut through the haze of hunger and gave him enough clarity to crush some sacred herbs and rub the paste on his nose. The sharp, acrid scent cut through the tempting aroma and allowed him to think clearly.

Something in these trees wanted him to eat the stuff, likely so it could then eat him. There was no question that the stuff was tainted. It might also be poisonous. Orsin wasn't going to test it to find out.

Then he saw the things moving through the trees, long trails of sap or slime clinging to them but in no way impeding their movements as it had Orsin's. They looked like massive sloths, each easily as large as he was. They moved slowly, occasionally reached down to bring a clawful of sap to their mouths to chew greedily on.

Anger flared in Orsin's chest. He wanted nothing more than to charge headlong at the creatures and rip them limb from limb, part of the expiation of the guilt the entire species bore for the death of Torben. But he knew better. The stuff would cling to him and he'd end up stuck in it, easy prey for the creatures that could move through it effortlessly, no matter how slow they might appear right now.

He instead began to shift carefully around the edge of the small swamp of delicious smelling ooze. One or two of the creatures noticed him, but though they began to move toward him, they did so with such slowness he was able to easily outpace them. It was only as he neared the edge on the other side of the patch of ooze that there was a creature close enough to the edge to be a danger to him.

Could Orsin have fled the thing? Yes. But he was as thirsty for vengeance as much as he was hungry for a solid meal.

So Orsin stayed near the edge of the swamp, allowing the sloth thing to move toward him. It showed no fear as it came. It probably hadn't had to actually fight anything as long as it had lived. It dwelled within a trap, deep within herd territory. What could possibly threaten it? Few Fursja even penetrated this far, and if they did it was usually in an army that burned everything as it went.

There was no way this thing had ever faced anything like that. Never faced any threat of any kind at all. So Orsin let it come, let it creep closer and closer until it was within reach. Then Muinnajhr lashed out, the full force of Orsin's weight behind it, counterbalanced by Hjarsurung.

The axe slid into the sloth-thing's skull like a knife into soft cheese. Though the action released a potent whiff of a smell so heavenly Orsin very nearly threw himself bodily into the swamp to devour the sloth thing whole. Only the sacred herbs in his nostrils kept him from doing just that, the faint acrid tinge to the nearby air just enough to allow him to hold on to his sanity by one desperate claw.

Orsin yanked his axe free from the skull of the giant sloth-like herd creature. It came out with a wet squelch and several gobbets of brain stuck to it. Seemed like the creature had as much sap in its veins as it had on its body.

He shook the flesh free from his blade, cleaned it with a few well-placed blows on a nearby tree, felling it in the process, and then moved forward. The scent of fresh air teased his nostrils and he quickened his step. Another patch of tundra? It would be welcome.

In short order Orsin found the clearing he sought, grey with snow, though at this depth in herd territory there was a wide ring of temperate grasses growing idly in the waste heat from the patches of herd-jungle. But what stopped him in his tracks was not the breath of fresh air or the prospect of another small bit of foraging, but instead the sight that revealed itself to his eyes.

It was the dome, the one he had spotted from the top of the tor.

The home of the herd queen and her attendant princes and who knew what else.

It rose high above the trees, and though it was still a fair way off, Orsin could now make out much more detail than he'd been able to previously. While from a distance it had looked like an expanse of unbroken grey stone, from this vantage point Orsin could see a curious mottling effect shot throughout the stone. Was it green? It was hard to tell at this distance and in this light. It would make sense if the herd had raised the structure with more of their strange ichor. It warped flesh, why not stone as well?

Or was the whole thing a giant mass of bone, fused together with the mutagenic shit that ran through the veins of every herd beast in existence?

He'd find out when he drew closer. For now he stood and watched, in case some clue as to the best way to approach the dome would reveal itself before he had to move further into the jungle and lose sight of it once more.

Nothing presented itself, though he did notice movement. There were spots across the dome, and from the way those spots seemed to alternately swallow and vomit forth small collections of dots, they were likely holes or some other kind of entrance or exit.

Orsin squinted. The dots were of varying sizes. If the smaller ones were the size of regular birds—doubtful at this distance—then the larger ones had to be truly massive. Orsin remembered the hulking size of the barons he'd faced. These had to be even bigger than that.

Particularly bulky or strong barons? Maybe even princes? Orsin's pulse quickened at the thought. But though he squinted and strained, he couldn't make out any further details from this distance.

Well. He'd found his destination. Now all he needed to do was find his way in. And then he'd kill himself a prince.

The herd would fucking pay.

Chapter 34

Orsin crouched amidst the leaves, moving as little as possible, watching spiders the size of mastiffs scuttle in and out of the tunnel across the clearing from him. His breath was hot and thick in the humid air all around him, and the jungle was cacophonous all around him, echoing with strange cries and guttural roars.

He was deep within herd territory, possibly only a couple days journey from the dome. All traces of tundra had been left far behind. He hadn't seen snow in days. Hadn't felt the comforting break in heat and humidity for even longer.

Orsin was hunting a baron, and while he'd spotted a few candidates, he thought the one that was lurking deep in the den across from him was probably his best bet. It commanded a host of lesser spiders, and when it spoke it did so with a clarity and purpose that had set a chill running through Orsin's blood.

This was no ordinary herd beast. This was a noble of high purpose. What that purpose was, he feared to discover, but he had overheard enough to know that something of value to the herd was kept in that den and the baron was in charge of it. It had even mentioned its last audience with its prince.

Orsin had only caught a snippet of that conversation. A wave of spiders had exited the den as he lurked nearby and he had been forced to withdraw or be discovered.

He had a good sense of their movements now, however. Each of the pack of spiders had subtle differences to their markings. He hadn't counted more than a couple dozen of them, not counting the baron.

The baron seemed to be an entirely different kind of spider, and it was huge, easily the largest baron Orsin had yet seen. It moved like a dancing blade, swift and efficient and deadly. Orsin had no doubt it could run him down easily, if it came to a chase.

A flurry of movement interrupted his thoughts. The smaller spiders were flooding out of the den and scurrying away down the trail leading from the clearing. Orsin counted quickly. He was fairly sure all but two were in the group. That would leave those two and the baron inside the den.

He could risk that.

Orsin waited a few minutes to be certain all the spiders were well and gone before moving carefully toward the den. He snuck in, keeping to the shadows. There was enough light pouring in the entryway that he could see. The walls were dirt, but coated with a green-black mass of webbing to reinforce it. Other than that, though, the passageway was clear. There were no hanging sheets of silk or the like to evade, a fact for which he sent a prayer of thanks to Weihlaris.

It was a simple den, really. There were no traps, no alarms. If there had been Orsin would have already tripped them. This deep in herd territory they must feel secure.

A deep, burning desire to fucking shatter that security rose within Orsin and he had to throttle it back. No, he couldn't attack now. He had a plan. He needed to stick to it.

He froze as a large shape suddenly loomed from one of the walls, but it wasn't one of the spiders. It was a large clump of webbing, a cocoon. It was bigger than he was, and Orsin wondered at what might be inside, but didn't pause to risk cutting it open. He needed to get deeper.

The den floor sloped down gently. Orsin saw more and more cocoons as he moved deeper, all generally of the same size and shape. Something about that tugged at his mind, but with so much attention going to not getting caught, he couldn't pause to put his finger on what about that was bothering him.

The gloom deepenend as he got further from the entrance, but his eyes adjusted as he went, and his other senses filled in the gaps. It was fortunate, actually, that the decrease in vision boosted his hearing, as otherwise he might have stumbled right into the main portion of the den and been discovered.

Instead, Orsin heard a voice—the voice of the baron—speaking to itself, or to the two remaining attendant spiders, from up ahead. He slowed and carefully crept forward. He could just make out the vast bulk of the baron shifting up ahead where the tunnel widened out into a large chamber.

Like the rest of the den, it was mostly open space. There was more webbing here, strong lines supporting the arched ceiling, and small webs that Orsin guessed were where the smaller spiders lived and slept. There were also several cocoons, all of the same general size and shape. This time, however, there was one that was open. A little light leaked down through veins in the ceiling, possibly for air circulation, and Orsin was finally able to see what was inside.

It was one of his people!

Slack-jawed and drooling a vicious green slime, Orsin could see from his hiding spot that the Fursja was still alive. Breath caused bubbles to form in the fizzing herd-venom around their mouth and a wheezing rattle of breath flowed in and out of the Fursja's mouth.

"Weak," the spider-baron said, its mandibles clacking. "You are weak. You can understand me, yes? This tongue of yours is primitive, and vile, but easy enough to master, yes."

The baron reached out with one massive leg and poked gently at the Fursja tangled in webbing before it. Orsin forced himself not to move, though his first impulse was to charge forward and attempt a rescue. It was a foolish thought. The green foam at the Fursja's mouth said they were already as good as dead.

"These are the strongest specimens you could find?" The baron said in its clacking, hissing voice to the two attendant spiders near to it.

Orsin hadn't noticed them at first. There was one to either side of the cocoon. Their legs held them in place on the wall, while each one used more delicate forelimbs to gently hold the cocoon open. They chittered in response to the baron, lacking the more advanced herd-beast's command of intelligible language, though that did not seem to be a barrier to communication.

"Yes, yes, every year a new crop of potential hosts, every year we hope to fulfill our queen's greatest desire to find one that is resilient enough to be a host for her eggs. Every year it is a failure, however. They all succumb to the incubation-venom too easily." The baron prodded the Fursja again. "Though this one showed some initial promise, it seems to be deteriorating at an increased rate. Perhaps it shall pull through and surprise us, but I am afraid we will be disappointed. Again."

Hissing in clear fury, the baron lashed out with its legs, turning its annoyance into quick, lethal-looking movements.

The spiders chittered at him.

"Yes, that is why I sent your siblings out on the hunt once again. Though the season is waning, and we have caught most of the specimens we are likely to catch, the stronger ones always last longer. Perhaps we shall be fortunate and your brethren will bring word of a likely candidate. We have not yet found the one that destroyed Kinu'Sahe." Hissing laughter filled the cavern. "Foolish fox. To let food destroy him so easily. He was weak. And yet—"

the spider shifted uneasily, "—to kill a baron, one of my peers, this specimen must be remarkable. If we can bring it down, inject it slowly, yes, yes, perhaps it would prove strong enough to host a queen's egg! Though even so, these tiny creatures are such poor sustenance. The larva will need so much food."

The spider clacked its chelicerae thoughtfully and went to prod gently at a few of the other cocoons.

"Though they have failed to resist the incubation-venom, the meat is still good. We shall keep it preserved, in case this year we are fortunate. Some stasis-jelly! Let us preserve the ones that have already succumbed before they mutate into proper awareness."

Orsin's mind whirled. Every one of these cocoons must house one of his peers! And why? For food. His people were being kept here as food. And as potential hosts for the herd queen's eggs?

So many cocoons. Had so many warriors fallen to the herd this year? Orsin couldn't believe it.

When the spiders opened a cocoon and old bones and fur fell out, he was relieved. Not all of these cocoons held living Fursja. But then, how many years had this been going on? How many of his people had suffered here in this horrible place?

A deep and implacable anger kindled in Orsin's stomach. He'd destroy this place if he could, burn it all to ash, rip the legs from the spiders and crush them beneath his heel. Even that fucking baron. A spider without legs was nothing.

"Clear out the bones! They are dry and have no marrow left in them," the baron commanded. "Haul them out to make room for fresher meat." It clacked in disappointment. "We shall have to send some of your siblings out to hunt fresher meat. We cannot risk eating any of these delicate morsels ourselves, not until we know whether or not the queen will have need of them." The spider-baron shifted uneasily. "We must succeed, and soon. My prince grows restless. If we succeed, he succeeds, and we rise with him. Yes, yes. We will find this baron-slayer and bring him in. Or perhaps one of our current subjects will rally. We have been surprised before. Never enough to achieve our goal, no, but some have rallied, near the end. Perhaps, perhaps we will be surprised."

The spiders were moving across the chamber toward him. There were cocoons hanging from the walls around him, part of what had been giving him cover this whole time. He needed to move. There was too great a chance he would be discovered, and while Orsin thought he had a good chance of meeting even this baron in equal combat, if he did he would either die or the baron would, and in either case he wouldn't get the battle with the prince he needed.

That Torben's memory demanded.

Orsin slowly backed away. He had what he had come for. He had learned several things that would be useful to him. Though his instincts screamed out at him to help the captive Fursja, they were already dead, pumped so full of herd-venom that their change was inevitable, if it had not already happened. There wasn't anything he could give them, except the release of death, but if he did that he would lose his best chance to get this baron to lead him to a prince. A plan was already forming in the back of his mind.

War required sacrifice. Sometimes truly terrible, gut-wrenching sacrifices. These Fursja were warriors, and though their fate was one worse than death, they would go to it having served the greater will of Weihlaris.

Orsin promised himself he would give them that much, at least.

CHAPTER 35

Orsin needed the baron to lead him to the prince. To get the baron to do such a thing, the baron needed a reason to go to the prince. And the herd beast would only do that if it was confident it had good news for its superior.

If it had what it thought was a proper vessel capable of hosting an egg that would hatch a herd queen.

The baron thought Orsin might be capable of such a thing, but there was no way in any blistering pit that he was going to allow himself to be captured. No. Then he would also need an escape plan reliable and effective enough to ensure he could slip away to follow the baron. That seemed like an unlikely prospect even under ideal circumstances.

No. What he needed was to trick the baron into thinking one of the Fursja currently being held captive was stronger than they actually were. If he already had his ideal specimen, he would not need to keep hunting for one, and Orsin wouldn't need to sacrifice any more of his people to this cause. One of the Fursja captives already present would just have to exhibit a sudden and miraculous ability to resist the herd venom, making them a tempting host.

And Orsin had an idea just how to do that.

He'd seen how the baron injected the Fursja in the den with what it called incubation-venom. It looked like a variant of the regular herd infection that mutated and warped ordinary life into twisted abominations, but seemed to have a slightly different effect. Orsin was counting on the fact that it was still a kind of herd venom, however. Because if it was, the sacred herbs he carried should have an effect. They should weaken the venom, make it seem like the host was stronger and more resilient than they actually were.

And if the baron thought it had a valid host, it would scurry off to report that fact in person to its prince.

Meaning Orsin could follow it right to his target.

It was a ruthless plan, and it turned Orsin's stomach to think of prolonging the suffering of any of his people, but he knew he would do it. He would do anything to achieve his goal. This was war, brutal and cruel. If their enemies would not hesitate to profane the most sacred of things, life itself, Orsin could not himself turn back from the hard choices.

Not if he wanted to achieve his goals.

It was a sacrifice he made, in a way, to his people and to Weihlaris. He sacrificed his morals, his scruples, even his fellow Fursja in this. But if he succeeded, if he managed to slay a herd prince and return to the Warlord with the knowledge he had gained in the process, it could alter the trajectory of the war.

Orsin could bear that burden. He would do the hard things so that the rest of his people might one day live free, and not have to make such terrible choices.

When the herd was dead and gone, eradicated from the world once and for all.

It was not glorious, what he intended here. It would not shower him with honour. It was an ugly, necessary thing, yes, and if it got him the chance to destroy a prince and pillar of the herd, he would do it.

That would be his chance at glory, though Orsin knew he would bear the bitter price of it down through the years until his death.

But he had no reservations about what he was doing. Nothing was going to divert his aim. Which was why he was here, sneaking into the baron's den once more, a small pill rolled of sacred herbs in his paw.

Twice before he'd done this, narrowly escaping notice. Each time he had dosed the Fursja he saw the first time he snuck into the den. All it took was a tiny packet of the herbs. He had seen light kindle in their eyes, an echo of the person they had once been. With the webbing of the cocoon and the flesh-warping nature of the herd-venom, Orsin could not be certain who it was, though a part of him knew it had to be one of his cohort. It had to be someone he already knew.

Someone he had fought beside, that first day, when the massed might of the Fursja warrior-hopefuls had spilled out form the gate and swept the monstrosities before them like chaff before the wind.

Orsin crept into the vast chamber. The baron was muttering to itself and inspecting several of the cocoons on the other side of the chamber. He had noticed it tended to hyper focus on whatever was in front of it, and paid little attention to anything outside that focus. Good for researching or uncovering oddities, but a terrible adaptation for surviving the battlefield or noticing when an invader was sneaking into your home.

Climbing the wall was the biggest challenge. Orsin had enough strength to do it easily, and the wall provided plentiful handholds, but he had to take great care of the webbing stuck to the wall. There were isolated clumps that were reinforcing the earth all around, and those were safe to touch. They weren't even that sticky, considering how much dirt clung to them, but there wer also larger guide-strands that the spiders used to move quickly around the chamber.

Once he had raised himself even with the cocoon, Orsin shot a nervous glance over his shoulder at the baron and its two attendants. They were all still engrossed in the contents of the cocoon they were investigating. Good.

Orsin quickly pried the strands of black silk apart with one claw. If he kept his fur away, the stuff wasn't too bad. He supposed his claws were enough like the ends of the spiders legs. All he needed was a small opening, big enough to pass the pill through and into the Fursja's mouth. They would swallow reflexively, something within them longing for the healing power of those herbs, though the dosage was far too weak to do anything about the sheer amount of venom coursing through their body. Then Orsin would squeeze the cocoon closed once more and descend.

"What? What is this?"

The shout of outrage nearly caused him to drop the pill. Orsin glanced back over his shoulder, but the baron was still not looking at him. It was waving its legs in agitation at something in the cocoon. Orsin could not see from this angle.

He was clearly running out of time, however.

Orsin shoved the pill in the Fursja's mouth. It snapped it down with more energy than it had the last two times. The herbs must be having a cumulative effect.

Too much of an effect. The Fursja in the cocoon groaned and growled as the herbs fizzed away at some of the venom infecting it. They began to struggle against the cocoon and Orsin had to lunge back, choosing to let go and risk making a noise when falling to the ground over getting ensnared by the web and becoming stuck to the wall for the baron to find at its leisure.

Orsin landed with a *whumph*.

"What's that? What's that?"

The baron. Orsin turned and sprinted back toward the tunnel, diving behind the first cocoon past the entrance to the chamber and crouching as near to the wall as he dared. He could hear the baron scurrying across the chamber. Was it toward him? Or was the baron heading toward the cocoon? Orsin could hear the Fursja within growling and groaning.

The sounds must have covered his retreat, for the baron did not immediately rush toward the tunnel in pursuit. Orsin took a slow, careful breath and slowly peered around the cocoon behind which he had taken cover.

The baron and its two attendants were standing before the cocoon with the Fursja he had been dosing. The baron was waving its legs and shouting orders at its attendant spiders. Carefully as Orsin watched the two attendants carefully drew back the cocoon while simultaneously drawing more silk from their abdomens to wrap the Fursja's limbs more tightly in place.

It occurred to Orsin then that he had never seen the baron produce silk of any kind. It was clear it was a different kind of spider at the core. Perhaps one that hunted rather than spun webs. Or maybe the herd-venom had burned away the ability to produce webs in exchange for the thing's excessive size and intelligence. There was no way to know what kind of trade offs the mutations made when a new herd beast was formed.

When their head was fully uncovered, the Fursja managed to growl in defiance at their captor, hatred sparking form their eyes. It was a mad, unfocused hatred, but still it was there and Orsin's heart ached to see even this much an echo of one of his people. But it was the reaction he needed and Orsin felt a grim satisfaction in that.

The baron was equally delighted, though for a far different reason.

"Good. Good! How unexpected. How fortunate." The baron rubbed its forelegs together in glee. "This one shows great promise, great promise indeed. Where did this well of hidden strength spring from, I wonder? Ah, but it does not matter. What matters is that I have a potential host. Do I not? Yes?"

The baron carefully prodded the Fursja, and they began to struggle, trying to pull free from the cocoon.

"Yes! Yes, yes. Most excellent! There is plenty of fight here. Enough to keep the host alive whilst the egg hatches and the juvenile queen eats her way free of the creature. And we have plenty of food, yes, good. Enough to see that the apotheosis is complete. Once she has achieved her form from this base matter, she can be fed on other meat."

The baron rushed around the chamber, checking on the other cocoons and muttering to itself about feeding and growth rates and other strange things. Orsin listened with half an ear, in case it let slip some secret that might be used to kill herd creatures more efficiently, but nothing of the sort presented itself, or if it did Orsin was not schooled enough to recognise it. Many of the words were unfamiliar, after all.

Once it had satisfied itself that all was to its liking, the baron ordered the two attendant spiders to carefully guard and care for their specimens, and to pass along those orders to their brethren when they returned from their latest hunt. Any new meat they brought was to be preserved right away, rather than tested with incubation-venom.

"We have our host, yes," the spider-baron all but cackled. "Yes. My prince must know! Must know! I shall go tell him of this now. Yes, yes."

Orsin backed quickly from the den, moving fast so he was out of sight when the baron rushed forth and headed for the dome.

It was fast. Terrifyingly so. And so eager that it threw much of its energy into an outright dash towards its destination.

Orsin had to sprint to keep up. Fortunately, the baron was too caught up in its excitement to report to its superior. Otherwise Orsin might have been discovered. There was no way to sprint quietly after the thing.

Right towards the dome the baron raced, with Orsin in pursuit. He was headed deeper into herd territory than any Fursja had been in years. The Warlord had made it this far, and some of his generation, but no others since.

If Orsin survived, he would return a part of an elite company.

But first, he had a prince to find.

CHAPTER 36

The heat only intensified as Orsin followed the baron closer and closer to the dome. The vegetation was thick and herd beasts scurried, scuttled, and slithered everywhere. Fortunately, the baron was a large and deadly presence. Not only did it leave a large pathway through the jungle greenery, other, lesser herd beasts fled its presence.

Orsin had seen barons devour lesser herd beasts to heal themselves. It was not surprising that the lesser beasts would avoid a herd noble unless ordered otherwise. And it was a blessing sent from Weihlaris himself as it allowed him to follow the baron with minimal danger of being discovered.

By lesser herd beasts, at least.

The baron was still a danger, looming large and deadly before him. Fortunately, the thing seemed absorbed in carrying its news to its prince Orsin could even hear it muttering to itself about it as it went.

In this manner Orsin made it through the jungle undiscovered and unscathed. The greenery was so thick, too, that when the base of the dome suddenly loomed ahead, it was a surprise. One moment there had been nothing but greenery, next the baron was scuttling up the mottled grey-green surface of the dome, headed for the largest of the nearby holes.

The passageway was easily five times larger than the baron's already substantial bulk. Orsin was unsurprised. Herd Princes were reportedly vast monsters, deadly, massive, and hideous to behold.

He'd know soon enough.

The baron disappeared into the passageway. Orsin mentally cursed and picked up his speed. There was no way to know if the tunnels inside would branch. He had to move closer to his quarry if he wanted to follow it to the prince.

Just inside he was surprised by a pair of spiders, mastiff-sized ones. They were unlike those the baron kept, and instead had red hourglass markings on their abdomens. They had not fled, but they were clearly surprised by his presence.

Before they could raise the alarm, Orsin lashed out with Muinnajhr and Hjarsurung, ending the beasts with a ruthless efficiency. Luckily there was plenty of vegetation in the tunnel, vile green moss that stank of herd infection. Orsin bundled the bodies off to the side and covered them quickly, before running down the tunnel to try and find the baron.

The tunnel did branch, but all the branches were smaller ones, so Orsin gambled that the baron would stick to the largest passageway. It paid off. He quickly caught up, following the sound of clacking legs, and caught sight of a massive form moving through the gloom.

After several minutes, Orsin spotted light up ahead. It was a sickly, pale thing, phosphorescent and faintly green. Nearing it, he saw it came from several strange, fungal growths. They looked almost like twisted paws, thrusting up out of the thick rot at the edges of the tunnel. They outlined a generally circular exit to the tunnel.

The baron rushed through, but Orsin paused at the exit of the passageway, to look ahead and see what he might be about to rush into.

The tunnel widened into a large chamber. It was thickly festooned with the trailing moss he had seen in the tunnel and shrouded with webbing at the edges. Smaller forms moved here and there at the edges, spiders that served the prince no doubt. He could make out two more tunnels, ringed with glowing mushrooms as they were.

From the form of the baron and its servants, as well as the herd beasts he had encountered thus far, Orsin had expected the prince would look like a giant spider of some kind, even larger than the baron.

It did not. Oh, it was massive, to be certain, but it didn't look like a spider. It was...alien was the only word for it. All the herd beasts Orsin had encountered, or were described in the tales, looked like a slightly twisted version of a real living thing, or a conglomeration of those things. Often those aspects were mutated but by the herd infection, almost beyond recognition, but they were, in the end, a warping of the natural order of things.

The prince looked like something that did not come from this world. It was truly other, a vile existence that seemed to make the world around it scream with the unnatural wrongness of it all. Orsin's eyes hurt just looking at it and a headache began to gnaw at him almost immediately, as if his mind was attempting to understand something that just didn't *fit* with the natural geometries of the world around it.

The Prince was a giant figure, with two arms and two legs, and what looked to be a head and a torso, not too dissimilar to the general shape of a Fursja or most of the other intelligent peoples of the world. It's skin was sharp and chitinous with exoskeleton, and the whole of the body was an intense shade of something like green that reminded Orsin of nothing so much as the look of herd-venom. Like he was made entirely of the stuff.

A massive, cancerous-looking hump twisted the prince's back, and the thing was riddled with holes. The Prince sat enthroned on a massive bench, a twist of the same stone like material as made the dome, pulled up and sculpted from the floor. Of course, with that kind of hump there would be no way for it to sit in the kind of chair the Fursja preferred. If it even knew what such things looked like.

It had three eyes, though they were more like pure red slits in the green carapace of the abomination, and the mouth that curved under them was a wicked gash filled with a yawning abyss of fangs. They looked even sharper than the seven claws that glittered at the end of each of its limbs. Limbs that, now that Orsin was looking more closely, appeared to have one too many joints in them.

His mind was a blade and he sharpened it on everything he was seeing, drawing it together and honing a plan. The moment was nearing, this would be his best chance at facing a prince. He'd have to take out the baron as well, but that should be simple. He had the advantage of surprise and plenty of time to have studied its weaknesses.

The unknown numbers of herd beasts scurrying around in the webbing that lined the chamber was another factor to consider, but not one Orsin spent a lot of time on. He knew how flammamble herd-venom webbing could be, and he had everything he needed with him to set the stuff aflame. That should burn most of the monstrosities lurking in the background to a crisp.

Orsin knew part of his brain was focusing on the details of his plan to avoid focusing on the presence of the Prince in front of him. The thing was monstrous. Not only in the aura of power it exuded or the lethal strength and grace that infused every fibre of its being, but in the way it screamed out at him as being something not of this world. It's very existence reached out and set a dissonance surging deep into his bones. His stomach twisted and threatened to disgorge its contents whenever he looked at the prince for too long.

There was no way such a thing could ever rest easily upon the earth of this world. That must be why it dwelled here in this dome, surrounded by layer after layer of rock and stone twisted and infused with herd-infection, to the point that it could hold court like this.

Orsin tasted copper and ozone on his tongue. He could feel the thrumming hatred in his being for this blight upon existence. Weihlaris called for its destruction, as did every ounce of flesh on his bones. Muinnajhr and Hjarsurung were eager at his side.

He would end this infection here, at the source. He would purge it by lancing the walking boil that was the herd prince. And then he would go home, content in the glory he had won and the vengeance he had wrested from the herd for all the wrongs they had done to him.

Standing here, in the presence of a prince, even the thought of facing a queen was nearly enough to cause him to vomit his feet up through his entire body. No. If Orsin was ever going to face the herd queen, he would do it after completing his Trial and with the full berserker blessing of Weihlaris.

But before he could do any of that he needed to execute his plan, escape this place, and return home. And Orsin was becoming increasingly homesick by the minute. It was past time he settled this.

Moving quickly, he retrieved the things he needed from his supplies. He had enough to make three flaming brands that should set the webbing alight when they hit. There were some large clumps scattered throughout the cavern that would make ideal targets. As soon as those were prepared, Orsin took one last look at the cavern.

The baron was still chittering to the prince and waving its legs. Now was as good a time as any he would have.

He did not roar his battle cry. There was no advantage to betraying himself that way. Instead he struck fire to the torches and flung them at his pre-selected targets as fast as he could, so the light did not betray him.

The webwork caught immediately and flames raced around the cavern. Shrieks of agony went up from the spider-beasts within and several bodies fell twitching to the floor.

Orsin paid them no heed. He was already in motion, axe and hammer at the ready. He launched himself from the tunnel, the sight elevation providing him the extra edge he needed to launch himself up in an a deadly arc that ended with him coming down, hard, right on top of the baron. A blow from his hammer sent it reeling, its head slamming to one side and exposing its neck to the follow up slash from Orsin's axe. The blade bit deep, driven not only by momentum but also by righteous fury and the pent up frustration of a Fursja warrior who had had to restrain his natural instincts for far too long in order to follow the accursed beast here, to his true prey.

The prince.

The baron's head went flying across the cavern and Orsin kept from the body as it twitched and spasmed, the legs desperately trying to slice into him. Without its head, however, the body was unable to do anything. Orsin landed several lengths away and flicked his weapons to clear the herd-ichor from them.

All around him the cavern burned and spider-beasts died. The prince had barely had time to react, Orsin's initial attack had been so swift and ruthless. But now, with the chaff dealt with, Orsin was free to focus on the main event.

"Come at me and meet your death, bug," he roared, feeling the deep sparks of a battle fury beginning to rise in his stomach.

The prince did not move. For a long moment it was locked in place. Orsin could feel its eyes on him, however. It was as if he were being weighed and measured, examined with a dispassionate interest like unto a mild curiosity.

It was not the feeling of a being that felt they were under threat.

"You are a blight upon this land," Orsin said, levelling his axe at the prince. "A living infection that taints everything it touches. I am here to end that taint, to cut out the infection and burn away all traces of it. I've killed three barons, single-handedly. You will be no different. I will leave this place with your head, consecrate it to the might of Weihlaris, and, when I return, and return I will, mark my words, it will be to destroy your queen."

Where before there had been dispassionate disinterest, or at most mild intrigue, Orsin's threat to the queen lit a fire beneath the thing. It hissed at his words, hatred suddenly a nearly-palpable weight throughout the room.

"Foolish Fursja," the prince said, speaking in a voice that clawed at the edges of Orsin's sanity, a strange, trebled crooning that echoed disharmoniously with itself. "You are brave to come here, I grant you that, but this room shall become your grave. I, the Great God Bylroth-Bal proclaim it. Here ends your insolent life!"

Then the Prince attacked!

CHAPTER 37

The herd prince roared as it lunged for Orsin. The sound reverberated throughout the chamber and rattled the Fursja warrior's bones. All around them flaming motes of ash floated, spider-corpses crackled and popped, and shadows surged in the flickering light.

Bylroth-Bal lashed out with its wicked claws, its multi-jointed arms flashing in the flickering light, as lethal as swords. Orsin swung Muinnajhr, aiming to cut the hand that dared raise itself against him, but the blade of the axe only struck sparks from the exoskeletal chitin on the prince's arm.

The thing was *tough*. And it was smart. The beast showed true signs of intelligence, as did all other noble-ranked abominations. Each had been an increase in power, so Orsin had to assume an increase in intelligence came along with that as well.

The thing was certainly even more resilient than the barons he had killed so far.

Well, if he couldn't easily slice into the thing, perhaps he could crack it open. Hjarsurung whirled in his grip and as the prince lashed out again, Orsin brought the warhammer swinging down in a brutal blow aimed at crushing the nearest joint.

The hammer struck home and Bylroth-Bal's flesh rang like a bell. Orsin couldn't tell if it had done much damage, but again he had deflected the blow. A feral grin stole its way across his face. The prince was lethal, and fast, but not so fast that Orsin couldn't hope to match it.

The prince had every natural advantage that the venom running through its veins could grant. It had size and strength and speed to spare. It was a perfect predator.

Orsin, by contrast, had the mighty frame of a Fursja warrior, but his claws could not compare to the natural weapons of the prince, his hide was nowhere nearly so tough and damage resistant, and he stood here, in the heart of herd territory, alone.

No. Not alone. Orsin brought Hjarsurung up to his face. Torben was with him. He held the weapon of his fallen friend. A drop of Torben's blood was forever forged into Muinnajhr.

Torben was with him.

Weihlaris was with him.

Orsin was a one-bear army.

Motes of fire flickered at the edges of his vision, the crimson thread at the edges suddenly sparking to life as righteous fury kindled into the beginnings of a true berserker rage. The herd had plagued his people, had plagued this world for too long. They had taken his best friend from him.

It was past time that Orsin inflicted some of that same pain on them.

"Who dares touch this mortal?" Bylroth-Bal hissed a sudden tension running through it. "Lord of Fury, is that you? Your touch will not save this pathetic servant of yours!"

The world flickered redly. The prince, perhaps sensing the flicker of divine energy at the heart of Orsin's burgeoning rage, suddenly flexed the hump on its back. From the myriad holes suppurating there, a horde of tiny spiders emerged, each trailing a long thread of silk behind them. The silk ballooned out and several of them began floating away toward the two tunnels that Orsin had noticed as alternate exits when he first examined the place.

The prince was calling in reinforcements!

Rather than fear Orsin felt a flicker of fierce exultation mix and send the rising rage into a frothing sea of pure power.

The prince feared him!

Before the battle-fury took him totally and his entire world narrowed to his battle with the prince, Orsin darted around his foe and ran along and then up the wall, Muinnajhr flashing as he went. Long streamers of moss and vines, tangled and thick, freed from where they anchored themselves, crashed down blocking first one, and then the other, exit. Reinforcements would take time to cut through the downed and tangled vegetation.

By then the prince would be dead and no more than a memory.

Bylroth-Bal howled out a challenge, and the spiders floating through the air in the cavern swelled, doubling and then tripling in size. They were still no larger than one of his fingers, but the things practically glowed with herd venom and their fangs would be large enough to break his skin if too many of them got close.

Muinnajhr whirled and Orsin cut through a few of them and waved away others with Hjarsurung. Still, spider after spider landed on his body and scuttled across his flesh, sinking their fangs in where they could. With their venom came something else.

The voice of Bylroth-Bal echoing in the vaults of his mind.

"You will fall before me, worthless scrap of fur. You are nothing before the divine might of the rulers of the Herd. I shall hollow you out and squat in your mind, and you shall carry me back across your worthless wall and I shall use your body to spread the might of my people throughout your lands. You will become the instrument of your own people's destruction."

The prince continued to whisper, that strange, disharmonic voice attacking all of Orsin's fears and weaknesses, burrowing through his memories and mocking him with petty slights and moments of shame.

Orsin roared in defiance at the voice in his head. He roared his disdain for the sting of herd-poison pumping through his veins, and he shrugged off the pain.

The pain was nothing. The herd-venom coursing through his body was nothing. Bylroth-Bal was nothing. All of his focus now was on the sea of rage crashing against the shores of his soul and the hated figure of his foe in front of him. It was as if the divine voice of Weihlaris spoke to him in the depths of his being and set his weapons free.

Destroy.

Orsin howled and launched himself at the prince. Axe met claws, and body blows were exchanged for hammer strikes. Orsin and the prince stood all but toe-to-toe, in spite of the abomination's massive size advantage, as they traded blows.

The Fursja warrior was forced to duck and dodge as much as he blocked. The herd prince was terrifically strong, a fact that was made abundantly clear when Orsin first failed to block an incoming blow. The force of it was enough to send him flying across the chamber to slam bodily into the wall.

The breath was driven out of him, and were he not in the grips of a primal rage blessed by Weihlaris himself, it might have been the end of the battle then and there as he was stunned by the lack of breath in his lungs. As it was, instead, Orsin just took a ragged gulping breath, forcing the air into his lungs by main strength and will alone and leapt immediately into a counter-attack, charging at his foe and bringing hammer and axe down to exact bloody, ichorous vengeance.

Bylroth-Bal's exoskeletal armour continued to protect him, however.

Orsin hammered at it. The hammer blows knocked the prince off balance, sparing him another blow like the last one which would have felled a lesser warrior, or indeed anyone not in the throes of berserker rage. Once or twice he managed to elicit a resounding crack from the stuff, but it was always on larger, flatter portions of the body. Though there might be cracks, they were small enough that Orsin could not easily target them for repeated blows, and the body was thick enough that not even Muinnajhr would easily pierce the flesh beneath.

Orsin dodged another blow and felt yet another small set of fangs pierce his flesh. Herd-venom pulsed in his veins, but the fury burning in his blood seemed to boil it away, or at least hold it at arm's length for as long as he raged. The whispers of Bylroth-Bal in his mind were no match for the white-hot fury of Weihlaris.

The Fursja dodged a sweeping roundhouse blow, falling to the ground and rolling away and behind the prince to come up for another attack from its blind spot. The motion crushed the spiders clinging to him and gave him the chance to attempt to hamstring the prince.

If it had hamstrings. The way its legs bent was inconclusive. Orsin whirled, a hurricane of fury, his hammer attacking one joint at the same time his axe slammed into the other. The weapons hit home and his foe stumbled forward.

"You will pay for that, Fursja scum!" Bylroth-Bal hissed like a spider and its eyes glimmered with hatred.

Orsin was caught in the grips of rage so tightly the prince might as well have said nothing. Was that a crack on the left joint? Orsin couldn't quite make it out in the unreliable light. Still, the prince seemed unduly angered by the blow. It either hurt or otherwise damaged the thing.

He had to be sure. Orsin threw himself forward, attempting to target the same joint, this time from the front as the prince had whirled around to face him. He wasn't counting on the blow doing anything, really, but it did get him what he needed. A bit of insight.

The prince flinched back. The movement was slight, but Orsin, all of his senses driven into hyper-stimulation by the rage consuming him, caught it easily. The prince had weak spots, places where the armour was weak because it needed to move.

He had been right to target the joints. And the joint that afforded the most movement?

The neck.

That would be the place the prince was the most vulnerable. Orsin would see how well even a prince of the herd was able to function without its head.

He threw himself once more into the attack. Hammer and axe flew, driven by pure, righteous rage. Orsin chipped away at the prince's defenses, striking body blows frequently, and, more rarely, a blow at the joint. Faster and faster each of them flew, the frenzy of battle filling their veins and the sound of their conflict echoing through the cavern around them.

Orsin roared in pain as Bylroth-Bal finally pierced his defense. Those sword-like claws pierced him through the shoulder, exploding out of his back in a spray of blood, ribbons of flesh and fur trailing from the tips of those lethal claws.

He felt no pain. Rather, he took it as an opportunity. With the prince's arm buried in his flesh, Orsin flexed and twisted his arm up and over, bringing Hjarsurung down in a lock on the prince's limb. Then, with the prince's second elbow exposed at the joint, Orsin brought Muinnajhr down like the fury of a thunderbolt.

The axe struck true, and with the joint exposed and bent nearly backward by the pressure Orsin was exerting with Torben's hammer, the prince's arm was severed from its body.

Orsin flipped his axe up into the air, ripped the prince's arm free from his own shoulder, threw it with the full force of his rage-enhanced strength at the prince, and then caught Muinnajhr as it came down, all in one smooth motion. The arm flew across the intervening space and one of the prince's own claws lanced at its neck before it could bat the projectile away.

There was a brief keening sound of pain before it was cut off and the prince swatted the offending flesh away.

"How dare—"

That was it. An opening. While Bylroth-Bal was distracted by the affront of having its own flesh used as a weapon against it, Orsin roared with fury and charged forward. His eyes trailed streamers of red light like flame as the power of Weihlaris suffused him and his strength surged to that of at least ten Fursja warriors. He slammed into the prince, low and powerful, and with a howl of exertion, he lifted the abomination entirely free from the ground and body slammed it down.

The prince's body flattened and Bylroth-Bal shrieked, green ichor running in streams from beneath it. Orsin must have crashed uncounted spiders still living in the thing's back. The Fursja warrior raised himself up above his foe and that's when he spotted it.

The chitin at the prince's neck was cracked, weak. But even so, Orsin did not have the strength to simply rip the prince's head free. No. This would take something more.

He knew exactly what to do. It was crystal clear in his rage fumed mind.

With a roar, Orsin raised Muinnajhr and brought the weapon down in a glittering arc to bite deeply into the weak spot at the prince's throat. The axe bit deep into the cracked chitin, but was not enough, on its own, to sever the head.

That's where Hjarsurung came in. Once, twice, thrice, Orsin brought the warhammer down on the haft of Muinnajhr, where the haft connected to the axe blade. The force of the blows drove the axe deeper and deeper into the prince's throat until finally, with the last blow, his weapon and Torben's moving in perfect concert, Bylroth-Bal's head parted its body and went tumbling away.

The body immediately went limp and began to liquify. Orsin jumped free and liquid herd-venom, steaming and stinking to a degree he had never before experienced, flowed across the floor of the cavern, tendrils of it reaching out to try and bind itself to any living flesh or vegetation it could find.

Fortunately, there was not much that still fit that description.

The head, however, the head remained. Even as the light within its eyes died, that hateful, disharmonious voice spoke again and Orsin felt his blood curdle.

"Petty, pitiful Fursja! You may have slain this unworthy form, but this is but one of many bodies I wear. You shall—"

Whatever threat the head was going to speak was lost as the last vestiges of life fled from the flesh. A dark, rippling shadow, so dense as to be almost a tangible form, poured from the thing's mouth and darted away down the nearest tunnel and into the darkness.

Orsin didn't tarry. A fierce, joyful fury burned in his bones. He reached out to collect the prince's head, and roared out a cry of victory that equal parts prayer to Weihlaris and ululation for Torben.

He had done it. He had slain a prince of the herd.

Now all he needed to do was escape with his life and bear this glory back home to his people.

Chapter 38

Orsin caught up the severed head of the herd prince and turned to run. He had achieved his goal, and jubilation threatened to unseat his berserker rage. He did not allow it to go to his head, however. He was still deep within herd territory, in the dome, surrounded by who knew how many abominations. His ears flicked, hearing a rising cacophony of howls of outrage and calls for reinforcements. Long limbs were tearing madly at the blockage he had dropped in front of two of the three tunnels leading to this chamber.

He needed to get out of here and fast.

So Orsin ran, letting the rage and energy that filled him fuel his steps. The prince's head was quickly tied off with a length of vine and slung out of his way so he had both hands free to fight, as encounters with herd beasts was going to be an inevitability.

He had no time to properly treat his wounds and herd venom burned in his veins, thick and hot. All he could do was shove a handful of sacred herbs into his mouth, chew, and pray to Weihlaris as he got out of the dome as quickly as he could.

It would be days of travel before he'd reach the safety of some Fursja ruins or the field of herd-repelling sacred herbs that grew near the tor.

Orsin sprinted along the tunnel. It was still mostly empty, the inhabitants driven away but the baron's passage earlier. Twice he ran into spiders scuttling out of smaller tunnels, but he caught them by surprise and easily crushed them without slowing his pace. He didn't slow until he reached the point where the tunnel exited the dome.

Then, Orsin paused, peering out carefully before charging into the jungle beyond. The nearby greenery shook with the passage of all manner of agitated herd beasts. His slaughter of the prince had clearly had an effect. Escape would be a trial all its own, though it would only add to the glory he would receive in passing it.

If he passed it.

The rage that had filled him during his battle with the prince was gone. And it was a good thing Orsin would need all of his wits to escape this situation alive. The battle fury was priceless in the heat of a chaotic battle, but it did not lend itself to wise decisions or calculated strategy.

He would make his way back along the pathway the baron had followed. It was the most reliable route and the only one he knew, rather than guessed at. He'd move fast, speed over stealth. He was too close to the dome and the herd contained too many wild cards. Who knew what senses there might be that could pick him out.

The weight of the prince's head at his hip suddenly seemed titanic, almost too much to carry.

Orsin shook his head.

"We did it, Torben," he said softly to himself. "We have struck a dire blow. You—" the words threatened to catch in his throat, but Orsin had bested a herd prince and he would not be stopped by a dry throat or a painful memory. "You have been avenged."

With that thought, Orsin launched himself out of the dome and into the greenery, thankful for once for the thickness of it. It would help hide him from prying eyes, and the ever-present scent was strong enough to help hide him that way as well.

The loam was soft beneath his paws as he ran, though he was wary of any treacherous footing. He almost missed a herd serpent, mistaking it for yet another ring hanging streamer of moss. Its fangs sank deep into his unwounded shoulder before he managed to slice the thing in half with Muinnajhr.

Swearing, Orsin paused long enough to retrieve more of his supply of sacred herbs, chewing them into a quick makeshift paste and applying it as he moved quickly along the pathway he was following. It was rough and ready field medicine, but it would have to do.

His vision blurred slightly, his body feeling the effects of weeks of foraging and subsistence eating, of near-constant battle, and the wounds he was still carrying from his battle with the prince. Orsin stumbled slightly, but pushed on. He couldn't stop now. He wouldn't.

He had to make it home.

Though as he moved through the jungle, hiding and skirmishing as best he could, the thought kept eating at him, as the herd venom ate at his veins: what if he didn't make it back?

He had achieved amazing things, yes, but Orsin couldn't shake the feeling that he had used up a lifetime of good fortune and more in these past few weeks. His life was balanced on the edge of a razor right now, and any bit of ill luck could doom him.

Orsin could very easily die out here, and none would know of what he had accomplished. The battle with the prince, all of his triumphs over the barons and other herd nobility, none would ever know. His name would pass into oblivion, unremembered save by his parents, and swiftly forgotten once they themselves passed on.

As would Torben's. None would know of his valiant final stand, or the role his hammer had played in the death of none other than a prince of the herd.

Orsin growled, his eyes narrowing. No! he had fought too hard, he had lost too much, he wouldn't lose this as well! There was no way he would allow anything to stand between him and his safe return home! He had made it this far into herd territory and slain a prince! He would make it home. His story would be known, his glory would be known.

Torben would be remembered.

At that moment, Orsin tasted the ghost of honey-mead upon his tongue and thought he heard the voice of his friend, laughing and whispering upon the air.

Then get moving. You don't have all season! You're carrying more than glory, my friend, you're carrying hope. So move!

And Orsin did.

Hope. That was a strange thought, but a true one. Princes did not fall lightly, nor often. If he survived to bear the severed head of their enemy back to the gates of Vaeggdor it would set off a celebration such as had not been seen in a generation. The head was a symbol of what they could achieve, both alone as warriors of Weihlaris, and as a people.

A twisted arctic fox leapt from concealment, yipping in startlement as Orsin's appearance. The Fursja warrior freed his axe and in one smooth movement hauled back and flung it at the thing, the force of the throw and the weight of the axe allowing it to blast through the herd beast's body, sending a spray of blood and entrails scattering across the jungle floor.

Orsin shifted his pace slightly, grabbed Muinnajhr as he ran past, and carried on.

The jungle presented more dangers, but each one he met with axe and hammer, with determination and fury and the memory of Torben. He gathered a few more wounds, and was nearly out of his store of sacred herbs when he finally made it far enough out of herd territory to find himself crossing patches of tundra with any regularity once more.

Though it was out of his way, Orsin backtracked his way to the tor. It was the best place to restore his supply of sacred herbs before they ran out and left him vulnerable to the herd venom that still beat within his veins. He could feel it, the hatred of the prince living on within him even though he had severed the thing's head and ended its life.

It was going to take more than the field medicine he could practice to be fully rid of it. It would take the expertise of the shamans of his home city or the touch of Weihlaris himself, neither of which seemed to be forthcoming anytime soon.

So Orsin found a safe spot to camp at the base of the tor, treated his wounds and slept off the worst of his injuries, though the herd venom in his veins slowed his healing greatly. It was as persistent as it was vicious.

Then he was forced to scale it once again and pick out a return path. One that included returning to the place he had interred Torben's remains. He refused to leave him out here alone to face the frozen tundra for eternity.

Orsin made it back to the grave site just in time. A pack of scavengers had excavated nearly to Torben's flesh when he arrived. Orsin killed half a dozen of them in his first furious charge, the berserker rage flaring within him like a flame. The rest fled. Then, though exhausted by the effort, Orsin retrieved Torben's remains and carefully bundled them up in the pelt of a caribou he had hunted down and slain after ensuring it bore not even the slightest hint of herd taint.

It got easier and easier as he went, the battles less and less dangers and fewer and further between. The closer he came to his home territory, the fewer herd beasts he faced, and many of those that did appear would pause and sniff the air before fleeing nervously.

The scent of a dead herd prince was apparently a powerful ward against attack by lesser beasts, at least when they were far from another herd noble.

"Not far now," Orsin said. He had taken to talking to Torben's remains as he carried them on his back. Though even as he did so, he felt there was far more of the life of his best friend bound up in the weapons at his side: Muinnajhr which held a drop of Torben's blood, and Hjarsurung which had been forged by Torben's paws alone.

When he delivered the remains to their final resting place after they had been cleansed, the weapons would remain, and he would carry Torben with him in three ways: in the hammer, in the axe, and in his heart.

"No," Torben's voice agreed, the rotting head that sat at the top of the pack moving its jaw in a grim mockery of life. "Not long now."

Orsin growled and retrieved another pawful of sacred herbs to chew on. The herd venom still flared in his veins. It was in an eternal war with the sacred herbs and Orsin's own iron will. While he refused to let it win, that didn't mean the venom had not managed to figure out ways it could fight back. Ways it could try to hurt him.

The hallucinations had gotten particularly vivid and distracting.

Thankfully, the venom was just that. Venom. While it might carry a residual hive intelligence with it, it was not self-aware or self-directing. It wasn't smart enough to lead him astray.

He had to believe that. He had to trust in himself and Weihlaris. He would see his family again—what was left of it.

And then he crested a small rise and here they were, the gates he had passed through untold weeks ago, when his trial began.

The way home.

CHAPTER 39

Orsin remembered making his way through the gates, stumbling and nearly exhausted. He could have been aided, but he insisted he make it under his own power. Though the Trial was completed as soon as he reached the sheltering might of Vaeggdor, Orsin felt he had to walk through the gateway for it to really count. He could not dissuade himself of this, so he stumbled forward, the head of the herd prince held aloft in dizzy triumph as he did so.

Everything after that was a blur or a dark void. He remembered chanting, and the sharp scent and taste of the sacred herbs. Not that he could ever forget it after the Trial. He had consumed so much of it, had so much of it pasted across his flesh.

The network of scars criss-crossing his body was extensive. Orsin had spent far too long tracing them with a cautious paw. Each one told a tale of glory and of pain, of honor won at the cost of blood and pain. The largest was the star-shaped mass of scar tissue on his shoulder where the herd prince had wounded him. That one still ached and it occasionally looked nauseatingly green in the light, as if some of the herd venom still lurked within it.

The shamans assured him that was not the case, that all of the foul stuff had been driven from his veins by their ministrations and the grace of Weihlaris.

There were others, most of them minor. The most interesting were the small round scars left from where he'd been pierced by the claws of the tainted Fursja that Torben had died beheading. Those small wounds ached in a peculiar way whenever the weather was about to turn and deliver a blizzard.

Orsin chuckled wryly. If he were ever wounded too greatly to fight, at least he would have a place predicting the weather. That had to be good for begging a few tankards.

His parents had been overjoyed to see him and have him home safe, though that joy was made bittersweet by the news and the remains he bore with him. The loss of Torben would be a scar that the whole family would have to bear, though it would weigh heaviest on Orsin's heart.

He glanced over to the Fursja that stood next to him. Torben should be standing next to him, right now. The survivors of the Trial were assembled before the Warlord and the Chief Shaman, prepared to receive the blessing of Weihlaris in recognition for their deeds.

It was a proud moment, but at best it was bittersweet. Looking up and down the assembled ranks of the Fursja that had returned from the Trial, Orsin could see that perhaps only one in three had survived to make it back through the gates. He'd known the Trial would be a winnowing and a harrowing, but to see so few faces amongst his cohort, to know how many he would never see again—faces he had laughed and quarreled with, had passed in the market and generally *lived* with all his young life.

It was a loss. Those that had survived had been forged in the hardest of crucibles and would rise in strength and power to carry the burden of their entire people on their backs, but Orsin, having lost Torben, was not certain if the price was truly worth it. And for that, more than anything, he burned to crush the herd once and for all, to remove this steady loss and sorrow from his people. There had been other Trials, after all, before the coming of the herd. And while the point of a Trial was to be hard—it had to be, if it was to be worth anything—this seemed excessive.

"Warriors!" The Warlord's voice echoed out over the assembled Fursja—the Trial cohort, their family and friends, the community that gathered for the sacred ceremony, all of them. "You have braced the enemy on their turf, you have faced them alone, with only your might and the grace of the gods to sustain you. That you stand here before me is potent testament to your prowess as warriors."

The warlord went on with his speech, praising their resilience, their determination, and their skill in battle. War stories of his own Trial were recounted and, when the warlord was done speaking, Chief Shaman Thuridral was called upon to invoke the gods and explain the importance of the holy rite as an affirmation of the results of the Trial. What was left unspoken was the judgement of Weihlaris that would come with the ceremony.

Each member of Orsin's cohort would face a shaman and they would be anointed with a paint or paste made from sacred herbs and blessed specially by the shamans. The process would connect each of the scars received during the Trial into an intricate pattern that, once complete, would act as a conduit for Weihlaris's divine power. Orsin didn't know precisely what happened, but somehow the process weighed the achievements of the Fursja warrior and then Weihlaris's Mark would appear somewhere on the Fursja's body.

Every mark was technically slightly different, tailored specifically to the Fursja who bore it and an expression of the trials they had undergone to achieve it. Once the mark appeared, the shaman would announce a small litany of the candidate's achievements and reveal to the assembled crowd a bit of the power that the god had bestowed upon the worthy warrior.

Later, after the ceremony, there would be consultations with the shamans and elder warriors of the Fursja, to help Orsin and his cohort better understand how to master the power the mark granted them, and how to uncover all of the abilities it conveyed. Not everything was revealed by the god Weihlaris to his shamans.

Some things were personal between a warrior and their god, after all, and it would not do to have all one's secrets known to the public. Any enemy might be able to pick them up that way.

The first of Orsin's cohort to undergo the ceremony was a lean warrior clutching a pair of wickedly serrated daggers. His name escaped Orsin, if the warrior had ever known it. There were plenty of candidates pulled in from the nearby villages that he would not have known personally.

This one had few scars so it did not take the shaman long to trace the pattern. There was a moment when the lean Fursja froze, and the paint seemed to writhe across his body, flashing into a new configuration before sinking into the flesh and becoming a part of him. As the Mark of Weihlaris manifested, the lesser scars accumulated during the trial faded from view, consumed or changed to produce the mark.

Not all scars vanished, however. Older warriors said the most important ones—for whatever reason—tended to stay. The lean Fursja didn't keep any. It could mean he was skilled enough not to have collected any, or simply that he had faced too few battles that really tested his limits. Or maybe he was simply lucky. Whatever the case, it was between him and the gods. None of the assembled would make judgements. The Fursja had fought the herd for too long for that kind of judgement or infighting. Some drunken tongues might wag, but the lean Fursja had survived his Trial and bore the Mark of Weihlaris's favor.

That was enough.

Then the ceremony continued, the shamans working their way down the line. The Chief Shaman was among them, and Orsin noticed that he tended to choose those he attended to personally somewhat at random. Well, at random or at the unheard prompting of Weihlaris.

Finally, it was Orsin's turn. Thuridral, the Chief Shaman, stood before him, cowled and enigmatic. Orsin stretched proudly, the scars scattered across his body a testament to what he had undergone as part of his Trial.

The shaman's face was a rigid mask, impossible for Orsin to read. Muttering prayers, he slowly traced a design all across Orsin's body, from scar to scar in sharp, brutal lines. The scent of the herbs, fresh and crisp, rose to Orsin's nostrils and brought memory after memory of the trial flooding back to him. The first time he needed to treat himself, the confrontation with the fox-lord, the fields of herbs surrounding the tor, the taste of the herbs as he desperately chewed the things all the way back from his battle with the prince—the smell brought all of it rushing to the forefront of his mind, and all the while the shaman traced lines across Orsin's body with an implacable expression on his face.

It took longer for Orsin than for many of the others. Eventually, however, the pattern was complete. The shaman raised his arms and called out to Weihlaris for the god's blessing—and judgement—and as the god had for every other Fursja warrior assembled, Weihlaris answered.

Orsin froze in place, every muscle seizing and unable to move. Every single moment of pain and privation he had undergone throughout the Trial suddenly flooded his body, burning all thought away, stoking that flame into a white-hot heat, and hammering his soul into a new, purer shape with the fire. That shape suddenly coalesced into a runic pattern that he could see in his mind's eye, a white-hot tracery of flame that suddenly flashed green. For a moment, it held the same shade as the herd venom, but then Weihlaris's fire purified it, tempering it to a deep, natural green, the colour of deep forests and old growth trees, untouched by time or taint.

Then that selfsame fire erupted across his body as the runic marking, the blessing of Weihlaris, manifested. The agony was the most intense thing Orsin had ever experienced, making the conflict with the herd prince pale in comparison. Yet still he could not move. All his muscles were locked in place, even his throat muscles. Not even a sound was he permitted to vent the agony. Every iota he had to simply endure.

Then it was over as quickly as it had begun. The Chief Shaman had placed a paw on Orsin's boulder and a soothing energy seemed to radiate from that contact. It was like the warming heat of a gentle fire rather than the roaring inferno he had just experienced and Orsin wondered if the energy was the shaman's connection to Weihlaris.

Then Orsin met the shaman's eyes and he blinked. Was that a flicker of respect? How unexpected. Orsin didn't think the old Fursja had it in him to respect anyone other than the gods.

"Behold," the shaman rumbled, "a blessed warrior of Weihlaris, bearing the greatest Mark of His Favour in seven generations! With the touch of our god upon him, this warrior will be a force of destruction like unto the blizzard itself. He will feel no pain nor tolerate no touch of poison upon her person or within his body. When the fury rages, it shall burn all taint and illness away! For none like shall be able to persist in the face of Weihlaris's divine fire! Rejoice, for we have gained a mighty warrior!"

The shaman raised his arms and the crowd roared in approval.

Orsin almost rocked back on his heels from the force of it. But his eyes locked with those of his parents, and their pride and love anchored him. And then, amidst all the sound and the fury, he thought he heard Torben's voice echoing from Muinnajhr, strapped as it was to his back.

Well done brother. Well done. You are a Prince among Fursja.

Then it seemed the voice of Torben snickered as it faded away.

The world seemed to take on a fuzzy quality. The shaman's description of his mark, was it even possible? So much power! Orsin had not heard of any mark so powerful amongst a returning cohort. He had slain a prince, yes, but he did not think it would result in this much of the god's favor! That thought, the roars of approval, the respectful nod he received from the Warlord, the feeling of Weihlaris's approval, all of it swept away Orsin's ability to think clearly. The remainder of the ceremony passed in a blur. It was only when the Warlord finished his speech to a truly world-shaking round of approval from the assembled Fursja that Orsin was shocked back to the present.

"Now, let us feast!" The Warlord roared.

The crowd roared back, joy and celebration rocking the very air around them all.

CHAPTER 40

Great bonfires cast leaping golden light across tables groaning beneath the weight of food and drink. The great celebratory feast commemorating the successful return of the Trial candidates had been raging for awhile, but it showed little sign of abating. Many of Orsin's cohort had gone weeks without proper food or drink. Their hunger was deep and not easily filled. There were a great deal of reserves to refill. And, of course, many of them had enhanced constitutions thanks to the newly manifested Marks of Weihlaris amongst them.

It would be many hours still until all the Fursja present were sated.

Orsin tore the flesh from a massive roasted rib of GauVark with relish, remembering the trouble he had gone to to trap one of the beasts in order to bait the fox-lord. He much preferred confronting the bulk of the beast like this. Safer and better tasting, if nothing else.

He had already had a sip of honey-mead and it had made him morose. He watched the cubs running and playing amidst the tables and his thoughts drifted, like a silly old bear, to the past, to when he and his friend had no greater concern than whether or not they would get caught raiding his mother's larder.

Those were simpler times.

By rights, Torben should be seated here with him. His friend had been as mighty and as determined as Orsin was. He was skilled with his warhammer and if he was not so constant in his faith to Weihlaris, he was still no apostate or heretic. He had been a breath of fresh air and buoyed the mood of all around him.

The world was a colder, sadder place without him.

Orsin stole another sip of honey-mead and rather than drinking, surreptitiously poured it to the ground with a whispered prayer that it find its way to Torben in the Halls of Weihlaris. And then, because that was the kind of relationship they had had, Orsin dipped his toes in the mead, for a little extra flavour.

Torben would have found it funny. After roaring in fury for an hour at being tricked. That was Torben. He was a true friend that never let anything get in the way of what was really important, like their friendship.

He'd even shadowed Orsin from the fringes, doing what he could to ease the burden for the Trial. It was keeping very much to the letter of the law, and skirting just a bit the edges of the spirit of things, but that, too, was Torben. He was always looking for a good angle.

Orsin looked over the table. There were a good dozen of his cohort here. None he knew well, but that would change in the near future as they began to train together in earnest. Passing the Trial was only the beginning, after all.

He couldn't help but wonder, however, who they had lost. How many Fursja thought as Torben did? How many went right up to the line and did what they could to ease the Trial of others of their cohort, while hewing also to the line drawn in the snow by Weihlaris, that the Trial was a thing to be undertaken and passed alone?

Orsin would never know. And it was likely that even if anyone else had a similar friendly ghost wandering the edges of their Trial, it would not be something they would ever realise. He was certain Torben would never have spoken of it, had he survived.

There was something to that, Orsin felt, now that the world was blurry with drink and he was flush with the heady highs of success. That action—shadowing and helping from the edges—was similar to how the Fursja worked together as a people. They were all the children of Weihlaris, but they were a collection of individuals, at least in terms of their martial prowess. They worked hard to excel individually, but their individuality was also tuned to a common purpose, uniting them into something greater without turning them into a faceless mass where individual freedom and liberty was crushed out by the greater will of the rulers. That was what the herd did, and it made sense that the Fursja would not act like their ancient enemy.

It might even be the key to their victory. Did they perhaps need to think of things this way more? To find those boundaries and the spaces where each individual warrior could support all the others around them without fouling or contradicting the individual talents and prowess of their fellows?

It was something to think about. Orsin grinned then as the ground beneath him suddenly seemed to wiggle. Something to think about when he had had less to drink and could talk to someone more sensible than he was.

A whisper caught his attention and Orsin glanced down to the other end of the table. Higrun and Mathajara were talking to one another, shooting him glances and laughing as they did so. And Orsin suddenly flashed back to that evening, not so terribly long ago, where he and Torben had been drinking and carousing at a feast very like this one. Where they had tried to win over those very Fursja.

It seemed like an entire lifetime ago.

For Torben, it was. Orsin shook off the thought and instead raised his tankard in a salute to Higrun and Mathajara. Maybe he'd try to talk to them again later.

Not now, though. Now he was still very much tied up dealing with the copious amounts of ale and honey-mead that were flowing toward him. He needed to make sure he drank Torben's memory under the table first.

Then there were the heavier thoughts. Orsin suddenly found himself beyond the Trial. All of his life to this point had been focused on passing the Trial. His thoughts as to what to do beyond it had been nebulous at best, but now here he was, facing down the rest of his life with very little idea of what it would actually look like, beyond the assumptions he'd carried with him from stories and hearsay from old warriors.

None of his wildest imaginings ever included him actually slaying a herd prince single-handedly. There were implications to that, and to the powerful Mark of Weihlaris which he now bore. It was a responsibility as well as an opportunity. The warlord himself had approached him earlier, saying that they would speak soon, once the festivities had passed and everyone had recovered from the celebrations.

In fact, Orsin had been receiving quite a lot of attention tonight. It wasn't just Higrun and Mathajara that had been shooting him glances. In fact, the only people that were treating him normally were his parents. They had embraced him, and, after a few celebratory drinks, had withdrawn home to allow him to celebrate in his own way, among his own generation. Their love he could feel was unaltered.

He had slain a herd prince. People knew. It had been recounted by the shamans as part of the ceremony. Orsin hadn't paid much attention to it at the time, consumed as he was by the touch of his god, but it was clear his feat had had an effect.

And he'd known it would, but knowing was different from living. Orsin was not prepared for the sudden feeling of being set apart from the rest of the Fursja around him. He wasn't sure he liked the feeling, for all it was the direct result of his prowess and the glory he had rightfully earned.

Glory he'd much rather be sharing with Torben.

It all began to swirl around in his head, a distracting concoction far more dangerous than any alcohol he'd consumed so far. The questions about his future, the regrets he had over the past, the unease of not knowing his true place amongst his people any more, the excitement at the Warlord's direct attention—there was so much to grapple with!

Orsin took another long pull form his tankard and speared several juicy looking mushrooms on his claws, nearly emptying the nearby platter of the delicacies. If he had tried to pull a stunt like this before the Trial, he would have been roundly shamed for his gluttony, but now, one of the victorious Returned, he could get away with it.

For this feast at least, and Orsin intended to take full advantage.

Besides, he had reserves to replenish.

It was also a welcome distraction from his thoughts. Eventually, though, Orsin chased them into the corners of his mind and firmly locked the doors on them. There would be plenty of time later to deal with these things. That was not what tonight was for.

Tonight was for feasting and celebration, for tales of battle and remembrances of the fallen. That was the secret of the feast, for it was held in honour of *all* who attempted Weihlaris's Trial, the successful and the dead. As much as Orsin was celebrating his return and being celebrated, he was also mourning the loss of his best friend.

Everyone here was caught in that same strange mix of joy and sorrow. Such was the life of the Fursja. They had fought and they had won, even if there had been losses along the way. It was no reason not to celebrate, but neither would it be right to truly forget those who had fallen along the way.

Like Torben.

"A toast," Orsin roared, raising his tankard high above his head and slopping the contents liberally on himself in the process. "A toast to the memory of those we have lost, warriors fallen in service to Weihlaris as they drove back the threat of the herd. I had a brother, dear to me as anyone in the world. He was called Torben. I'm sure many of you here knew him. You knew his ready smile and the terrible jokes he told—you know the ones! And how confident he was that they were better than any you'd have off a bard."

There was a rumble of laughter scattered around him at that.

"Torben always had my back. There was not a greater friend or ally anyone could ask for. I know a part of him will always be with me, and with us—" The axe and warhammer strapped to Orsin's back seemed to pulse in concert with a smug satisfaction at that, but surely that was just the drinking he'd been doing. "—but I will miss him every day of my life until we are reunited in the Halls of Weihlaris! May it be long after the scourge of the herd has been burned from the world, never again to return! To our lost brothers and sisters!"

Orsin drained the tankard in one great draught, loosing a massive belch as soon as he had finished. He roared in triumph and slammed the tankard to the ground, shattering it into dozens of pieces.

"Come! Let us drink and be merry! Many of our friends are not here with us, and we must be sure to drink their share, to live for they cannot, to love for those are the ties that will bind them to us, now and forever!"

Another tankard appeared in Orsin's paw, as if by magic. He hefted it into the air and called out another toast.

"To our fallen brothers and sisters! To those we fight for! To Torben!"

The massed voices of the nearby Fursja celebrants came back, a glorious chorus.

"To Torben!"

AFTERWORD

Thank you for reading and I hope you enjoyed the first book. If you want to support me , please leave a review. I would really appreciate it. You can follow me on my social media for more news and updates about book 2 (Twitter): @noel_traver.

ACKNOWLEDGEMENTS

I would like to thank my girlfriend for always supporting me in each and every area and making me a better person in life.

Thank you to Jordan for being a dear friend to me and helping me build the world of Primal Fury.

Thank you to Kian N. Ardalan for being the first to retweet the cover of my book and putting it out there and being a cool and kind person in general.

Also a big thank you to Petrik Leo for supporting and promoting self published authors in general and mentioning Primal Fury: Trial of the Berserker without me even asking. I appreciate it and looking forward to more of your booktube content.

Thank you to Boe Kelley for inviting me in the Indie Accords discord. The community there is very kind and welcoming.

Thank you to the rest of the people who showed a lot of interest and excitement. It means a lot to me.

Printed in Great Britain
by Amazon